KNIGHTS IN SHINING A

A ROOKERY CASTLE M

Book 1

By Eliza Helen Holimold

The story is set in the fictitious village of Heathbrook which is situated near to the Staffordshire – Derbyshire border.

It is a typical village where everyone knows everyone and somewhere down the historical line, most of them are related. It has a post office, a chemist. The Raven Arms Pub, St John's Church and last but not least a haunted castle.

Knights in Shining Armour is the first in a series of books and has many twists and turns as you get to know the characters. It tells you how the Knight family came to live in Rookery Castle and why someone is trying to bump off the ladies of the WI.

Audrey Knight had looked longingly at Rookery Castle for many years and each time she saw that it was up for sale, yet again, she vowed that if she ever came up on the Lottery she would buy it and move her family in, make it a proper home. She deserved it, her family deserved it and so did Rookery Castle.

Little did she know, her dream was going to be a reality and she was unaware that the reality, at times, would turn into a nightmare.

This cosy mystery is full of laugh out loud humour, fascinating mysteries and some spooky goings on, as the Knight family try to turn Rookery Castle into a home and business.

Table of Contents

Characters.

<u>The Family</u>

Audrey – Matriarch.

Ned – Patriarch.

Greg. Eldest Son - Married to Louisa children Liz, Holly & Theo.

Pete. Middle Son –single.

Bobby. Youngest son – single.

Celia – Louisa's mother and Audrey's friend.

Jack Jnr – Louisa's nephew and Celia's grandchild.

<u>In the Gatehouse</u>

April Belle.

May Belle.

Vicar June Belle.

<u>In the Village</u>

Mr & Mrs Gahir – Post Office.

Julie Tattershall – Chemist.

Caroline Chen – Area Manager Cornwallis Chemists.

Patricia and Roger Swinger – Landlords of the Raven Arms.

Victoria Swinger – Roger's mother.

Sarah – Barmaid.

Jemima – Waitress.

Tom Belle – Father of the Belle sisters.

James – Choir Master.

Larry O'Leary – Vet.

Suki Ryan – Forensics.

Donald Scott – Doctor.

<u>Police</u>

DS Bob Sergeant.

Constable Robin Sergeant.

Support Officer Mandy Riley.

PROLOGUE

He couldn't wait to get away from the dinner table, it was torture sitting trying to contain his excitement.

He sat at the end of the table in the place of honour which was befitting the man of the house, his fiery battle-axe of a wife sat to his right and to his left was the bane of his life, his son, the pathetic mummy's boy, did he really father this pitiful bag of bones. If sheeee spent half the time fussing around him as she did that little wimp, he wouldn't have to be looking elsewhere, but looking elsewhere was so much fun.

Mrs. Shufflebotham, the cook, had done them proud again, her cooking was always outstanding, her baking sublime, what a pity she was old or he would have loved to take her while she was bending over a mixing bowl, but his attentions had always gravitated towards much younger commoners.

The three-course dinner was at last over, they retired to the sitting room where James Ayre, his butler, held open a box of his favourite cigars. Once he had chosen one and rolled it between his fingers several times, he clipped the end and Ayre, who seemed to appear from nowhere, reached towards him with a silver gas lighter, flicking the top a few times until a tall yellow flame extended from it. The butler held the device steady whilst the Duke puffed eagerly until it was alight. The smell and the aroma of the expensive cigar he enjoyed so much was a delight.

At last, his glass of port was empty, downed more quickly than etiquette allowed, but he couldn't wait to be free. Getting up from the large leather armchair, he kissed his wife's forehead; she was drinking her sherry and tapping away at a tapestry frame in front of her. He shook his son's hand and retired for the night.

They had always had separate bedrooms, theirs being a marriage of convenience, he had the title, her family had money, a match made in heaven or so he thought at the time. However, he quickly realized that despite many attempts at getting his hands on her family fortune his wife would not be parted from her inheritance. She allowed him a pittance for his pleasure; he had to resort to sending Ayre into London on occasions to sell pieces of the artwork and silver, which he had been hidden away in the attic of the large noble residence.

Heavy breathing and much coughing and cursing would have been heard, if anyone had been around. His solitary comical figure hunched over, his short bowlegs taking long cumbersome strides as he rushed along the winding corridors, up several flights of stairs and through heavy carved wooden doors with sturdy metal hinges and fine ornate locks.

"I'm late, I'm late I'm late," he muttered sounding very much like the Mad Hatter from Alice in Wonderland. He stopped, thinking he could hear footsteps behind him; he held his breath to listen, but could hear nothing.

"No it must be my imagination, silly old fool," he said scolding himself.

It was such a rambling old dwelling; no one apart from his butler and the valet, George, would know he wasn't in his rooms. He went through the hidden door at the back of his closet and entered the secret passage that one of his ancestors had wisely secured as an escape, just in case the castle was invaded. It had many hiding places and exits some of which even he had never found. His hurried footsteps pounded along the dark gloomy passageway, echoing like a herd of wild horses. It seemed like an eternity before he eventually unlocked and unbolted the door to his secret boudoir, at last his journey had ended. His breathing slowed, he blew his nose into a beautifully monogrammed handkerchief throwing it carelessly on the bed.

"So let it begin," he sniggered.

Opening the wardrobe door he surveyed the outfits in front of him, none of these would do by Jove no, he turned around and saw the new outfit standing in the corner, "tee he, that is the one that will entice my little princess to my bed," he said out loud.

The costume had been especially made, he told Rubin his tailor it was for a fancy dress party he was attending. The original had been standing in the reception room for centuries; it was far too heavy and cumbersome. He had tried on the unique suit of armour, with the help of the faithful Ayre, but he couldn't move in it, let alone chase the young maid around the four-poster bed. This new lightweight version was just the ticket; it still looked the part, shiny and bright. It took what seemed like an age to struggle single handedly into the outfit he had chosen, but at last he surveyed himself as best he could in the large full length mirror, only being able to see a silhouette due to the lack of light.

"Damn and blast this dark room he muttered. Normally he would light the candles but in his haste to leave the dinner table and scurry to his sanctuary, he had forgotten to ask Ayre for a box of matches, in future he would keep a box on the table next to the paraffin lamp.

He stood eagerly awaiting his pure innocent princess, dressed especially for the occasion he knew this would please her, this is what she had requested and he would do anything to get his hands on the buxom child. Already the fantasies were running around in his head, he was conscious of beads of sweat running down his back causing him to shudder and wriggle. The room was in shadows, just a narrow beam of light shining through a crack in the stone wall. No electric lighting, never got around to putting any of those new-fangled inventions in, the workers may have disclosed his retreat to his family or even worse the farmers in the village.

He could think of so many more things he could use his money on, a strumpet, streetwalker, slut, lady of the night, call them what you might, they gave him pleasure, but not as much as his little princess was going to.

He belonged to a gentleman's club in town, a small group of select members very often frequented a new style of establishment which was filled with jazz music, where young girls dressed in skimpy clothes, throwing themselves around the dancefloor with gay abandon, leaving nothing to the imagination. The new age women he believed were referred to as flappers, they certainly were erotic, he had on occasions plied the girls with drinks and enjoyed their company, but they were too willing, too obvious, no fight, no struggle, no games, no fun.

He could just about see the outline of the unlit candles sitting majestically on the old sturdy dressing table and the paraffin lamp standing alone on the table in the corner. Looking around and listening for the tell-tale echo of her tiny feet on the well-worn steps he looked with glee at the massive oak wardrobe that contained the secrets to his pleasure. The hand carved four poster bed, grand and sumptuous with its delicate hand carvings, the red luxurious hand embroidered canopy was elegant and the silk sheets were exciting him beyond measure. Almost unable to contain himself he went to listen at the door.

Did he hear something? Was she on her way? Unable to rein in his excitement any longer he flung open the door, the smell of stagnant icy cold air taking his breath away for a moment. Was she hiding to play a little trick on him, perhaps she'd started the game already; he chuckled to himself, the anticipation almost too much to take.

"Hello my little damsel, are you hiding from your knight in shining armour," he whispered leaning over to peer into the darkness, he heard a rustling behind him and as he turned and felt a hand on his shoulder.

Where was he? His head was throbbing, his whole body contorted and in great pain. He opened his eyes, could he see a small blurred shadow, a face close to his. "Who was that?"

"Who are you? What..." He realized he was lying at the bottom of the steps.

He heard bolts being squeakily pulled across on the other side of the imposing door, which led to the servants' quarters, it creaked and groaned as it opened slowly and unsteadily, a beam of light shone into the small hallway at the bottom of the steps that led to the bedchamber above. He tried to turn to see who it was, but couldn't say anything, he felt a huge weight pressing down, crushing his chest, his breath coming in short shallow gasps. His heart pounding against his ribcage, so fast he thought it was going to burst out at any moment. His body was now bathed in a cold sweat, he let out a gurgling sound and the light went out of his eyes. He was no more.

CHAPTER 1

White rabbits. White rabbits. White rabbits.

"White Rabbits, White Rabbits, White Rabbits," Audrey mumbled as she yawned and stretched.

The Sun was streaming through the bedroom window. Oh well, she said to herself another day, waking up is always a good sign, particularly when you think of the alternative. She wondered downstairs to see Ned, her husband of forty two years sitting in the living room of their three bedroom Victorian town house, his wild grey hair sticking up in all directions, a bit like a nutty professor, which he was really. His paper was balancing on his knee, coffee cup in one hand and pencil in the other, the cup was at a precarious angle, the milky liquid just waiting for another degree of movement before it would slide gently from the cup onto his paper.

Oh yesssss there it goes, Audrey thought to herself. Before Ned could come out with any profanities, she said

"White rabbits. White rabbits. White rabbits."

He looked up, his eyes just visible above the glasses, which were perched on the end of his nose; the gold frames a little worse for wear, the arm being taped together with a cream plaster to hold the frame together. He'd sat on them so many times everyone wondered just how long he could keep them from falling apart.

"White rabbits.White rabbits. White rabbits and good morning to you to Audrey, is it the 1st of the month already."

"No" she replied, "I said it just to confuse you. Of course it's the 1st of the month, the 1st comes around every month without fail 12 months of the year; I really don't understand why it's such a surprise to you."

"Oomph," he grunted, eyes down looking at his crossword again, trying to look at the clues, which were now becoming increasingly difficult to see due to the beige coffee stains.

"Are the dogs out Ned?"

"Yes Audrey they're chasing the white rabbits around in the yard."

She turned to see him smile cheekily with a look of smug satisfaction at his response. She growled at him and then turned, only allowing herself to smile once she was out of his sight.

Audrey opened the back door; the three border collies greeted her with smiling faces and waggy tales just before they herded her back into the kitchen. She gave them all a little treat from the cupboard and then felt the cat, Cinders brushing up against her legs, "don't worry Cinders, I haven't forgotten you," she said bending down to give her a little catnip.

Having made herself a coffee she walked into the tiny conservatory, which looked out over the apology for a garden, it was actually a yard with a few flower tubs. Just catching a brief glimpse of her own reflection in the glass door, she stopped and looked at herself, tall and upright or she was after she'd first seen the slouch looking back at her. Long shoulder length silver hair, which had once been almost black. She wasn't a beauty by any stretch of the imagination, but quite attractive in a homely sort of way. Wrapping the fluffy dressing gown tightly around her, she pulled the belt just a little tighter around her slim waist; it was quite cool being only 7am.

She shuffled over, in her monkey slippers that her eldest daughter Marcia had bought her last Christmas, to one of the two wicker chairs that were squeezed into the tiny conservatory, they called it a conservatory, it was a porch really, but conservatory sounded so much better. Audrey sat and looked out, sipping the warm black liquid from the mug she held in her cupped hands.

The dogs started barking furiously and throwing themselves at the front door. Post woman, she thought to herself, probably another bill. Never mind she really didn't need new slippers, these would do, even though she kept tripping over the monkey tail. The money can be spent keeping the gas and electric on and the larder stocked.

What had happened to our retirement plans? She thought. "Silly me," she said aloud, she knew what had happened, Ned's pension fund had collapsed and they'd had six children to keep clothed and fed for the first twenty odd years of their lives.

Six children, how did that happen? She chuckled to herself, of course she knew how it had happened, too many chases around the kitchen table and she just wasn't quick enough. There was still an occasional chase around the table but rather slower nowadays, she virtually has to stop so that Ned could catch up.

A gloomy shadow passed over her as she thought of how things should have been. They would have been more than a little comfortable, if things had gone differently, a cottage by the sea, a new car, or even cars, holidays abroad. That was the plan, before realising there was no private pension, no lump sum to treat the children, no extra money to pamper themselves. As it was, they just managed to visit the girls, who were spread across the UK, once or twice a year, but only for a few days. Still they were happy days, filled with laughter, spending precious time with the grandchildren. She pondered; she really did wish they lived closer.

"Ohhhh Audrey really, chin up girl, think of the good things, you have a wonderfully eccentric husband, three handsome boys and three beautiful girls, a multitude of the cutest grandchildren ever produced. How blessed are you."She said aloud. "Still this isn't getting the baby a new bonnet, upwards and onwards Audrey old girl, upwards and onwards."

With that Audrey went to the front door to see what demon bill had been pushed through the letterbox. Surprise, surprise as Cilla would have said, a brown envelope from gov.com was calling for her attention. She stood looking at it for a moment or two; it can't be toooo bad can it. Be brave woman, go for it and with that she tore open the envelope and read the few lines, 'Dear Mrs,' not even a name, that's a good start, even gov.com doesn't grace me with a name? 'Due to an error in calculating your tax in the year 2003, we have overcharged you blah blah blah, and therefore a cheque is enclosed. We are sorry for any inconvenience etc., etc.'

A cheque she thought gleefully, looking at the amount, she really couldn't believe her eyes. Walking nonchalantly into the living room where Ned had dropped off whilst doing the crossword, she shouted his name. "Ned. Ned. Ned wake up. We've got a cheque."

"What...Where...when ah." He muttered shaking himself awake.

"You were asleep Ned."

"No I wasn't, I was just resting my eyes."

"We have a cheque from the Income Tax people." Audrey waved the cheque under his nose.

"Really, how much? Are you sure it's not an April fools prank," he asked.

"£11.23!"Audrey replied.

"Umph, no one would play an April fool's joke for £11.23, are you sure you haven't missed a few zeros of the end." He looked over to see her shaking her head. "I think I'll go back to sleep then." He yawned and stretched.

"You mean you'll go back to resting your eyes?" She looked at him eyebrows raised questioningly.

"Exactly," he said with exasperation.

Well not to be sneezed at, it's obviously an omen, my lucky day, she thought. White rabbits, white rabbits white rabbits, not just once but twice today and a cheque from gov.com, can't be bad. I think this calls for a lottery ticket, maybe two, that is of course if there's any money left over from the shopping. I know I'll take Ned with me to the supermarket, he hates going to the supermarket. That'll teach Mr Grumpy to be so dismal.

"Ned, Ned *come* on get suited and booted we're off to the supermarket, you can help me carry the shopping, your good deed for the day."

"Do I have to?" he pleaded

"No you could stay at home put the vacuum on and mop the kitchen floor." Audrey said with a hint of sarcasm.

"The supermarket it is then," he groaned

By 9am Audrey was driving their old and somewhat decrepit car to Cheadle the nearest big shopping centre about 10 miles from Heathbrook.

The small village where Audrey and Ned lived only had a few shops. The lovely Mr & Mrs Gahir ran the Post Office, which sold just about anything and everything. There was also a chemist, which only opened when the pharmacist, Julie Tattershall was sober enough to make it down the stairs from her flat above.

The village pub was run by the local letch, very aptly named Roger Swinger. He ran the Raven Arms with his overbearing and right up her own bottom spouse, Patricia. Victoria, Roger's 95 year old demented mother lived with them, much to the annoyance of the Swingers.

Just about a 100yards away from the high street, there was the village hall, which was attached to St John's Church. There had been a right hullabaloo 15years ago when the old vicar died and a local girl took over, June Belle moved from a small cottage she and her sisters shared with their dad, into the Gatehouse, a large detached residence that belonged to the Castle.

Oh and of course, the village had a Castle, Rookery Castle a 13th century historic residence, complete with several outbuildings and a Moat.

On their way to do the weekly supermarket shop they passed through the village and continued along the lanes, past St John's Church, its beautiful old stone structure and stained glass windows were an imposing sight when driving along the lane that led out of the village, it was contained within the original hand built stone walls. Just past this picture of rural perfection, huge arched wrought iron gates came into view, supported by sturdy stone pillars, just beyond the tree lined driveway you could glimpse the turrets of the Castle.

A large wooden sign hung from the gates.

"It's for sale **again,"** Audrey said to Ned who seemed to have his nose glued to the crossword yet again.

"What's for sale?" he replied.

"Rookery Castle, for goodness sake darling don't you notice anything?" Audrey said irritably.

"I think that should be, do you notice nothing, but I'm not certain," he said sarcastically "I'll look it up."

Audrey sighed. Then a smile lit up her face, "When we come up on the lottery we'll buy Rookery Castle and we'll all move in."

"Yes dear, of course we will, when we win the lottery," he said patronisingly.

"Promise Ned."

"Yes Audrey promise."

They managed to get everything on Audrey's shopping list and as they were leaving, she stopped off at the front desk to get the Lottery tickets. The boys would be over tomorrow for Sunday lunch, Hunters chicken, everyone's favourite. Ned had loaded all the bags into the boot of the car and the Lottery tickets were securely tucked into Audrey's purse, so they started on their homeward journey.

The sun was shining; the radio was playing some good old hits of the 60's, all was well with the matriarch and patriarch of the Knight family. On the familiar journey home, they followed the twists and turns of the lanes, past Ned's Council allotment, they waved to Marjorie who was digging holes for her Charlotte potatoes, Ned always called her his allotment girlfriend to make Audrey jealous, it didn't work. Travelling a few hundred yards more, Audrey saw a very familiar Pink Volkswagen Beetle on the side of the road with the vicar looking at it in despair.

"Ohhhh goodness" Audrey exclaimed, "its June, looks like the old bangers' broken down again."

"I thought she was a friend of yours Audrey. Fancy calling her an old banger!" Ned commented.

"How on earth you can sit there straight faced and say something so predictably unfunny as that is beyond me Ned Knight," Audrey said biting her lip so as not to laugh.

June the Vicar was a friend of the family, she and her two sisters and brothers had been born in the village. They had all attended the same school as Audrey.

April was the oldest, she was in Audrey's class, very dependable, organised and as honest as the day is long. May was the middle sister and the year below, but as Audrey and May got older they found they had so many things in common, including a sort of intuition, a sixth sense about people and things that happened, they became best friends. The two boys Julius and Augustus came next they very rarely made an appearance in the village and if they did call in for some special occasion they didn't stay long. Then there was June who more than ten years younger than May, she was in the same class as Audrey's brother Liam; the vicar had never married and was without any shadow of doubt the most unlikely vicar you could possibly meet. According to May, their mother could never make up her mind about anything, she was very indecisive, and naming children was no exception. When she started producing them at a fair rate of knots, the last thing she wanted to do was waste her energy thinking of baby names and so named them all after the month they were born. May was actually born in December but her mother couldn't think of a girl's name similar to December so followed April with May.

"Hi Audrey, hi Ned sorry to be a pain could you give me a lift home, I think poor Puff is on her last legs." June said tearfully

"Sorry to hear that Vicar, does she live in the village, how old is she?" Ned mused.

June and Audrey said in unison, "Puff the tragic wagon is the car Ned."

His face was poker straight but Audrey could tell he was joking because his shoulders were jiggling up and down uncontrollably. June threw her rotund body into the back of the car, causing the front to rise off the ground slightly. Although one of her dearest and oldest friends, it had to be said

June tended to pant and puff her way through life, and she definitely looked a little like a cuddly weeble, you could push her, but she would never fall down.

Audrey tried to change the subject so as not to give Ned the opportunity to do any more leg pulling. “Rookery Castle’s up for sale again then June.”

“Yes it is, and it really is a nuisance getting used to new neighbours yet again. You put all your time and effort into putting together a welcome basket and before the fruit can go mouldy they’ve gone.”

June and her two sisters live in the Gatehouse, it was a stone’s throw from the Castle, and it had been loaned to the church by the owners back in the 1920’s, so every Vicar since then had been given the imposing four bedded property to live in rent free. It has been said that there was a tunnel running from the Castle to the Gatehouse for some illicit or illegal reason, but no one who had lived there had ever been able been able to find it.

“Why do you think there have been so many owners of the castle June? Is it the size or the condition do you think?” said Audrey.

“Well Aud.”June is the only person allowed to get away with shortening Audrey’s name; it began when June was a very young child and couldn’t pronounce her ‘r’s. Audwey just didn’t sound right and June’s brothers and sisters, along with all the other village children, ribbed her mercilessly about it, Audrey felt sorry for her and said she could call her Aud because she was a very special little girl.

“There have been some very peculiar goings on since I moved into the Gatehouse, particularly when I've been taking Satan for a walk in the evening. I've seen lights going on and off and strange noises. April says it’s all in my imagination, trees rustling shadows from the moon and such like.” June replied.

June stopped herself abruptly before she could say anymore; after all, she didn’t want to appear to be a gossip. The area manager, Mr Cleese, of the Superior Hotel and Fitness Chain, who were now selling Rookery Castle, had told her they were having problems keeping builders on the site; there had been some scary situations and freak accidents, which resulted in the contractors pulling out of the deal. He had asked her not to breathe a word, so if she told Aud that would have been breaking a confidence.

A few days after her conversation with Mr Cleese, she saw six burly builders running down the driveway throwing their tools, and themselves into their big white van; she had thought to herself at the time, this isn't looking good. A few days later, the 'For Sale' sign appeared on the gate.

Audrey's voice interrupted June's thoughts. "Strange, no one seems to last there long isn't it, but life is strange don't you think June?"

"Umm certainly is." June replied. Not trusting herself to say much more.

Audrey really didn't like silence when she and Ned had company; you never knew what he was going to say. He was a lovely man, but tended to put his foot in his mouth whenever he was trying to make conversation. In fact, he tended to do that even in general conversation; it was an endearing trait, which seemed to be in the family genes, the role now being taken over by their youngest son Bobby. I wonder what goes through Ned's mind when he's making those inappropriate comments, she thought to herself. Oh. Oh He's taking a deep breath in, his mouth is opening, he's going to speak, nooooo. I know, a song, that'll do the trick.

"Luck be a lady tooonight.
Luck be a lady toooonight.
Luck if you've been a lady to begin with.
Luck be a lady toniiiight."

Audrey sang with great enthusiasm but unfortunately completely out of tune.

Ned said, "What was that noise Audrey?"

"Didn't you recognise it Ned, Luck be a lady tonight. Frank Sinatra. Did you recognise it June?" Audrey said looking in the driving mirror, trying to see her friend who was sitting in the back.

"Well Aud dear, if I'm going to be perfectly truthful, the words I did recognise, but the tune is a most definite no." June bleated apologetically.

Umph, Audrey thought, the sisters were all the same. May let her join the choir because she felt sorry for her, but made her promise just to mouth the words, April said she couldn't sing anywhere near her because it put her off key. Apparently June had no idea what tune she was singing but it definitely, positively, wasn't Luck be a Lady tonight. Some friends they are.

"I feel sooooo lucky today, June I've bought two lottery tickets. I've used the children's birthdays. Ned has promised, when my numbers come up this evening and we win we're going to buy Rookery Castle. So we'll be your neighbours, how lucky are you June, no more strangers moving in, the Knight family coming to live next door to you, we'll be like your Knights in shining armour." enthused Audrey.

"Only two tickets Audrey, how did you manage that with so many children," June exclaimed.

She had no time to reply as a female teenage Goth stepped out in front of the car, she was looking intently at her mobile phone, fingers moving with speed and expertise over the screen.

Ned screamed and closed his eyes. Well really, Audrey thought. I don't know why he screamed and closed his eyes; after all closing one's eyes does not mean that the event won't take place and screaming really doesn't resolve the situation.

She looked at the young girl whose eyes were still glued to the screen of her mobile device. She seemed to be totally oblivious of the fact that her life had almost come to a very premature end. Audrey decided that because the girl hadn't come to any harm, presuming of course that the look of annoyance, at being interrupted mid text meant that no immediate action had to be taken. She concentrated her attention on her husband. "Come; come now Ned I think you can stop flinging your arms around and screaming, I really don't think that sort of language is suitable on a sunny Saturday afternoon, please remember the Vicar is in the car."

She looked around at June who seemed to be taking things quite well, considering her beloved God's name was being shouted at full throttle in the same breath as someone having sexual intercourse with their mother. Ned really did watch too many American detective films, no-one in a civilised country like England would say something like that, she said to herself oh no, heaven forbid.

June, who was sitting on the back seat looking slightly pale, her dark bob looked as though it had slid forward a couple of inches, completely concealing her face, she raised her hands to part the curtain of hair, revealed bulging dark brown eyes which had a look of sheer terror. Audrey thought the look was attributed to the emergency stop she'd just made, after bumping up the kerb and manoeuvring onto the pavement in front of the Post Office. She felt quite proud at this point that she had actually bought the car to a stop. If they hadn't stopped, she would have had to make a decision, as to whether the car was going to hit the black and white pedestrian pole, risking the orange ball ending up on her knee. Alternatively, ploughing into the post office window and possibly having Mr or Mrs Gahir, or even both of them sitting on the bonnet of the car. For some reason, perhaps it was shock; she had a vivid picture of the distressed pair sitting on the bonnet of the old grey Mondeo, offering her a cup of tea and a fruit scone. At that moment, she would have preferred a very large scotch, but if the picture was real and not a mirage, she would have settled for tea if there was no scotch on offer and the scone did look quite inviting, sitting on its Royal Doulton fine bone china plate.

June bolted from the back seat of the car saying she felt like some fresh air and would walk the rest of the way; it was only a few steps. Ned said he would join her but Audrey hit the child lock so he couldn't get out. After only a few moments, she managed to negotiate without any major incident her exit from the pavement. They were on their way home again, Audrey was unaffected by the experience, however Ned's eyes were tightly shut and for the first time in a long time she heard him muttering the Lord's Prayer. Most of the words were incoherent, but "deliver us from evil" was repeated in a clear rational voice several times.

All the shopping was unpacked and put away, Audrey managed to cook the tea without any mishaps, Steak and Chips, it was always Steak and Chips on a Saturday. Friday night was curry night, Saturday was steak night, Sunday roast dinner and the rest of the week was whatever was on special at the supermarket on the Saturday. The Knight family were definitely creatures of habit, but habit is good, good and predictable. Still Audrey wasn't quite so predictable today, two lottery tickets, not one but two of the little gems.

Audrey looked at the clock on the wall and realised the Lottery show had started. "Oh bugger, wrong channel," she said aloud. Switch over Audrey, she thought. Wait, be patient, it'll be announced soon. Steak was very nice tonight; she liked Ribeye, very tender and flavoursome.

Audrey really didn't like clearing the table and washing the dishes, she didn't know why, it just seemed like a waste of time, like housework, you clean and it gets dirty again, so you clean it, then it gets dirty again and so on. The dishwasher that the children had bought her for her birthday last year was sitting there and all the clean dishes were drying in it. She must tell the family one of these days that she didn't know how to work it, anyway it was just as easy to wash the dishes and let them drip dry in there, at least they were out of sight if they had visitors and it did save on tea towel washing and drying.

The Lottery show was just starting, so she sat down to watch it, tickets in front of her, the man seemed to go on and on. "Oh just get on with it man, no one wants to be listening to your inane chatter." Audrey said taking a sip of her Saturday Night glass of Chardonnay.

About time he shut up, first number out that's Bobby's birthday, second number, come on just do it. Great that's Jan's Birthday. Mmmmm this is exciting. Must breathe, that's Greg's birthday, she thought to herself.

Ok. Ok. Don't panic. Do not panic, good grief, she thought, I'm sounding just like Jonesy out of Dad's Army. It's only a few numbers. I mean really how scary can numbers be?

She stared out of the window, just too frightened to turn again to look at the TV screen. She was willing herself to turn her head just a fraction. No, as much as she tried, she couldn't do it. Reaching for the TV remote, she pointed it at where she thought the screen was and pressed the pause button. Just looking out of the corner of her eye to make sure the screen was still. No movement, none at all that was good. Three numbers had been drawn, three to go. Don't sweat you idiot it's most unbecoming and makes you slithery and smell like a polecat, or do ladies just perspire? I wonder at what age does perspire turn into a glow or is it the other way around. Was she really so stupid as to be rambling incoherently even though it was only in her own head. I'm not stupid am I? She thought. I know the chances that the other three numbers coming up are millions to one. Press the play button you coward.

A thousand times, she seemed to repeat that statement, eventually her index finger developed a will of its own, took over, and pressed the play button. Five minutes later she was still sitting there eyes transfixed to the screen unable to move, speak or think. Then she heard an inhuman almost hysterical, ear-piercing scream, which brought her back from the brink of insanity, or had it? The noise continued, then the realisation hit her with the force of a steam train, the unearthly noise was coming from her mouth.

CHAPTER 2

Rags to Riches.

And that is how the Knight family came to be standing outside the enormous arched doorway of their new home, Rookery Castle.

Ten of them, plus three Border Collies and a very disgruntled black cat had loaded themselves into seven cars and travelled to the outskirts of Heathbrook. Ned had turned the key in the huge padlock on the arched wrought iron gates, and then they had driven along the winding driveway in a convoy. The one removal van that was following them was packed with 14 suitcases, some sentimental personal belongings, and the kitchen table. The castle had been furnished to a high standard when the previous owners had tried to turn it into a Spa and Fitness Hotel, but everyone agreed it was better to move in before deciding what to do with the décor and furnishings.

The boys, Greg, Pete, and Bobby had jumped at the chance of living in the castle, and to complete the little band of homemakers, standing in awe were Greg's wife Louisa, the children Liz, Holly and Theo, and Audrey's friend, Louisa's mother, Celia. The Knight girls, daughters Marcia, Janine, and Nancy had decided to remain at a respectable distance from each other, which considering they didn't get on well, was a very good idea.

Having won £24 million on the Lottery, Audrey and Ned decided to employ a cleaning company, to give the place a good dusting before everyone moved in. It would have taken weeks if they'd chosen to open up all the rooms, so 'Dolly Maids' only cleaned the main areas and the rooms the family had claimed as their own. Celia, Liz, Holly, Louisa and Audrey had been on a shopping spree in Manchester, they bought all new bedding. Nearly all the packing cases had been emptied, which meant that some homely touches had been added to their rooms after the big clean-up had finished. The castle was ready to move into, unbelievably only six weeks after their good fortune.

The family stood for several minutes, mesmerised by the sheer vastness, which stood before them, glued to the spot, no one moving or speaking, their eyes trying to take in the majesty of the sight in front of them. The first person to speak was Theo, the youngest of Greg and Louisa's children. Clearing his throat he said, his voice flipping between high and low, "Is there a dungeon?"

They all turned to look at the tall muscular thirteen year old. Then totally ignoring him they walked up the steps to the front door of their new home. Ned unlocked the door, allowing Audrey and the other women to walk over the threshold first. He followed them and then the rest of the family spilled into the grand reception room at once, Greg being the natural leader told everyone to go to their rooms and unpack.

"Back down here in one hour for coffee and biscuits," he said.

No one questioned him; in fact they all nodded obediently and scurried off to follow his instructions. Apart from the dogs, they stayed downstairs sniffing into every corner barking and chasing each other from room to room. The cat, however, just sat on the marble floor in the middle of the reception room, hissing and spitting at the stairs, obviously making an indignant stand against being removed from the house she had known as home for the last sixteen years.

Sixty minutes later Audrey arrived in the kitchen to find Celia had just put the kettle on; between the two of them they filled coffee cups and opened packets of biscuits. The others all seemed to arrive at once; the girls and Ned were grabbing the now filled cups putting in sugar and milk, and shovelling handfuls of biscuits onto plates. They looked around for somewhere to sit, but there were no chairs to be seen. The kitchen, which was the size of a small barn, was obviously set out for commercial use, but the women all agreed they could convert it to something a little more homely without too much effort. Everyone was wondering where the boys were, when the kitchen door burst open and in strode the missing family members, carrying ten chairs and Audrey's cherished kitchen table.

Whilst they were packing for the big move, the boys had suggested that they took the very old and a little battered table to the dump, but Audrey insisted that it was going with them and nothing would persuade her to part with it. They all groaned but the table brought back very good memories: they'd had many family dinners, birthday parties and other celebrations sitting around that table. It had served the family well for changing nappies and dressing wounds. The children and grandchildren had put big sheets over it and pretended it was a tent, when it was too cold or wet to play outside. Audrey smiled and looked over at Ned. Little did the boys know but that table had been instrumental in their conception and in fact thinking back, some of them could actually have been conceived on it. That table was a part of their family and it was here to stay, no amount of moaning or groaning was going to change that.

It took a couple of weeks to get settled into a routine. Coffee and biscuits were served every morning at 11am, all of the family sitting around the kitchen table for half an hour or so talking about what they'd done to the castle and grounds, and what they were going to do. There was such a lot of work to be done especially to the moat and land, which seemed to have been neglected. So far, they hadn't even had the opportunity to explore all the nooks and crannies, even Theo hadn't investigated the dungeons. Quite a lot of the rooms were locked and although they had a huge set of keys, they could see no point in opening rooms until they needed them. The prospect of cleaning, decorating and sorting fifty plus rooms was too much, as far as the dust and mess was concerned, out of sight out of mind was the policy, they would concentrate on what they needed to work on, in order to live a comfortable family life.

The boys and Louisa had given up their jobs to concentrate on making the castle into a home, it all seemed like an exciting adventure, a dream that they didn't want to wake up from. The dogs, Duke, Sky and the pup Sheppie thought they had died and gone to heaven, the grounds were vast, over 50 acres, they followed Ned and Pete, as father and son walked around the land making notes of fences that needed fixing, making plans for the moat. Ned had always wanted a pond full of Koi carp and they had seen just the spot, a shallow pool fed by the moat, it could be fenced off and would be ideal.

The dogs still hadn't ventured upstairs, the hairs on their backs bristled when they got to the first landing and they shot back down again, making their way to the place they had made their own, a large square porch, about the size of the living room in the old home. It was ideally situated next to the kitchen, and lead into the orangery, it also had a door leading to the outside of the building. The men decided this was going to be the cloakroom, boots and dog beds littered the floor, and from the hooks on the walls hung waterproof, coats, scarves, hats, and brollies. A variety of torches and lanterns sat in size and strength order, on a shelf above the coat hooks, along with several neatly folded old and well-used towels.

The only member of the family who really hadn't settled was Cinders, the black furry moggie; she continued to hiss and spit, refusing to enter most of the rooms. Generally, you could find her curled up on her bed next to the dogs, or prowling around the kitchen, chasing shadows. Her main hobby seemed to be scratching the tiled kitchen floor, in the corner by the sink. She had even taken to climbing into the cupboard, sniffing and hissing. This had caused some disturbing moments, when the family had gone into the cupboard and been confronted with a pair of large green eyes jumping out at them. The tiles in front of the brand new Aga, which had pride of place under the side window, seemed to get a lot of attention from the aging cat, as if she were attempting to tunnel her way out. Everyone found this very amusing and put it down to her age.

It was Thursday, the 1st of the month, almost three weeks since they'd moved in. That morning they had all greeted each other with the customary, White rabbits, White rabbits, White rabbits, and after eating breakfast, they went about their early morning tasks. Four hours later the family were gathered around the kitchen table again, for their usual elevenses of coffee and biscuits, when Celia made an entrance, with a small four-year-old boy, he was dragging his feet and making an awful scraping noise. It was Celia's grandson Jack Jnr; he was the son of Louisa's sister, Janet and her husband Jack Snr. They all turned, the look of horror on everybody's faces was clearly visible. Only Audrey and Ned stayed sitting, while the rest of the family disappeared very quickly out of the back door, coffee cups and half empty plates abandoned, followed very closely by the dogs and an extremely nervous cat.

"Hi Jack Jr it's nice to see you." Audrey said looking at the boy fondly.

Celia pulling a slightly apologetic face said, “His dad’s dropped him off, he’s on his way to work and Janet’s working nights. I usually look after him on Thursday morning just until noon when he goes to activity classes. I’ve had him in my room playing games since 8am but he’s a bit bored, hope you don’t mind.”

Audrey gave her a knowing look; smiling in sympathy, she shook her head. ”Jack would you like juice?”

“Yes please,” said Jack Jnr pulling at his sweater, as if he was trying to stretch it to fit a grown man. He obviously had something on his mind.

“Is something wrong Jack?” Audrey said with concern pouring him some juice in a colourful plastic mug.

“I was thinking, I don’t know what to call you, so can I call you Nana Audrey like Theo does please?”

Laughing Audrey replied “I think that would be a very good idea young man.”

Audrey new that Theo was Jack juniors hero, he followed him everywhere, hanging on his every word, the fact that Jack could copy Theo and call Audrey Nana, seemed to fill the little boy with sheer delight.

Jack ran over to the table where Ned was sitting, knelt on a stool that had been put in position for him by Celia, with the juice placed in front of him. He put both elbows on the table, leaned forward head in hands and with a look of determination on his face, silently stared at Ned, who as usual had his paper in front of him with his old battered dictionary trying to solve the crossword puzzle. After a while Ned looked up and Jack held his gaze looking directly into Ned’s eyes, Ned responded with his normal growl and then as the silence grew longer and longer, he gave in and said,

“Ok Jack you have my permission”

“What’s permission mean?” Jack answered.

“Well it means that he’s giving you the ok,” said Audrey

“Ok for what,” Jack said, continuing to look deeply into Ned’s eyes, his face screwed up in concentration.

“It means that it’s ok for you to call me Grandad Ned like Theo does,” Ned said not looking up from his crossword.

“Theo doesn’t call you Grandad Ned, neither do Holly and Liz” shouted Jack indignantly raising his body to an upright position.

“Really what do they call me then?” came the curious reply.

“Everyone calls you Grumpsy,” mumbled Jack, getting down from the stool and standing legs apart, hands on hips, striking his superman pose.

“No they don’t,” said Ned sticking his chin out and puckering his lips.

“No, **e v e r y b o d y** doesn’t call you Grumpsy,” said Jack quite innocently “Nana Audrey calls you Mr Grumpsy and sometimes Mr know it all Grumpsy and sometimes she even puts a swear word in.”

With that Celia snatched up some of the remaining biscuits with one hand and grabbed one of Jack’s hands with the other, Audrey quickly caught hold of Jack’s remaining free hand.

“Time to feed the ducks Jack,” they said in unison lifting him off the floor and swinging him towards the door.

“Yippee more swings, more swings,” Jack squealed at the top of his voice.

All three left at some speed through the door into the garden, almost running towards the widest part of the moat, where the ducks waited.

Celia and Audrey sat by the moat congratulating themselves on their coordination, resulting in a speedy exit and watched Jack feed the ducks. Audrey stood and looked around to see if the coast was clear, she did a 360 degree turn in search of Ned’s familiar frame, but thank the Lord it was nowhere to be seen.

“I think we should get back to start lunch,” said Audrey with some reluctance.

Celia said, "I have to take Jack to his activity class, but I should be back by 12.30 to help out." Audrey went reluctantly back into the Castle to face the wrath that was Ned. Luckily, he was nowhere to be seen, so she raided the larder and decided on baked potatoes and baked beans with a salad for lunch.

Once everyone was assembled and lunch was being devoured by all ten diners, Audrey sprang into action.

"We've been settling in now for a little while, we've got each one of our bedrooms and bathrooms arranged the way we all want them, the kitchen is looking reasonably cosy and the sitting room is just perfect."

When they first looked into the sitting room, which was at the front of the property, it had astounded them. Three, four seater red leather sofas were arranged in front of an old Victorian fireplace, the room had all its original features. Ornate coving framed the two large ceiling roses each one having a chandelier hanging from the middle. High white skirting boards surrounded the new laminate flooring and a few very expensive blue and red patterned rugs were scattered around. A large square antique coffee table was placed in front of the fire and in-between the three sofas, which made it a lovely family area for conversation in the evening. They had all agreed it was perfect, the sun streamed through a large bay window in the early evening that lit up the scene of tranquillity and splendour.

"So I'm thinking about Christmas, I know we said we wouldn't open up rooms until we needed them, but I've invited the girls, with their families for Christmas lunch and a stopover on Christmas Eve and Christmas night. They've all accepted and I'm really looking forward to having the entire family under one roof for the first time in years," continued Audrey.

After a minute's silence everyone joined in with, "Christmas is months away."

"I know it is guys, but I like to think ahead, we will need at least six, maybe seven bedrooms opening up. There will be five adults, unless Jan has lassoed an unsuspecting male plus eight children. We may have to redecorate and we most definitely will have to clean each room, buy new bedding etc. The kitchen only sits ten of us; maybe we could fit another four at the most, which means we are going to have to open up another room on this level that will seat twenty-three people. All in all I don't think that is going to take five minutes do you?" said Audrey eyebrows raised willing anyone to actually answer the question or argue the point.

Louisa cleared her throat and said in a small apologetic voice, "I'm afraid we have a few more than that," her face was contorted into a grimace and a smile.

All eyes were now on Louisa, who was very slim and only just a smidgen over 5ft tall, a complete opposite to her husband's large 6ft frame. Greg was looking at her in complete puzzlement.

"Mmmmm well errrr, Janet and Jack sorta, kinda like, invited themselves around for Christmas lunch and of course Jjjjack Jnr," stuttered Louisa.

The sentence started as a slow foxtrot and ended up as a quickstep, almost as though the quicker she said the last part, the more likely the statement would escape everyone's notice.

Sensing her daughter-in-law's nervousness and predicting the rest of the family's reactions, Audrey said cheerily, "oh no problem, the more the merrier, another three won't make any difference, more people to help with the clearing up operation after we've eaten."

Louisa looked relieved; she smiled sweetly and mouthed the words "thank yooouuuu" to Audrey and blew her a kiss. Audrey winked back at her and sneaked out a little grin.

Ned growled.

Greg looked around in disbelief, everyone else was stunned into silence, not for long however, the room broke into a buzz until Audrey took charge again explaining her plan of action.

"This afternoon I will go with Celia and Louisa, we'll open the doors we can open with the keys we've got from the Estate Agents, do an inventory of each room on this floor and the one above to see if we can find some suitable dining room furniture. The old games room next to the drawing room may be the best option for a new dining room, but I'm not sure it would fit twenty six of us, I'll measure it to see."

"Surely the dining room would have been on this floor not on the one above, imagine trying to carry your dinner upstairs, it'd be cold by the time you got to sit down?" Holly queried.

"Not necessarily they used to have dumb waiters to hoist food up from the kitchen, but I haven't seen one in here." Celia commented.

"In those days Holly, they had servants, cooks and butlers to do all the fetching and carrying, the gentry wouldn't have had to do any fetching or carrying, Butlers would serve you drinks, maids would wait on tables and bring your meals to your bedrooms if you didn't fancy getting out of bed," replied Audrey.

"What's a dumb waiter?" Said Holly bemused.

Theo felt the need to chip in at this point. "It's a waiter that's dumb stupid. Can we have butlers and maids and stuff Nana?"

Holly batted him across the head and Audrey threw him a look, which said over my dead body. Theo knowing Audrey well, just shrugged his shoulders and continued playing on his mobile phone.

"Liz, Holly, Theo can you go to the second floor and make a plan of which bedrooms you think would be the easiest to do up and possibly could fit three or four beds in, perhaps we could have a girls dorm and a boys dorm. If you could make a note of which doors are locked I'll go up later and see if any of the keys fit," Audrey turned and gave out large notepads and pens to Celia and Louisa.

The three ladies went through the door and into the hallway leading to the stairs, as they left the room they heard Liz and Holly humming the theme tune from Star Wars while Theo said in a deep voice, "Rookery Castle: the final frontier. These are the voyages of the Knight family. Their continuing mission: to explore strange new worlds, to seek out new life and new civilizations, to boldly go where no human has gone before."

The women went methodically from room to room, Audrey tried each key in all the doors and when one fitted she left that door open with the key in the lock. Louisa drew a plan of each open room, doors and windows sketched in, an open padlock indicating which doors were unlocked and a closed padlock signified which ones weren't. Each room had a reference number put on the plan, the same number was then written on a sticky note stuck to the door. Celia put a tag on the keys that opened the doors with the same reference number that was on the door and the plans.

They found a library that was filled floor to ceiling with books, in the centre was a large oak desk and a leather chair. It looked as if someone at some time had started to log the books as there were several piles in one corner; a clipboard, paper and pen were perched on the top.

"Some of these books look really old, I bet they're worth a penny or two," said Celia admiringly. "Perhaps we could start cataloguing them, what do you think Audrey?"

"It would be a huge job; maybe we could persuade the other ladies from the WI to help until we can get someone in?" said Audrey as she was walking around caressing the books, that was until she found several spiders webs and an awful lot of dust.

Celia and Louisa thought it was a good idea, they agreed to bring it up at the meeting. Audrey immediately sent a text message to the WI ladies in the village asking them to meet at the manor instead of the back room of the pub.

CHAPTER 3

The Lion. The Witches and the Wardrobe.

Theo led his sisters along the corridors, having insisted on taking the lift up; the builders had got as far as installing a lift before they abandoned the project, even if it did only take four people. Well it said it took four people, but that depended on how big the people were, if the vicar got in that would take up at least three spaces, I really don't think anyone else would be able to breathe for the whole of the journey, Theo thought to himself.

Theo went straight to his Nana and Grandad's room for a quick nosy before starting to do the job of bedroom hunting. The room was very big with an old-fashioned bed; two ornate oak wardrobes and a big chest of drawers, there were two old fashioned lights on the wall above the bed, with little light pulls on them. In the corner was a door, which led to a bathroom with a big bathtub and a walk in shower. On the far wall of the bedroom was large oak door. On opening it the children realised it was another bedroom, which was slightly smaller, but when you opened up one of the wardrobe doors, you walked into a dressing room with rails of clothes and a couple of full length mirrors. Another door led into an ultra-modern bathroom with a Jacuzzi and a door by the bed led from the room into the hallway again; it was right opposite the door to the master bedroom.

"This is so cool, it must be Nana Audrey's room, I've heard her talk about her escape room when Grumpsy's snoring gets too loud. I wonder if Grandads got another room." Liz had no time to finish what she was going to say, because when she looked around Theo and Holly were just disappearing through the door into the master bedroom.

Theo opened the wardrobes but only found clothes; he started rooting through boxes stacked on the floor of the monstrous wardrobe, but on leaning in, Holly kicked his bottom and he fell forward head first into the space, head-butting the back of the wardrobe.

"It's hollow," he said banging on the panel at the back, his fist picked out what seemed like a drawer with a small round knob in the middle. He struggled for a minute or two but eventually managed to pull the handle and a drawer opened. In it was a small old-fashioned key, it looked green and a gold sort of colour. He turned the key a few times in his palm and noticed his fingers had turned a strange shade of green.

He held the prized key up in the air with a look of pride on his beaming face. "I wonder what this opens," he smiled and turned disappearing into the wardrobe, throwing clothes, shoes and boxes at Holly and Liz, "Do something with these you two, I'm going exploring."

"OHHH Yesssssss" Theo exclaimed, "I've found the hole, looks like it's been filled with chewing gum or something, I think this is a hidden door". He reached into his pocket for his treasured penknife that his Dad had bought him for Christmas, and started to burrow into the hole and pick out the substance, which was blocking it.

"Don't do that Theo. Nana said to find bedrooms for the family when they stay over Christmas," Holly whined. "We're going to get into some serious trouble."

"Mmmmm I know, but there could be a bedroom behind here just like Nan's getaway. That's it I've cleared it out and the key fits, just a little turn and hey presto."

Holly pulled him out of the way and stood in front of the door. "This is not a good idea; you are going to get us all into mega trouble."

"I'm going in no matter what you say Holly, so I suggest you get out of my way unless you want to get hurt," Theo said menacingly.

"So you are determined to open this door?" Holly said.

"Yes of course I am, it's an opportunity I can't pass by," Theo chuckled.

"Well, I won't let you." Holly stood facing Theo in the doorway of the wardrobe.

He looked at her, jaw set, his teeth clenched, and his eyes looking like a demons in his light olive face.

Holly said with resolve in her voice, “if you continue to try and get us into trouble, I will scream and scream until I can’t scream anymore; it will deafen you and raise the whole house.”

“Mmmmm, I believe you would,” he said, eyes twinkling with mischief. He started to turn towards Liz as if he’d given up; she was sitting on the bed amidst a mountain of clothes, seemingly disinterested. Theo muttered, “But I think you should be very aware of a gigantic spider just about to crawl into your hair.”

With this, she definitely did scream, running like a whirling dervish in the direction of the hallway, rushing past her older sister and desperately trying to shake the imaginary spider out of her hair.

“Holly, he’s only winding you up, oh god you are so gullible,” Liz said as she looked over Theo’s shoulder to see how far he’d got in opening the hidden door.

The door creaked open and Theo, followed by Liz and closely bringing up the rear was a very dishevelled Holly. They stepped through the frame and into a narrow corridor. “Come on you witches, get on your broomsticks and follow me,” laughed Theo.

There was no lighting, so all three of them took out their mobiles, turned on the torch app to see where they were going. They crept slowly along a long dark corridor, very aware of their own breathing. It seemed like an eternity before they came to a small landing and there was a door that was slightly ajar. Very little light adorned the room just a glow from a slit in the wall. They looked around at the old dark furniture; a four-poster bed seemed to take up most of the room and at the top of each of the four pillars was a carved lion's head. Their mobiles' torches picked out a few pieces of bedroom furniture, all covered in dust.

“This looks like Miss Havisham’s house in Great Expectations,” whispered Liz in a slightly wobbly tone.

The torches scanned the room and picked out an open door. They all crept over, Theo first, Liz next and still at the rear Holly. The young boy leaned over and shone the torch down a twisty flight of stone steps, even their breathing seemed to echo. Without speaking, one by one, they edged slowly down the steps and around a corner, there was a small landing and on the wall facing them a stone carving of a male lion had been etched into a manmade crevice. Seeing the lion gave Theo an idea, he took a big deep breath in and then let out a loud **roar**, followed by an evil laugh. A scream escaped from Holly's mouth, she jumped back up one of the steps, becoming entangled in a spider's web, with a spider still in it. Things happened very quickly but in slow motion if that's at all possible. Holly continued to scream and Liz dropped her phone, which did several somersaults down the stairs before landing on Theo's head, this made him lose his footing and go tumbling down the remaining few steps. He landed on something hard and from the glow of his mobile phone he thought it looked like a silver body, the torch started to fade as it began losing its power.

Theo rose as if by levitation from the silver body, he turned and ran up the stairs all in one swift movement his feet seemingly not touching the steps at all. He leapfrogged over Liz who was bending down retrieving her mobile; he then got stuck in the doorway with Holly as they both tried to exit at the same time. It seemed ages before they managed to unravel themselves, then all three of them fled back down the passageway with an icy white mist following them, footsteps echoing, bouncing off the walls. Just before they hurled themselves through the door at the back of the wardrobe, they heard two doors slam loudly in quick succession behind them. They hastily closed the door in the back of the wardrobe, locked it and stood there for a few moments panting; mouths open, unable to speak, frozen with fear.

One by one, they stepped out of the bedroom, shutting the door carefully behind them and started towards the stairs as if in a trance. Walking slowly and silently down the staircase, all thoughts of the lift had disappeared from their minds; they made their way down to the grand reception room.

As soon as the children had disappeared on their adventure to find bedrooms, the ladies started looking through some of the first floor rooms which had already been opened, very quickly deciding there was nothing in those of any interest. One double door was locked, trying several keys they eventually found one that fitted, it turned easily in the lock, they opened the door and walked inside. "Perfect" Audrey said, Louisa and Celia agreed this really was perfect, they'd found the old dining room. Standing in the middle was a large mahogany banqueting table with twenty blue and gold upholstered chairs, the room itself was long enough to seat quite a few more. Everywhere was thick with dust and would probably take a couple of days to give it a good clean.

On one wall was a tall sturdy serving dresser with lots of drawers and doors in it. It stood a little proud from the wall and so Louisa took a peak behind. "There's a door here Audrey I wonder where that leads to?"

The three ladies tried to move the obstruction, but it wouldn't budge.

"We'll have to get the boys in to look at this, I think big guns are needed," Louisa laughed as she looked in all the drawers and cupboards.

The women looked and felt grubby and so it was decided a break was needed.

"Perhaps if we go on the internet we could get a similar but much smaller table and another six chairs to match the ones already in there," Audrey said as they headed towards the kitchen for a cuppa and a conflab.

They passed through the reception room and were greeted with the sight of the children standing at the bottom of the stairs.

Celia said, "What's wrong with you? You look as if you've seen a ghost."

With that, all three of them started to cry and were babbling their story most incoherently. After a couple minutes of wailing, many tears and a few hysterical screams, a voice boomed in the background and Greg appeared in the doorway.

"Enough" he said with authority, "Calm down everyone, let's all go to the kitchen." With no hint of objection, they trooped in a straight line out of the reception room, down the hallway and into the kitchen.

Greg was not pleased by any stretch of the imagination; he didn't have time for this sort of nonsense. Towering head and shoulders over everyone, legs spread apart, hands on hips he said, "Right what's going on, I want the short version, no frills or exaggerations, just the facts."

The three children all started to talk at once, until Greg held his hand up in a stop motion, giving them a withering look at the same time. "Liz you take the helm please," he said.

Liz took control being the eldest, "Well the short version is, Nana sent us upstairs to look at the bedrooms, Theo started to nosey around Nana and Grumpsy's bedroom," she was cut off in mid-sentence.

"I was trying to find a bedroom like Nana's, with a secret room in it," said Theo indignantly.

Greg threw him 'the look', and he shut up. He looked over at Theo and Holly, "if anyone else interrupts they will have to leave the room, and they'll be grounded for a week, you can all have your say later." He looked at Liz nodding for her to continue.

"Theo found a door in the back of Grumpsy's wardrobe, he opened it, and we all went down a dark passageway, through a door, into a room, and down some creepy steps. Theo slipped and landed on a body. We ran back along the passageway and we heard footsteps behind us, it was very cold and a white cloud followed us, two doors slammed. We locked the secret door, came downstairs and started to tell everyone what had happened, that's when you came in," Liz smiled smugly feeling very proud that she'd explained it all so well in such a short space of time.

"Ok well done Liz, I think we should investigate this hidden room, but we can't all go there, so I'll just take Theo and mum, Theo you lead the way."

Greg got three powerful torches from the cloakroom and then threw out an arm in the direction of the hallway door, Theo went striding through it and Audrey saluted Greg as she disappeared towards the lift.

Audrey was appalled when she saw the state of the bedroom, clothes and shoeboxes strewn over the bed and floor, she bristled and tutted as she looked at the boy.

Theo looking suitably chastised went over to the wardrobe, turned the key in the lock and opened the hidden door. The boy stepped nervously into the corridor, followed by Greg and Audrey; it was dark, damp and eerie. They shone their torches up and down the walls, ceiling and floor, as they proceeded, trying to take in the full picture of this old stone passageway.

Eventually after a couple of minutes, their torches picked out an open door and they all went in, the light from the torches threw shadows around the room, giving the impression of movement even though there was none. In the room they saw a huge four-poster bed, a giant carved wardrobe and a chest of drawers with candles, everything thick with dust and cobwebs, definitely not an inviting site. Theo refused to go anywhere near the stairs and so Greg and Audrey went to investigate. The two powerful torches picked out 'the body', which was an old suit of armour. Just to the right of the armour at the bottom of the steps, was a huge door with ornate hinges, it was slightly ajar. Greg tried to peer around it, but even shining the torch through the gap, he couldn't see anything. He tried to pull the door open, but only managed to move it a few inches. Nevertheless, that was enough for him to brace his back against the wall and push it open further. The door creaked and groaned then started to sway. Just in time, he pushed himself through the opening. The door came crashing down on top of the armour, missing Audrey by a few inches. She coughed as years of dust rose and started to choke her; she got a handkerchief out of her pocket and held it over her mouth.

"Are you ok Mum," Greg said with concern as he peered up the stairs to where Audrey was sitting. She nodded her head unable to speak in case the dust went into her throat.

Whoosh, a cold white misty cloud rose from underneath the fallen door. Audrey sat transfixed; she knew just what the children were talking about. The icy cold cloud went right through her, making her whole body tingle and then it seemed to float to the top of the steps disappearing from sight.

She heard footsteps echoing and gradually fading as they seemed to get farther and farther away.

“Wow mum look at this” Greg shouted beckoning her over. “It looks like the old servants' quarters.”

Four small rickety beds were in a row, only a few inches between each one. A cracked mirror was anchored to the wall opposite with a large nail. A rail was constructed in the corner; it looked as though it could have been a wardrobe at one time. A chest of four drawers stood with a washbowl and jug on top with one solitary candle in a rusty holder. Everything was covered in cobwebs and a mouse went scurrying across the room.

Greg tried the handle of another door, which was situated opposite the one that had just collapsed. It wouldn’t budge, the handle turned but there was no give in the door at all. He turned to Audrey and said, “I wonder if any of those keys you have will fit this lock?”

“Not sure darling, perhaps we should try them tomorrow. I think I need a shower and I would like to be around when and if, you open that door.”

They both backtracked using the fallen door as a bridge over the first few steps, climbed the remaining winding stairs and through the room with the four-poster bed. Theo was nowhere in sight, so they both presumed he had run, when he heard the door collapse. They proceeded along the passageway, and started through the concealed door into the wardrobe, Audrey heard the slamming of two doors, and she turned to see the mist, hanging like a cloud in the passageway just behind them, they locked the door and stood for a moment in the Master bedroom. Theo appeared in the doorway with Louisa and Celia, “is everything alright? Theo said there was a loud bang, he ran downstairs to get us,” Louisa said with great concern in her voice.

“We’re fine Hun don’t worry, a door fell off its hinges, I was trying to murder mum but she moved too fast,” Greg said, his teeth seemed to be even whiter now that his face was two shades darker with dirt.

Audrey had been quiet and deep in thought on the journey, completely ignoring Greg's conversation about what could be on the other side of the door. When they got back into the kitchen, Pete, Bobby and Ned had returned and after hearing Liz and Holly's story of 'the body', Pete and Bobby couldn't stop laughing. Ned just said "Poppycock" and made yet another attempt at his crossword.

"Well Dad," said Liz "Did you see it, the body, did you, did you?"

All three children were eager to get their fathers opinion of the situation.

Greg took centre stage, "The body was a suit of armour," the three children sighed with both disappointment and relief at the same time. "There was a door at the bottom that collapsed when I tried to move it, which means the armour is probably completely crushed. There is a bedroom down there that looks as though it could have been servant's quarters and another door that we couldn't open, we're going to try the spare keys tomorrow and do some investigating. We went along a passageway that seemed to slope down and the stairs went on for quite a way. It definitely looked like servants quarters, so I should imagine there are more steps which could lead to a basement, we will have to wait and see." Greg continued, "In the meantime, Theo, Holly, Liz, go upstairs and tidy up that bedroom you've completely demolished, it's now 4 o'clock and dinner is in two hours, you don't eat until I've inspected the bomb site and Grandad Ned is happy with your efforts."

"But did you feel the cold and see the white mist, did you hear the footsteps Dad?" said Theo with an eager look on his face.

"Theo, it is a very old castle, it's very draughty and of course you are going to feel cold chills when you open up a room that has been closed for years, the mist was probably dust that you disturbed. I think the footsteps you heard were your own, the passageway and the room echoed when we spoke, so it wasn't all in your imagination. You were frightened and I don't blame you, it isn't the sort of place that oozes tranquillity. Don't go reading something into nothing, now upstairs please." Greg replied.

He escorted the children to the bottom of the stairs and pointed upward. Audrey went with them; she thought of it as damage limitation. She got them organised giving them all different jobs.

"Liz, hang the clothes in the other wardrobe, it's almost empty. Holly, jumpers and cardigans you can fold and put in a neat pile on top of the dressing table; I'll find a place for them later. Theo, put all the shoeboxes under the bed out of the way."

It's a good opportunity to throw some of Ned's old woollies away without him knowing, Audrey thought to herself.

They just about made it downstairs ready for dinner and after they'd eaten and while the children were clearing away Greg went to answer the front door; the bell had been rung numerous times followed by several loud knocks. Greg opened the door and was confronted by Heathbrooke's WI, led by the obnoxious Patricia, landlady of the village public house.

"Thought you weren't going to answer you took that long," Patricia bellowed, pushing past an open-mouthed Greg. Someone at some time had likened her to a raging bull in a black shroud, nobody had ever thought of a comparison more suited. She stood a little over six feet tall and if anyone had said she was an all in wrestler, no one would have batted an eyelid. Her greasy black hair was cut in a short urchin style, however an urchin she definitely didn't resemble.

Greg was almost knocked off his feet by Patricia Swinger and had only just gained his balance as Mrs Gahir the postmistress breezed in, a huge smile on her chubby face, salt and pepper hair scraped back and held in a bun at the nape of her neck. "You look lovely Mrs Gahir, beautiful outfit." Audrey said pointing to the turquoise and gold sari.

"Oh I like to make an effort dear, I don't get out much nowadays. The shop opens 7am to 11pm seven days a week, I have to rely on him indoors to take over for a few hours when I need to get out, but thank you for the compliment it is very much appreciated," she beamed as she stood in the reception room.

Julie the pharmacist tripped up the step as she staggered through the door, "Hope I'm not late. Are there refreshments served during this meeting? I'm parched," she slurred, blinking her eyes as if she were trying to focus.

"Hope you enjoyed your trip Mrs Tattershall," Greg said stifling a snigger.

She scowled at him and followed Audrey and Mrs Gahir into the Library. Just as they had entered the room the three Belle sisters who had come in through the back door followed them in. Patricia had made herself at home in the only chair. After a few minutes of greetings and polite chit chat, Celia and Louisa came in with a trolley of tea, coffee and biscuits.

"Anything stronger on offer, I've got a sore throat coming on," Julie said rubbing the front of her neck.

Audrey closed the door, "Not just at the moment Julie, perhaps a coffee will help to soothe your throat, or I do believe I have some cough sweets in the first aid cabinet."

Julie waved her hand dismissively. Everyone helped themselves to the refreshments and Julie resigned herself to a couple of hours of sobriety.

The meeting went well, all the women agreed to help organise the Library, cataloguing all the books and putting them on a computer database. Audrey closed the meeting; Patricia said she would draw up a rota when she got back to the pub and send an email out with her suggestions.

As all the visitors were leaving, Audrey took May to one side explaining the situation with the hidden rooms; she really wanted both of them to investigate the mist and footsteps before anyone else went down there. May said she would come along with her sisters the following morning declaring that there was strength in numbers.

Dinner went without event but everyone was feeling a little anxious. Louisa and Celia continued to scold the children explaining the dangers they had been in. They could have been trapped in that room for days. That seemed to do the trick and they promised that they wouldn't do anything like that again, although Theo had his fingers crossed behind his back.

A few hours later everyone went their separate ways; Audrey found herself on her own and so poured herself a very large nightcap and retired to the Kings Suite, the rooms she and Ned had chosen for themselves. Sitting in the bay window on a luxurious window seat, she sipped her whisky and pondered on the events of the day. After draining the golden liquid from the glass Audrey started to walk towards the door to the small getaway room, stopping just short of the door she turned and looked at Ned snuggled down under the blue shiny cover, his breathing deep and even. Smiling she got undressed and put on a long white sleep shirt with the words 'I'M NOT BOSSY. I'M THE BOSS' printed on the front; she slipped under the covers next to Ned cuddling up to his back. She sighed and thought how blessed she was to have such a wonderful family and such supportive and unusual friends. Audrey slipped off into a deep sleep contented and happy.

CHAPTER 4

Ghost Hunting.

Early the following morning Audrey was just washing the breakfast dishes when the three sisters breezed in. April in her normal attire, classically cut tailored cream trousers and a cream M&S sweater, her short, wavy, fair hair immaculate as usual. May floated in, blond hair loose around bare shoulders, her long pale yellow gypsy dress flowing around her slim figure.

"What's happening Aud?" Said June as she barged past her two sisters knocking them out of the way, her black cassock swaying from side to side as she stomped into the kitchen. "Hope you don't mind, I've bought Satan with me, can I leave him in the cloakroom with your pooches?"

"No problem June, Pete will be taking them for a walk in a while, I'm sure one more dog won't make any difference," Audrey made four cups of coffee and explained what had happened the previous day.

"Did the mist go around you, or through you Audrey?" Said May head tilted to one side, deep lines appearing on her forehead as she frowned.

"Definitely went through me, I felt a weird muscle spasm, a sort of tingle that lasted a few seconds, my legs went very weak, and I had a feeling I was going to vomit. Luckily no one was paying any attention to me at the time, so they didn't notice and I definitely heard the footsteps walking quickly away from the room." Audrey said with an involuntary shiver.

April stood up, pushing the chair back she said. "Well come on girls we'll risk it for a biscuit, let's go and see what this spirit is up to, lead the way Gunga Din and don't forget your set of keys, everyone grab a torch." She bit a perfect crescent shape out of the chocolate digestive she was holding, returning the remains to the plate. Picking up a torch, she swallowed her mouthful of crumbly chocolate and she said in a loud enthusiastic voice "Wagons Rollllll." She strode out along the hallway and bounded up the stairs, stopping abruptly when she realized she didn't' know where she was going. Looking behind her she saw the others standing at the bottom of the stairs looking up at her. Audrey pointed towards the lift and April joined them just as the lift doors opened. They all managed to squeeze into the small space, but it was very cozy and June thought to herself perhaps it was time to go on a diet.

They made their way to the Kings suite, through the wardrobe into the sloping passageway; the sisters looked in wonder at the stone walls, light from the torches going in all directions. Perhaps Greg could rig up some lights on the walls, Audrey thought. But that was in the future, at that moment the passageway was dark and musty, the stone walls and floor where shiny with condensation, the slightest movement was echoed and magnified a hundred times, just the breathing and footsteps of the four adventurers sounded like a gaggle of geese in chaotic chatter.

The large door stood in front of them slightly ajar, Audrey whispered, "I'm sure we shut that when we left the room yesterday." The sisters seeing the chamber for the first time stared around; it was as though the space was stuck in a time warp, everything as it would have been left many years ago. It was difficult to age the room, seemingly a mish mash of different decades. May was drawn towards the four-poster bed; she laid her hands on the wooden posts caressing them and then put her arms around each one, hugging them in turn. Her eyes closed as if willing them to speak. After a few minutes, she leaned over and reached for a small white piece of cloth, it was dirty and yellow with age but she could just make out some hand-embroidered initials on the corner, it looked like BAB. She crunched it up in her hand and raised it to her nose, sniffed it and then placed it on her cheek.

A whirlwind entered the room, bouncing off the walls and a white mist swirled around them, similar to a low-lying fog on marshland. They all jumped and stood wide-eyed watching the mist travel around them, as if by an unseen hand, the piece of cloth was snatched from May and it fluttered down resting on the bed where it had laid for so many years. May sat on the bed and put her hand on top of the cloth again; a gust of wind hit her and threw her back on the bed.

"That's quite enough thank you," said May, sounding confident. "I don't know who or what you are, but I can assure you that we will find out with or without your help. So it's your decision are you going to help us or not?"

For what seemed like a very long time the women stood and sat completely still, the mist seemed to calm down and gently swirled around the room, a very quiet chuckle startled them, they looked around at each other. Audrey went over and sat with May on the bed, they held hands and the laughter got louder. The mist gathered in front of them and the shape of a man took form, small portly with a paunch, just an outline nothing very defined, as quickly as it had appeared, it disappeared again, just leaving the echoing footsteps leading away from the room.

"Well I can't say I'm sorry to see that go," said June in a very high-pitched voice, it sounded as if she had something stuck in the back of her throat. "Right, let's go before it comes back, I'm all of a sweat, my nerves are shattered, I don't think I'm cut out for this sort of thing, I need to go and have a word with the Lord to calm myself down."

The three women looked at her and then each other. Audrey was the first person to speak. "No June, we all need to stick together, I'm not going anywhere until I've done some more investigating, who's with me?" Two hands shot up straight away, they all looked at June who timidly and reluctantly raised her arm very slowly.

April relieved some of the tension in the room by saying to June, "I'm sure the lord won't mind where you are when you have a few words with him, so here is just as good a place as anywhere else." All four of them tiptoed down the steps, negotiating their way over the fallen door.

"Did you hear something?" June whispered with a degree of hysteria.

"Like what?" April's voice boomed.

"When we stepped on the door I thought I heard a moan." June's voice got even quieter.

"Probably just the door putting pressure on something underneath, nothing to worry about let's get on." answered April in a very matter of fact voice.

They went through the doorway and slowly shuffled across the dormitory style room over to the door on the other side. Audrey tried several keys before she found one that fitted, it was a large brass key very similar to the old key that opened the church door. She tried to turn it, but it only turned half way and then stuck, she tried with all her effort but it wouldn't budge. April fished in her small cream leather bag and bought out a shiny silver pen. "Try this as a lever," she said while holding her torch directly on the key and lock. Audrey put the pen into the ring at the top of the key, but couldn't quite get the leverage she needed. June took over, she said a quick prayer and with one almighty effort, the key finally did a complete turn and the door opened.

They walked into a small room with only a tiny window for light, it was sparsely furnished with a rickety old table and chairs, by the style and type of wood, Audrey estimated it could have been made in the early 1900's, as was the furniture in the dormitory bedroom next door. A cabinet stood on its own, with a few plates and cups sitting on a faded lace doily, next to it a very battered easy chair, which looked as if it were an apartment block for the local mice population, apart from that the room was cold, bare and uninviting. April walked over to a door set on the opposite side of the window, carefully pulling the handle, slowly and noisily it jerked open inch by inch to reveal another set of steps very similar to the ones they had just descended. Audrey looked at her mobile phone, "does anyone have a mobile signal?" she asked eyebrows raised.

After a few seconds, each person in the room said "No".

"In that case I really don't think we should go any further without some backup, if we get stuck no one will know we're here. Perhaps we should come up with a plan of action, making sure we can call someone in an emergency." Everyone agreed that it was an excellent idea, although they were all disappointed at not being able to get any further.

The room turned icy cold and the wind whipped up again, all the doors slammed shut.

"Or maybe we are a little tardy with that idea ladies," stated April.

June startled by the noise flew to the door leading to the dormitory, wrapping her chubby fingers in a tight grip around the handle, she tried to yank it open, it wouldn't budge; she looked around in panic hopping from one foot to the other.

May stood next to Audrey their fingers entwined and said with a look of boredom on her face "Ok whatever your name is, we'll call you BAB for the moment; you've had your little joke, as you can see we're all absolutely terrified, now open the door. As Queen Victoria would say, 'we are not amused' and we need to get back, it's time for tea and biscuits."

Obviously BAB was getting bored with the game, because the door to the bedroom was thrown open, the wind did a circuit around the room making the ladies look as if they'd all had a bad hair day, it then disappeared with a whoosh through the door leading to the stairs, just leaving behind the echo of footsteps.

June charged through the doors and up the stairs, never faltering until she reached the wardrobe, only then did she pause, eyes closed face looking towards the heavens and said a quick thank you to her savior. Seconds later the other three came tumbling out of the wardrobe.

"I was worried you might have slammed the wardrobe door and we would have been stuck in that passageway," said April angrily before uttering "stupid girl."

They all went down to the kitchen to grab a cuppa and a few biscuits; the rest of the family had already had eleveneses and had left to perform their various duties. All the dogs were exhausted after their hour long run and so after devouring water and a few doggy treats they lay down in the cloakroom to recover.

After several biscuits and many gulps of the hot, sweet, milky beverage, the women had a quick run through of what had happened and agreed that the mist must a restless spirit, someone who was unable to pass.

Audrey said, "Does anyone remember any stories attached to the castle?"

They all looked at her and shook their heads, June shook her head so vigorously that she looked a little like a cartoon character especially as her face was still white after her experience.

June half raised her arm as if asking for permission to speak. "I did see lights blinking on and off some nights when I was taking Satan for a walk, I've mentioned that to you before. There have been some quite hasty exits from the castle, by workpeople and owners alike, but nothing bad as far as I can remember, just a bit spooky."

"Perhaps I should start looking in the Library, there must be a record of previous owners," Audrey said taking her cup to the sink. "April you're good on the internet, I'm told there's lots of information on there if you know where to look. Perhaps you could search the local papers for someone who died under mysterious circumstances?"

"Certainly can do Audrey, no problem at all, I can also look at births deaths and marriages in the village to see if that would give us a clue." April said before disappearing out of the back door and marching along the driveway to 'The Gatehouse' to get her laptop.

"I could look through the Parish records to try and find information," June said pushing the last biscuit into her mouth before anyone could pinch it.

Audrey went to the old coach house where Ned and the boys stored tools and decorating equipment, it was very cramped, several unopened boxes adorned the floor. An almost new pink bike stood by the doors, Holly had insisted she would die if she couldn't have it last Christmas, unfortunately, she only ventured out a few times; it now stood abandoned.

Tool chests galore, in every size, shape and colour, all full of tools that were either rusty or no good, or brand new and never used. Greg wouldn't use anything that wasn't the most modern or up to date and Ned wouldn't throw anything away. There were several sets of ladders, some looking a little worse for wear, but hanging from a hook on the wall was a lightweight set of aluminum steps, about 6ft high, ideal she thought and unhooked them, carrying them with some difficulty across the back courtyard through the kitchen eventually entering into the library.

When she returned June had gone to look for some old paperwork in the Church, taking her dog with her. May had acquired some old rags from the cloakroom and a bowl of soapy water.

“Cleanliness is next to Godliness,” May said winking at Audrey as she started to wring out a cloth ready for action.

Audrey looked around the room, opposite the doorway was a large bay window, an old-fashioned desk sat proudly in the middle of the room, it had a green and gold leather inlay and a hole, which would have supported an ink well in days gone by. Shelving full of books and old papers took up two of the walls, going all the way up to the top of the high ceiling.

“I would suggest we start at the top and work down, but the ladders only go half way up, so I’ll just clear the shelves I can reach. The only things we are interested in are books about the property, diaries, land deeds etc., Anything else can be dusted off, the shelf wiped down and put back for the WI ladies to catalogue.” said Audrey as she started to climb the ladders. “If you can stand on a chair May I’ll pass everything down to you, if you can stack it all on that old desk please, once we’ve cleared a shelf we’ll start the sorting out.”

“Yes boss.” May said good-humouredly.

April joined them with her laptop, signed into the castles Wi-Fi and so the work commenced. They were all so engrossed in the task; no one noticed Louisa and Celia standing in the doorway.

“So this is where you’re hiding, we missed you at lunchtime Audrey, I’ve left you some soup on the stove and there’s a crusty cob.” Celia looked at them inquisitively.

Audrey jumped and held a hand to her heart, “Good grief you almost gave me a heart attack.”

“What are you ladies doing?” Louisa laughed as she looked at Audrey and May covered in dust and grime from head to foot.

“Mmmm well girls, it’s like this. We are trying to find some history about the castle; we’re sorting out and dividing everything in here into two categories, books about the castle and paperwork, all the other books we’re putting back for the WI to sort out. Oh and obviously we’re doing a little cleaning at the same time." Audrey dusted off her clothes and run a hand through her hair as she spoke.

Louisa smiled "The boys were talking about going back through the passageway to investigate, have you found those keys yet Audrey."

Audrey sneezed and trying to think quickly said, "I seem to have mislaid the keys for the moment, but I could do with the men being distracted for a couple of days. I don't want them going up there until I've found out a bit more about this place, I'm looking for old plans and any deeds to the castle, just so I can get a better perspective on what we are getting into when we explore, I think it will be less dangerous that way."

Celia and Louisa both said that was a sensible thing to do and went off in the direction of the kitchen to hatch a plan, something to distract the men's attention away from exploring. A few minutes later Celia entered the library with a trolley of fresh juice, coffee, three bowls of steaming hot soup and crusty bread spread generously with butter.

"Well done Celia, you really are a trooper." Audrey said climbing down the steps and grabbing a glass of juice. "Don't know about you lot but I'm starving, and I've got a throat like frog." Everyone laughed and helped themselves to bowls of soup and gulped down a very welcome beverage. It was after 3pm and enough was enough. They had sorted four shelves on one wall and they hadn't even scratched the surface.

"Think it's time for a break, let's stop for today and resume another day, if that's ok with you all. I feel shattered, I really must be so unfit, I need to start an exercise routine if I'm going to be wondering around this monster property. I will definitely need more energy than I've got now." A picture of the pink shiny new bike in the coach house entered her mind and she decided to look it out a little later. It was years since she'd ridden a bicycle. "How are you getting on April?" she croaked.

"Not too bad, I've traced the owners back to just after the war but it's a bit of a void before then, I think the castle was requisitioned for a few years by the army during and just after the war, but I can look further into that. There seems to have been an awful lot of people moving in and then selling up within a few years. Nothing of real interest, a couple of articles on some strange goings on, but nothing very definite and the information is extremely sketchy. You know what newspapers are like, full of fake news and sensationalism. Some of it is very interesting though, absolutely fascinating, I'll start again later this evening." replied April.

They had just returned to the kitchen and started washing up their lunch dishes when the back door flung open. Patricia ran in breathing heavily, arms flaying all over the place and clutching a piece of paper. Ro....rog....roger she stuttered.

"Calm down dear, you'll have a heart attack and then we'll never find out what you're babbling about," said April rather uncharitably, it was obvious to everyone that the two women didn't get on and they spied every opportunity to have a jibe at each other.

Audrey took Patricia outside to sit and calm herself down in the fresh air; she'd started to have a coughing fit. She sat gasping and panting, unbelievably reaching into her black bag and pulling out a packet of cigarettes and silver lighter with her initials engraved on it, P.M.S, Patricia Margaret Swinger.The publican had poured herself into a bright yellow jumpsuit which made her look like an oversized banana, it had Pat embroidered on the right breast pocket. Audrey wondered if anyone had actually taken the word as a command and if so would they have dared to pat the right breast of this formidable woman.

A cigarette in her right hand, she threw her hands up in the air in a dramatic gesture which caused ash to scatter about her person. Panic and a hint of excitement laced her voice. She took another long drag on her cigarette, as if instead of it being toxic fumes, it was in fact oxygen. She held her breath as though she wanted to keep the smoke a prisoner inside her lungs and then with her thin lips clenched and stretched into an inhuman grimace, a plume of smoke billowed from her nostrils, she really did look like a very angry dragon. After repeating this motion a few more times, she seemed to calm down, leaving the cigarette dangling from the corner of her lips, she stretched the piece of paper out and gave it to April with a look of smug satisfaction on her face.

"It's Roger's mums birth certificate, Victoria Edith born 21st April 1923 Mother Edith Mary Higginson, scullery maid. Father, Bertram Aynsley Beresford. Duke of Beresford."

The last few words came out very slowly and April looked up open mouthed, everyone looked aghast, momentarily stunned into silence, apart from Patricia who after lighting another cigarette seemed to get a second wind, smiling she said "I think we may just be entitled to the castle or at least some of the furnishings, if nothing else I think Roger deserves to have a title."

Other than 'The letch' you mean, said May.

Patricia ignored the remark, stuck her nose in the air and continued. "I'm going to look for a solicitor on Monday to see what's what, not that old fool Corbishley in the village; a good one. I will be here tomorrow straight after the church service, with Victoria, to help sort out the Library, after all I want to get familiar with the property, I may be moving in," with that she strutted down the driveway head in the air and disappeared out of sight.

CHAPTER 5

Seek and Ye Shall Find.

It was Sunday Morning and everyone was dressed appropriately for the church service. Even Holly and Liz had abandoned their jeans and t-shirts for summer frocks and Theo looked so handsome in his chinos and a checked short-sleeved shirt. All the boys and Ned wore their suits and Audrey, Celia and Louisa looked like an advert in Country Garden magazine. They entered the church and Audrey joined April, June and the other choir members in the seating at the side of the pulpit.

June welcomed everyone and started playing 'All things bright and beautiful' on the church organ. The choir really did sound beautiful, everyone singing with great enthusiasm, apart from Audrey, who was only allowed to mouth the words, but she did that with great feeling. James the choirmaster was leading the singers, belting out the words in his deep baritone. It was a small congregation of around forty people but they raised the roof with passionate harmony.

After a rousing sermon by June, a reading from Psalms given with great emotion by April, everyone strolled out of the church and into the Sunday summer sun. A good thirty minutes later, the Knight family arrived back at the castle; everyone changed out of their Sunday best and enjoyed their elevenses around the table in the kitchen. Discussions turned to Patricia's revelation about being related to 'The Duke'.

"What do you think Ned? Will she have a claim?" Audrey asked.

"I don't think so Audrey," said Ned smiling, "but it won't do any harm to get the solicitors involved, just to keep them up to speed. She's always tried to be a bit above her station; however, I do think that if there is anything in the castle that was an heirloom, something that belonged to that particular family, she may have a claim against it. Which if you are looking at some of the antique furniture, paintings etc., that could be worth a pretty penny."

Everyone around the table agreed that it was worth informing the solicitors, just in case the situation got out of hand.

“If there is anything in the property that the Swinger family is entitled to, it wouldn’t bother me letting it go. I’ve always felt quite sorry for Patricia, with what happened to her family.”

Everyone looked at Audrey questioningly.

“Don’t tell me you didn’t know?” Audrey gasped in disbelief.

The family looked at each other and shook their heads.

“Well they were quite wealthy at one time; they lived just outside Derby in a very large house. Apparently, Patricia and her mother were unbearably arrogant and they led the servants a right merry dance. They thought most people were beneath them and treated them like dirt. Then her father made some bad investments, got into a lot of debt, couldn’t cope with the situation and took his own life. Mother and daughter were thrown out of their home; it had to be sold to pay off some of his debts. They had to live in a council flat; they were penniless and had to get jobs to make ends meet, obviously never having to work before, they had no qualifications or experience, so the job market was limited. Patricia started working in the local pub and her mother got a job as a cleaner, a big upheaval for them and you can imagine what happened when they came across anyone they’d treated badly. I do believe they went through a really rough time.”

“What goes around comes round,” Louisa said.

“It sounds to me as though the title is more important to the Swingers than the money would be,” suggested Celia.

They all agreed that it would be an absolute nightmare for the villagers if ‘the letch’ and his wife gained titles.

“Well no use surmising. I don’t think it will affect us too much do you Audrey?” said Ned scraping his chair back and heading towards the back door. The dogs were smiling and crying knowing it was time for ‘walkies’.

“Whatever,” said Audrey, “it is what it is and we don’t know what’s going to happen.”

Celia and Louisa started the Sunday lunch telling everyone to be back in the kitchen by 3 o'clock. Greg announced he was going to look at running an extension cable from Ned's room, to see how far he could go. He'd already collected a few long extensions from the coach house and he'd been into town and got some garden lights from the cheap shop.

"I think you should take Pete and Bobby to help you, there's safety in numbers, I'll look for those keys when I've got a minute," Audrey said crossing her fingers behind her back.

"More like hindrance than help, but ok, if you want me to. Anything to keep you happy mum." Greg looked at his younger brothers' tutted and sighed and with a quick flick of his head, he motioned to the back door. Before they could make their exit, Ned came tumbling in through the doorway from the cloakroom, arms laden with reels and garden lights, followed by three very excited dogs and a grumpy cat. "Thought I'd give you a hand. I've left the other lights and extensions in the cloakroom, couldn't carry them all."

"Are you sure it's a wise decision to help the boys Ned, you know your DIY skills are a little lacking dear and it's going to be extremely dusty." Audrey said trying to get the boys out of a difficult situation.

"I'll be fine Audrey, I taught these boys all they know, I'll just be supervising."

It was the boys turn to let out a disappointed growl.

"The dogs are going to be upset, they thought they were going for a you know what." Audrey said touching her nose and raising her eyebrows.

"Oh ok Audrey, you win, come on Duke you lead the way, just a short one, can't leave the boys to do all the work." Ned followed Duke out of the house, closely followed by Sky and Sheppey; Cinders curled up on one of the dog beds and purred contentedly.

All three boys smiled at Audrey and said, "Well done." Laden with cables, reels, and lights they decided to put all the equipment in the lift and walk up. It would save making two or three journeys.

The Belle sisters weren't coming around today; it being the Sabbath. June frowned on any type of work other than prayers and singing. There was another service at 5.15pm and at 7.30pm; Audrey had declined to join the choir this evening, saying she had too much to do. Nobody would miss her anyway, she told James, since she didn't actually utter a sound.

Greg had put in a doorbell with a pretty ding, dong, ding. He hadn't been very happy when he found Theo trying to alter it to the theme from the Munsters but fortunately he hadn't succeeded. When the doorbell rang out Audrey answered it, finding Patricia, Victoria and Mrs Gahir on the doorstep. "Oh how lovely to see you all, do come in, but I thought you were doing this on a rota basis?"

"We are dear," said Mrs Gahir looking at Patricia, her face lit up with a wide smile.

"Well me and Victoria, or is it Victoria and I, thought we'd lend a hand for a couple of hours. I know it isn't our turn, but we thought it our duty with Roger being the heir and everything." Patricia replied rushing through the door with her mother-in-law in tow.

The window and the door in the library had been left open to let in some fresh air. It looked a little less gloomy and dirty today. Patricia eased her bulk around the desk and sat Victoria on the room's one and only chair. The elderly woman sat staring around with a questioning look on her face. "Where's the party? It's a bit glum in here," she said, her eyes screwed up as if trying to focus.

"I said it was a work party, mother-in-law, we're helping to sort the library out." shouted Patricia very slowly.

"What library? Where are we? Any cakes going? You can't have a party without cakes, it just ain't right."

Patricia frowned, "We are at Rookery Castle mother-in-law, you know the one your dad the Duke used to live in."

"Me dad, me dad, the Duke, well just listen to you Miss La de da. Me dad was a stable boy; mum said he died in a fire before I was born. Duke indeed." She laughed fit to burst, then she stopped suddenly, looked around and said "Where's the party, I want cake, is there any sherry?"

"I give up," said Patricia bristling. "Occasionally we get a few of hours of normality but then she goes back into her own world, never knows where she is from one day to another."

Audrey and the postmistress nodded and smiled sympathetically, although most of their sympathy was with Victoria, not her impatient daughter-in-law.

They all set to work sorting through books, Mrs Gahir was typing away on her laptop, putting in authors, titles and genre on a spreadsheet. About an hour or so after they'd started, Greg came in with an armful of old journals. "I found these under the floorboards in the dormitory, they were wrapped in a small blanket but it fell apart when I picked them up. The mice have been at them and they're faded, but you can still read some of the writing. The best one is the last one. It was under the others so it was fairly well protected. The first one is almost eaten away, thought you might want to look at them mum."

"I certainly do Greg, thank you for that. I'll save them until later. Are there any dates on them I wonder?" Audrey shuffled through the worn shabby books, the writing was childlike and each one had what looked like a date written on the cover. The first one was 192 but the fourth number couldn't be made out. Most of the pages were eaten away and the writing almost illegible apart from the occasional word. It'll take me ages to read these; I'll start with the first one and try to decipher it before I move onto the others. It will probably take me weeks."

Patricia looked at the books, picked up the last one, which was in much better condition than the others. "Why don't you start with this one - it's easier to read." She said flicking through the pages and stopping to read one which seemed to interest her.

"Because that isn't the way mum does things, she's a bit OCD about everything being in order. She goes mad when she takes Dad shopping," Greg said walking back towards the door.

"Well of course I do," snapped Audrey. "You have to shop up and down each aisle in order. Your dad keeps going off track and he misses aisles out. Then we only get half the shopping because I have to keep trying to find him, to bring him back to the place where he should be. Up, down, up down, up down, up down, simple."

"See what I mean," said Greg turning on his heel and filling the doorway as he walked through it. "Only one hour to dinner Mum, I'm going to wash up, can't be late or my mother- in-law won't stop moaning at me for a week."

Audrey's eyes followed her son as he left the room, when she turned around again Patricia was urgently putting books back on shelving, slamming them into position as if her life depended on it, she seemed to be very anxious and agitated. Victoria got up and started to roam around and so Patricia said she would have to take her home before she wandered off and got lost. She grabbed her mother-in-law's arm, none too gently, steering her to the front door. Victoria tried to pull herself away from Patricia's grasp, but to no avail; she was shouting about cake and sherry as they hurried through the front door, down the steps and into the car.

Mrs Gahir closed her laptop after reading a text message from her husband, her ever-smiling face turned to Audrey and said, "I have to get home to him indoors before he dies of starvation, apparently he's lost the kitchen, that is if he knew where it was in the first place. Mind you at least while he's in the shop, I know it's only his eyes that are wandering and nothing else."

"I can't imagine you having a lot of trouble in that direction Mrs Gahir; your husband seems such a quiet pleasant gentleman."

"Mmmmm the quiet ones are the worst. He's been known to have his head turned more than once. Have you seen the way he looks at you Audrey, like he's taking your clothes off, undressing you with his eyes?"

"Well I can't say I've noticed. I'm sure you must be imagining it. No-one has undressed me with their eyes for many a year, dear."

"Oh he's always had a thing for you Audrey, says you are a more glamorous version of the Queen."

They both laughed and hugged as they said their goodbyes. Audrey continued trying to read the beginning of the first journal but the light wasn't strong enough. She closed the window and left the room in search of Greg; a bright reading lamp was needed in the room and a couple of easy chairs.

It was time to eat. She didn't realise how hungry she was until a waft of deliciousness passed under her nose and she hurried to the washroom under the grand staircase, scrubbed her hands and washed her face. Only fifteen minutes to go to lunch she thought to herself. Where's Ned? I'll ask him to open a couple of bottles of wine; those journals are definitely something to celebrate. She went in search of her husband, bumping into him as he was coming out of the pantry by the kitchen. He was holding a bottle of white and a bottle of red wine, "Great minds think alike," she said taking the cold bottle of Pinot Grigio out of his hand. "Be a darling and go and get a bottle of Prosecco. Louisa loves the bubbles and I don't think I want to share the Pinot anyway." She laughed as she grabbed the bottle of red out of his other hand, spinning Ned around and pushing him back into the pantry with a quick flick of her hip on his bottom.

"Well done ladies, that dinner was absolutely fantastic, Roast Beef and Yorkshires are one of my favourites." Ned smiled as he rubbed his stomach that seemed to have grown in the last hour.

Audrey stood up and went over to the oven. She opened the door and with her crocodile oven gloves on her hands, bent over and extracted an extremely large apple crumble.

"Ohhhh," everyone exclaimed.

"Nana's special apple crumble," she said, putting it in the middle of the table in front of her husband. Celia handed out bowls and gave Ned a large spoon; he dished it out in even portions and Louisa placed steaming hot jugs of homemade custard at each end of the table.

By 5 o'clock Sunday dinner was over and all the wine consumed, even the youngest members of the family, Theo and Holly had sipped a small glass. Audrey and Ned had always allowed the children, once they got into double figures, a small glass of wine with Sunday dinner, they thought of it as responsible drinking. Once the children got into their middle teens, drinking wasn't a novelty and when all the other teenagers in the village were getting drunk and supporting hangovers, the Knight children were just having a good time.

"Well I'm as full as a bed tick," exclaimed Greg as he scraped his chair across the tile flooring and stretched. "I'm going to take the dogs for a long walk around the grounds, anyone joining me?" much to his surprise Ned, Pete, and Bobby stood up uttering their agreements. They all went into the cloakroom gathering the three very excited dogs as they passed through. They all disappeared out of the back door; the dogs weaved in and out behind the four men, as if herding them along the back courtyard and into the fields.

Theo, Holly and Liz were just sneaking through the kitchen door, hoping to slip out unnoticed to have a few hours on their mobiles, playing games or posting on social media. Then a voice boomed out stopping them in their tracks, a very loud voice for such a very petite person. "Dishes children, one clears and cleans the table, one fills the dishwasher and one can wash the saucepans. Then you can have a couple of hours to yourselves before you empty the dishwasher and put everything away. I'm going to sit outside with a coffee and brandy. Anyone joining me ladies?" The children groaned but knew it was completely pointless arguing with their mother. She was very placid, but when she spoke with the booming voice, they had learnt from experience resistance was futile.

Celia and Audrey smiled with approval and went to sit in the courtyard. They sipped their after dinner treats and chatted. Audrey said, "Have you devised a diversion for the men, to take their minds away from exploring?"

Celia and Louisa looked at each other and laughed, "Oh yes Audrey, we certainly have, Louisa could hardly stop laughing as she explained.

"I told Greg if he got the men to clear and clean the coach house, he could build shelving, workbenches and tool cupboards. Once all the toolboxes had been emptied, he would be able to see what tools he was missing and go shopping for some new toys."

They all laughed and agreed that once Greg had 'new toys' in his head, the other three men wouldn't stand a chance. Ned would have to be with him 24/7 so that his son didn't throw away any of the rusty old keepsakes. The other two boys would try to get out of the 'Coach House Spring Clean', but Greg and Ned would make avoidance impossible and so they would just resign themselves to the inevitable. The now cluttered, dirty and disorganised dumping area would be transformed into a clean, tidy and extremely well-organised work area, keeping all four of the men out of the house and busy for several days. Louisa had dropped in the words, workbenches and tools several times; her husband's mind had drifted off into DIY heaven.

It was gone 7 o'clock when the men returned. Greg had insisted on surveying the bombsite which was the coach house, making plans for the clear out and gave his father and siblings jobs to do the following morning.

"How did you get on with the electrics in the passageway Greg?" Audrey enquired.

"Good Mum, We've coupled a few heavy duty reels of cable from the bedroom through the passageway and attached small floodlights. Two in the passageway, one in the four-poster room, two on the stairs and one in the dormitory. We can see a lot better now, it's definitely less spooky. After we'd done it, we all agreed it needs a qualified electrician to put something more permanent in there. Have you looked for those keys yet?"

"A qualified electrician, the more I think about it the more I'm convinced that is the way to go Greg. Could you see to that? It will probably take a couple of weeks to get someone to start on it and in the meantime the temporary lights will do very nicely." Ned said helping himself to a port.

"I just haven't had time to look for the keys properly," Audrey said as they were walking through the reception area towards the sitting room. This lying was getting easier with practice she thought, not quite convincing herself.

The family all met in the sitting room after the children had finished their chores, spending a few hours chatting and laughing about everything and nothing. The youngsters drank hot chocolate and the adults held large tumblers of their favourite tipple. All happy and tired, one by one they drifted off to bed, Ned locking up before retiring for the night.

Audrey was the only one left, she bought the journals from the library into the sitting room, along with a torch and a magnifying glass she'd borrowed from Theo. The writing was almost illegible and so reading it was very difficult. The holes that the mice had made rendered some of the pages impossible to decipher and she could only make out a few words. Although she wasn't too sure, she thought it revolved around the writer starting to work, presumably at the castle. The kitchen was mentioned; she saw the words cook and Mrs Shufflebotham. After several pages a birthday was mentioned, 14years old, a card and a box of chocolates. Some reminiscence followed about their dad, who had died. Audrey couldn't read anymore, not only were her eyes closing but the next few pages were faded and half eaten away.

She laid the open book down on the coffee table, yawning and stretching as the grandfather clock in the reception area chimed midnight. Time for bed she thought. She leaned forward to pick up the book to put it back in the library when the room went cold and the pages started to flip over until it closed. An invisible hand started to write on the front cover, 'Edith', but as quickly as the writing appeared, it faded. "Thank you for that information Sir, I'm very grateful, is there anything else you think I should know?" she said to the empty room. A quiet sniffle could just be heard, as though someone had a cold or was crying. The room came up to temperature again, she stood up book in hand and returned it to the library. She decided it was time to go to bed, tomorrow was another day and hopefully she would be able to solve some of the mysteries of the castle. She remembered Victoria's birth certificate that Patricia had showed them the day before. The mother was Edith. Could it be too much of a coincidence for there to be another Edith working in the castle? It was quite a common name in the early 1900's; Audrey's mother had a Aunt called Edith and so did Ned's father, so that was a possibility.

She took the lift to the second floor. Whilst the metal contraption ambled slowly upwards Audrey remembered the pink bicycle, she made a mental note to try to ride it tomorrow and that should be fun. She attempted to remember the last time she'd done any cycling and recalled it was probably when she was a teenager, before she'd learnt how to drive.

Audrey lay on the bed listening to the rhythm of Ned's snoring in the other room. She snuggled into a white candlewick dressing gown that was pulled tightly around her body. She was feeling a little apprehensive about the keep fit malarkey she'd talked herself into, but drifted off after a few minutes into a deep and dreamless sleep.

CHAPTER 6

I want to ride my bicycle; I want to ride my bike.

Monday morning and Theo and Holly went to school. School was breaking up in a few weeks and the children just couldn't wait. It was Liz's day off; the salon didn't open again until Tuesday. Liz had decided when her mother finished work she was still going to carry on and finish her apprenticeship, so she continued working at 'The Hair Hub' in the nearby town, transport wasn't a problem she had passed her test a year ago, and bought herself car. Liz really wanted to open her own salon. She hadn't approached her mum or nana yet, but she was sure they would help her fund it, fingers crossed.

Audrey extracted the pink bicycle from the Coach House, just as Greg and his three unwilling helpers arrived.

"Audrey, surely you're not going to try and ride that," said Ned as he looked disapprovingly at the pink cycle.

"No of course I'm not Ned, I thought I'd pull it apart and make a Lamborghini out of it," Audrey replied curtly.

Louisa came running over with the pink helmet she'd found in Holly's wardrobe, handing it over with a flourish to Audrey, who plonked it on her head. She adjusted the helmet strap and at the same time threw her leg over the seat, straggled the machine as though she was a veteran rider. Well veteran she was, but a rider she definitely wasn't.

"Careful Audrey you're bound to fall off," called Ned as she pushed herself away from the onlookers.

"No.....I...won't," she said very slowly, but before she'd finished the last word the bicycle swayed from side to side and then tipped over, leaving Audrey in a heap on the floor.

"Told you so," said Ned, starting to walk away quite quickly, before Audrey had time to gather herself and take revenge.

“Perhaps more practice on the grass Audrey, that’s how we taught the kids. It saved on plasters, disinfectant and tears,” Louisa said supportively.

The men retired to the coach house to start their clear out, Louisa went indoors to start her days work and Audrey continued to practice on the grass. After an hour or so Audrey was a lot more confident and was riding up and down the driveway quite safely.

Elevenses were served and everyone sat around discussing their plans for the day. Greg had managed to find an electrician who was arriving this afternoon around 5pm to look at the job.

“Well done,” said Ned, devouring his third biscuit and second cup of coffee, “How did you manage that? I thought electricians were in great demand. I expected to have to wait weeks to get one out here.”

“Simple dad, I used my initiative. Tom Belle was an electrician before he retired a few years ago. In fact he lectured at the sixth form college until his wife died. He took it so badly he sort of gave up on life for a while. I spoke to April about it and she said it would be a good project for him, give him something to do to occupy himself.”

“What a wonderful idea Greg; he’s such a lovely man and still very bright and active despite being an octogenarian.” Audrey smiled at her son with approval. “I won’t be here for dinner this evening, its choir practice and then we’re all going to the pub for a quick drink. The sisters are coming over this afternoon and so I thought we’d sit in the back courtyard and have some scones and jam before we go.”

Ned was just getting up to go back to the coach house when a thought struck him. “Oh by the way, I’ve telephoned the solicitor and given him the low down on the ‘Swingers’. He says he doesn’t think we’ll have any problems but he will look into it. He’s more of a conveyancing man but he knows someone who can do the research and give us an answer.”

Everyone nodded their recognition of the information and dispersed leaving Audrey, Louisa and Celia to clear up. Louisa was deep in thought and Audrey asked her if something was the matter.

"Oh Audrey, I know I gave up work to help with the house but I am missing it so much. It's lovely here, but I miss the interaction with the girls at the salon. I don't want to let you down, leaving you with all this work."

Audrey gave her a big hug and said "Why don't you just work a couple of days a week it will do you good to get away. I realise this project is quite a daunting task and after all there's no hurry, we have a lifetime of exploration and designing to look forward to. In fact think about opening your own salon with Liz next year. I know that's what she wants and Gill Braydon is close to retirement - perhaps you could consider taking over?"

Louisa jumped up and down with excitement. "How wonderful, but wouldn't that mean you and mum having to do more work?"

"If push came to shove we could well afford to take someone on from the village. They could do some of the more mundane work and you have to do what is right for you. I was only thinking the other day, that even when we've sorted all the rooms to our liking the day-to-day cleaning is going to be a humungous task. I think I may just enjoy putting my feet up and watching someone else work." Audrey laughed and left mother and daughter to continue their plans while she went to practice on her new pet project.

Audrey and the Belle sisters had just finished coffee and scones in the garden when they heard someone approaching. There was no doubt in their minds who it was, they heard 'Always look on the bright side of life', being whistled before he'd even come into sight.

"Hi Tom, how are you doing honey? Come and join us I'll get another cup, there's plenty of biscuits left," Audrey said, hugging him.

"Don't mind if I do, ta duck," he took in a breath and everyone knew what was coming as he started his rendition of 'Buddy can you spare a dime'.

Tom had worked for many years with Audrey's father Harold and his cousin Ronnie. Like Tom they liked to sing but unfortunately they only knew all the words to one song. Every Sunday lunchtime at the Potteries Workingmen's club in the middle of Hanley, Harold, Ronnie and Tom would get up and do a turn. They sang many songs, very rarely with the right lyrics, they seemed to make them up as they went along, if they ran out of steam the song ended up with a la la la or a do do do, or a whistle. The only one they ever completed word perfect was this one. Whenever Tom saw Audrey, he seized the opportunity to sing at her and today was going to be no exception.

Tom finished the last verse and then turned to his eldest daughter April.

"Oh no," she said knowing what was about to happen.

Tom began.

Though April showers may come your way.
They bring the flowers that bloom in May.

As soon as he finished the last word, he spun around to catch May's hand just as she was starting to make a hasty retreat.

Maybelle, ma bell.
These are words that go together well
My Maybelle
Maybelle, ma bell
Whistle, Whistle, Whistle

Just before June could escape from the inevitable, without faltering or even taking a breath, he started his performance,

June is bustin' out all over.
All over the meadow and the hill.

La La La La, de deeeee.

Luckily, he paused taking in a deep breath; May expertly jammed a biscuit in his mouth. Everyone breathed a sigh of relief. The ordeal was over for now, but they all knew he would continue if they didn't keep him busy.

A text message came through on the women's phones. "Good grief," said April as she grabbed her cardigan. "Choir practice, see you down there."

"I'll join you in a few minutes; I'm just going to get my bike and helmet. Tom, Greg's in the kitchen I think, just go on in."

Tom sauntered into the castle whistling an obscure tune, to find Greg.

"Audrey, surely you aren't riding that to the church, it's only five minutes' walk away?"

"Yes I am May. We're going to the pub after and I want to see what it's like on the open road."

"It's less than a mile along country lanes Audrey, hardly Route 66. Keep death off the road I say, I'll take the car." May waved and did a little jog to catch up with June; April had already disappeared through the gates.

Audrey went to the bathroom to tidy herself up, and then sneaked out of the back door not wanting to face the men, who would definitely not have approved of her mode of transport.

The choir practice went well, it lasted for two hours, which is more than enough when you're singing full pelt. Not that Audrey was, but it took great skill to mouth all the words in perfect synchronisation. Patricia was the only one who hadn't attended, everyone else was very enthusiastic. When they were ready to leave James took all the music, words and notes, putting them in his small briefcase. "I think we need a bit more practice - perhaps we could meet on Thursday for an hour? I would really like to try out a new song. 'I can see clearly now' is so beautiful and I think it will fit in nicely with our other numbers for the Harvest Festival." Everyone nodded their agreement and exited the church.

June turned the electricity off and locked the door. It seems wrong locking a church, but I suppose it's a sign of the times she thought.

Eight choir members took two cars down to 'The Raven Arms', by the time they'd got there Audrey was already waiting, Pink helmet padlocked to the front wheel she threw her head in the air. "Soooo what happened to you lot?" She smiled and went through the front door into the lounge. "I'll have a gin and tonic please Sarah, I should be ok to ride back home with just one. You all on your own dear, where's Patricia and Roger?"

Sarah handed her a glass of gin and opened a bottle of tonic, "Patricia's upstairs with Victoria she's not feeling well, keeps wandering off, it's very difficult to keep her safe with all the stairs. Roger's gone to look at a nursing home, just for a few weeks respite. I think it's all getting too much for them now, Audrey."

"Yes I'm sure it is, I wondered why Patricia wasn't at choir practice."

Everyone else had come into the lounge by the time Audrey had finished her conversation and they sat chatting and drinking for a couple of hours.

"Anymore for anymore," said Sarah looking very bored, the choir were the only people in there.

"Not for me," said Audrey, "I have to be going I can't believe the time, it's getting dark over Bill's mothers, we must be in for a spot of rain. It's not normally this dark must be the cloud cover."

Audrey said her goodbyes and went outside, it had already started raining and she regretted not putting on a raincoat. I must put a pack-a-mac in the saddlebag for emergencies; she thought to herself as she put on her helmet and started along the lanes towards home. It was quite dark and the rain was coming down very heavily. She really didn't feel that safe and she'd forgotten to bring her mobile with her; she cursed her stupidity. She felt kind of excited by the wind on her face and the earthy fragrances that came with it. She was getting very sure of herself on the bike.

A dark green ford drove by towards the village, coming a little too close to Audrey and she jerked the bike from the gutter to the narrow pavement.

A car appeared going in the opposite direction towards the village, the driver honked his horn; she tried to peddle a little closer to the grass verge. The rain lashing down made the bike more difficult to ride but Audrey concentrated and seemed to be doing quite well.

Another car was coming towards her, she felt very unsteady. She was just thinking of getting off the bike and pushing it back home when she heard a car coming up behind her. It flew past her at some speed, she couldn't see what sort of car it was and visibility wasn't good. Oh, why was she so vain, why didn't she wear her glasses, she would be able to see a lot better. The car that had just passed her turned around, the headlights dazzling her;

perhaps it was someone offering her a lift. Oh, I do hope so she thought. Her legs were trembling and panic was creeping up her chest from her stomach. The car seemed to speed up and head for her, perhaps they couldn't see her. At the last minute the car swerved and sped past.

An engine sounded behind her, a smooth, powerful one. Her lights were on front and back, and her reflectors were clean she'd made sure of that.

The vehicle grew closer and would flash by soon enough. Audrey rode as near the edge as was safe.

She looked towards the bend up ahead and felt the bike bump and tip. The left handlebar bounded out of her hand but she grabbed it again.

The wheels slide sideways. The whole bike slid sideways while Audrey felt herself fall towards the gulley between the trees and the embankment.

It's going to be alright she said to herself but it was not all right. It was all wrong.

She started to scream.

Beneath her body she felt slime. A tree loomed. A jolt and the bike swung around on its side, the back wheel pointing downhill. The front wheel had slammed into that weathered tree trunk and stopped the slide.

Sitting up she thought she heard the car's engine. It seemed to have turned around again and then she saw the headlights coming towards her once more. Feeling very vulnerable, she sensed she was in grave danger and started to cry.

With all the effort she could muster, she climbed out of the ditch and into the field behind. There was a little wood at the far edge, Audrey recognised it; it led to the back road leading to the castle. She made it to the trees thinking she would feel safer there, but no it was dark and uninviting. Which way was it? Straight ahead of course, she thought, but which way was straight ahead. Audrey was bloodied and beaten but kept going. The branches and thorns clawed and scratched at her face as she breathlessly made her way through the dark, hoping she was going in the right direction, praying that home wasn't too far away. Exhausted she came to the edge of the wooded area and couldn't think which way to go; she was completely disorientated. It had started to hail now and she could feel the tiny hailstones stinging her face and hands. Unable to see more than a few feet ahead, she peered into the darkness, water dripping down her face and into her eyes. Her whole body was shaking partly through fear and partly through cold, she was drenched. Her feet seemed heavy as the sodden earth gripped at her shoes. The mud was boggy and she lost her footing, falling headlong down a steep embankment, hitting her head on something hard and cold. Her vision was blurred she felt sick and tired, unable to remain conscious any longer her eyes flickered and closed, she fell into a dark oblivion.

The phone rang next to April's bed; she looked at the clock it was 11.30, who was calling at this time. If it were one of those foreign sales calls, she'd give them a piece of her mind. "Yes," she said gruffly, it was not a good idea to disturb April unnecessarily, particularly at that time of night.

"April it's Ned," came the reply.

"Oh hello Ned, something wrong hun?" Her tone did a complete turnaround on hearing her neighbour's voice.

"Is Audrey there April? I've rung her mobile but she's left it on the hall table or I wouldn't have disturbed you."

"The last time I saw her, Ned, was at the pub that was around 9 o'clock she was going to ride her bike back to the castle. Have you tried looking around she may have fallen asleep in the sitting room?"

"I have searched everywhere, I've even looked in the coach house, the bike isn't there." Ned sounded very anxious.

"I'm sure there's a simple explanation, I'll wake the girls, we'll take the road to the pub, you get the boys and the dogs, search all the footpaths and shortcuts leading to the village. We'll all take our mobiles with us to keep in touch. We'll find her in no time I'm sure."

It was all hands on deck, a few minutes later the both families were out in force calling Audrey's name and travelling either on foot or in cars around the castle grounds and in the surrounding lanes.

Thirty minutes later there was still no sign of Audrey, the boys decided to split up taking a dog each with a plan to fan out in different directions. The girls and Theo stayed and continued their search of the house, calling Audrey's name and looking in all the unlocked rooms.

Ned's phone rang, it was Pete "Sheppie's found her, she's breathing but she's cold and unconscious and there's blood coming from her head. We're in a ditch about half a mile away. Head towards the woods by the lanes and I'll wave my torch and set Sheppie barking."

"Have you called an ambulance?" Ned asked running full steam towards the woods at the far end of the estate.

"No, I'll text Greg and ask him to do it, then I'll text everyone else and tell them where we are," Pete said.

The search party all converged within minutes and an ambulance was on its way. Audrey had blood all over her face and there was a deep gash on her head. The blood had congealed in her matted grey hair. The boys took their jackets off and covered her up. April, May and June went to the main road and spread out to tell the ambulance where to go. The blue light could be seen from the gatehouse several seconds before the ambulance turned up at the castle entrance. April opened the gates, directing the paramedics overland to the edge of the woods. May ran in front of the ambulance, over the fields, guiding their way. The ambulance stopped and the driver called to May, "we can't get any further than this, these vehicles aren't made for this type of terrain. Is it much further?"

"No it isn't. You can see the torches just over there, that's where she is," replied May her speech coming out in gasps due to the exertion of running across the field.

"No problem, we'll get the stretcher and walk the rest of the way. Can you walk in front of us with your torch, we don't want to trip over any mounds of debris while we're carrying this." he said unloading a metal stretcher. The two men grabbed each end of the stretcher and followed May, walking slowly to the embankment where Audrey was lying still unconscious.

"You took your time, she could have died while we were waiting for you to get here," Ned growled.

June touched Ned's arm and said in a soothing voice. "Quiet Ned, let them do their job."

After a thorough examination, the paramedics put a collar on Audrey before gently loading her on the cradle stretcher and carrying her up the embankment. The boys helped to steady them and the stretcher whilst they climbed, then they walked very quickly to the ambulance. Once installed they attached several wires to Audrey, clipping them onto machines on the wall of the ambulance. An oxygen mask was put on her face and she was wrapped in a foil blanket, they secured her head and body so there was no movement. The driver started up the engine. The other man stayed in the back and was writing information on a clipboard when Ned got in the back and perched on a small bench opposite Audrey, having secured his seatbelt. They made very slow progress across the fields, but once on the road the blue lights were turned on. They sped through the lanes and once on the main road, the sirens were turned on and continued blaring all the way to the hospital fifteen miles away.

Greg followed the ambulance in the car with Pete, Bobby and May. June and April went back to the gatehouse and everyone else took the dogs back home giving Sheppie lots of praise on the way. Once back home they told the children what had happened, the three dogs had treats and everyone else had coffee and biscuits. It was too late to think about the caffeine or getting back to sleep.

"Are we having a day off school tomorrow then? It's very late and I haven't been to sleep yet," Theo said to his mother.

"We'll see Theo. You and Holly get to bed now; I'll make the decision in the morning. See if you can get some sleep - if you can doze off now, you can get a couple of hours in."

Holly stormed out "I'm always left out of everything, it just isn't fair."

Theo looked more than a little disappointed, but thought it wasn't the right time to argue. Louisa, Celia and Liz curled up on the sofas in the sitting room waiting for news from the hospital.

A little past six in the morning the boys returned they wanted a shower, a change of clothes and some food, in that order. Ned had stayed with Audrey.

"No real news to speak of," announced Greg "They were taking her to X-ray and arranging scans when I left. She's still unconscious but her breathing is stable and her heart is strong. Fingers crossed we'll know more a little later. I think we should take it in turns to go to the hospital to be with Dad, he won't leave her. When I've had something to eat, I'll take him a sandwich and some fresh clothes. There's a coffee machine at the end of the corridor so at least we can all get a drink."

"I'll do a couple of bacon butties for you to take with you. How is he Greg?" Louisa asked in a concerned voice.

"Complaining about the coffee," he smiled and Louisa let out a little chuckle.

CHAPTER 7

I Can See Clearly Now The Rain Has Gone.

Ned and the boys were all at Audrey's bedside when the doctors arrived the following morning, twelve hours after the incident. The nurse ushered them out of the room and into the corridor to allow the medical staff to discuss the case in private. It was twenty minutes before the two men and a woman came out, but it seemed a lot longer to the waiting family.

The female doctor smiled at them and said, "There is no real change since she was admitted. All the scans and x-rays have come back and it looks as though the patient has come out of it quite lightly. She just has a simple linear fracture of the skull with no complications at all from what we can see. We have put her on a powerful dose of antibiotics due to the cut and the amount of soil embedded in the wound. Mrs Knight has been sedated to allow nature to take its course. Rest is a powerful healer. As soon as the medication has worn off we're going to investigate further. However, according to the results of the tests, there were no internal bleeds, or any signs of anything other than contusions and some minor cuts. If everything goes to plan she should be home in a few days, provided that she will rest and take her medication."

"Phew that's wonderful news," said Ned, obviously very relieved. "Don't worry we'll make sure she's well taken care of. She's a very special lady."

They all shook hands with the doctors and thanked them. Ned led the boys back into Audrey's room.

A few minutes later a young police constable arrived with an older plain-clothes detective. They introduced themselves as PC Sergeant and DS Sergeant.

The four men looked at the police officers. "So what's the problem? How come we have a visit from you lot?" Ned said questioningly.

"It's to do with the incident last night Sir; we would like to ask a few questions. Obviously Mrs Knight is in no fit state to be interviewed so I'll come back a little later. In the meantime the constable will stay with you and he'll inform me when your wife has regained consciousness."

The boys started talking all at once and Ned's voice rose above them all, "I can't see why you have to be involved. Audrey fell off her bike, got confused and hit her head, simple as that. I can't see why you need to be here. I'd have thought you had better things to do with your time."

The boys nodded and muttered in agreement looking quite aggressively at the young constable. They'd played football against him last year in a charity match and they were none too impressed when he ran rings around them.

"I'm not at liberty to divulge all the details at the moment, but suffice to say it could turn out to be a police matter. I beg you good day," said the detective before turning on his heel and striding out of the room.

The boys glowered at the constable, who then went out of the room and sat on a chair in the corridor.

"What's all the noise about? I've got a stunner of a headache and I'm thirsty, anymore gin in that bottle Sarah?" Audrey said, eyes still closed and the back of her hand resting on her forehead. Her tongue was darting in and out of her mouth trying to get moisture to her lips. "I think I have someone else's tongue in my mouth. I can't feel it but I know it's there."

"Audrey Knight it's about time you woke up. We've been here for hours while you've been in the land of nod. Now stop messing about and open your eyes," said Ned pressing the buzzer for the nurse.

Audrey was completely confused, she couldn't remember very much at all but the nurse said it was quite normal and things would probably come back bit by bit. Ned and the boys filled her in on what they thought had happened, while the nurse took her blood pressure and temperature. Within a few minutes the nurse had extracted some of her blood for testing and everything was entered very efficiently on a chart that was held in place on a plastic clipboard at the foot of the hospital bed.

Ned and two of the boys had gone home for some lunch; Greg sat with his mother whilst she flitted between sleep and consciousness. During her more alert moments she and Greg tried to piece the story together.

"So I've jotted a few things down mum. You left the pub at around 9pm and you'd only travelled half way home before you fell off the bike, probably because of the dark and lack of cycling experience. You must have become disorientated, tried to get home over the fields instead of along the lanes, missed your footing in the dark and fell down the embankment hitting your head on some rocks. Dad dozed off in the sitting room until around 10.30 when he started to look for you. When he couldn't find you or the bike, he called April at the Gatehouse, that was 11ish. We got a search party together and started to look for you, finding you a couple of hours later, which would be 1am. In fact it was Sheppie that sniffed you out. The ambulance got there at 1.15, but it took quite a while for them to go over the fields, so by the time they'd examined you and got you back to the ambulance it would be getting on for 2am. I remember looking at my watch when we arrived in A&E and it was 2.30."

"I'm sure there was more to it than that Greg. I remember being very frightened and running away from something. There were bright lights shining straight into my eyes. I couldn't see properly. I do wish I could remember more," said Audrey just as the PC came back into the room.

"It appears that you will be released in a few days Mrs Knight, which is very good news. DS Sergeant would like to visit you, but he's been delayed. I've been told to stay here until a replacement can take over. Someone will be here in the corridor until he says otherwise," he said smiling at Audrey and then turning his head to frown at Greg.

Greg stood up rising himself to his full six feet two inches. "We don't need you to do that, I'm here, you can go back to the station now."

"Sorry Sir, I've been given an order, that's what my boss wants and I don't have a choice. Before you say anything else, neither do you," he said with some force, almost standing on tiptoe to try to look directly into Greg's eyes.

Greg narrowed his eyes and jutted his chin forward; he was just about to speak when a little cough from his mother made him reconsider his actions.

Audrey smiled and thanked the constable for his consideration. Greg sat back down on the hospital chair, obviously not very happy at his mother's intervention. The PC turned with a look of victory on his face and left the room to sit in the corridor.

A female PCSO took over from the constable at around 10pm, just after Audrey had persuaded Greg to go home. She was a very cheery young woman who seemed to have acquired a uniform that was a size too small. She told Audrey she would be there until early the next morning. Ned telephoned the hospital just before midnight to be told that Audrey was sleeping soundly; she'd been given some sleeping tablets and should be out cold for most of the night. The nurse explained that she was going to be doing one hourly checks throughout the night and mentioned that there was still a police presence in the corridor outside Audrey's room. Ned was baffled by that last statement, but was so tired he didn't have the energy to argue or to ask for an explanation.

When the ladies from the WI arrived to visit Audrey on Wednesday afternoon, she was feeling more like her old self, although still battered and bruised, the scratches on her face and arms still visible. There was an elderly constable sitting in the corridor, who'd been there since 6am and it was almost time for someone else to take over. When he saw the ladies walking towards him, he stood up and turned to stand in front of Audrey's door.

"May I ask your names please ladies?" he said whilst taking a sheet of paper out of his uniform pocket.

"Why do you want our names? I presume you're not planning on arresting us or asking us out on a date?" April said with a roguish smile on her face.

"It's a bit like trying to get into Stringfellow's Nightclub madam. If your name's not on the list you can't come in," he chuckled at his quick-thinking response.

He checked their names and they all trooped through the door in single file. Patricia, Mrs Gahir, Julie and all three Belle sisters. The nurse who was taking Audrey's blood pressure frowned but thought better than to mention the 'two people per bed' rule. He knew these women were not to be challenged through past experience and so moved on to the next room where he could exert his authority without too much of a backlash.

Everyone started to speak at once, apart from Julie who sat there uncharacteristically silent.

"Are you alright Julie, you're very quiet?" said June with some concern.

"Alright, alright, you ask me if I'm alright. I will never be alright again," shouted Julie in an agitated voice.

"Well spit it out woman, obviously you have something on your mind. The stage is all yours," April said briskly.

"**S o m e o n e** in the village has reported me for being drunk whilst dispensing drugs. Drunk, I mean meeeee, drunk. I can't believe anyone would hate me so much as to tell such blatant lies," Julie said spitting the words out venomously before she sagged in her chair, where she held her head in her hands and let out a gut-wrenching sob.

"Oh my dear, there, there," said June rubbing her back.

Everyone else just looked at each other, not able to find the words to comment, considering Julie had been dispensing drugs whilst slightly tipsy for many years.

"Ummm so what is going to happen to the shop?" said Mrs Gahir, who for once did not have a smile on her face.

"It will still open. Can you believe they're sending a young girl from Head Office? She's going to take over until the enquiry has finished and the council has reached its decision." Julie took a long breath in before continuing. "I don't know who it was, probably one of you lot, but I hope you know, you've ruined me. I can't believe I thought you were my friends.

I hate you all," she hissed before brushing June out of the way and running out of the room.

June ran after her, but only reached the end of the corridor before she was gasping for breath. I really must go on a diet, she thought returning to the room. June plopped down on the chair and helped herself to a biscuit from the pile on the trolley in front of Audrey. "Anyone got a can of coke or something; I've got a throat like sandpaper?"

May passed her a bottle of water from her bag and June drank it as though she'd been in the desert for days. "I'll go to the vending machine, anyone want any water while I'm there?" No one replied. May reached in her bag to check her purse for change before leaving to get some bottled water. "I'll get a couple of bottles; I've got the feeling everyone will be thirsty once you've helped yourselves to Audrey's biscuit supply."

Everyone looked around at each other, just waiting for someone to start the inevitable conversation.

Patricia was the first one to speak "Well I'm not sure what that was all about. Why she suspects us is a mystery. We would never have gone behind her back."

"No, if I had anything to say I'd say it to her face, which I've done on many occasions. I don't agree with anyone going behind her back, but she really was an accident waiting to happen," April said raising her head high.

Mrs Gahir sat very quietly, with a sheepish grin on her face. She extracted a small hand-held fan out of her handbag, turning it on full blast. "These hot flushes are driving me mad, I really can't think clearly." she said with immense frustration. "It's so hot in here," her face was changing from dark olive to a deep maroon. "I think I'm going to have to leave you ladies and get some fresh air."

They all bid Mrs Gahir goodbye and May passed her in the doorway, giving the postmistress a hug and a look of sympathy. Audrey asked Patricia if she'd got any further with her enquiries, regarding the castle and Roger's ancestry.

“That’s for me to know and you to find out Audrey. I’m sure our solicitor will be in touch when he uncovers the truth,” said Patricia, nose in the air and a look of arrogance on her face.

After an hour and several biscuits later they all left. Just as Ned, Greg and Louisa stepped through the door.

“The boys wanted to come as well, but we decided it was better to follow a rota. They will be calling in later with mum,” said Louisa giving Audrey a hug and planting a very firm kiss on her cheek. She then took out a bottle of squash and a large bag of fruit from a carrier bag she was holding.

They brought Audrey up to date with the family’s activities over the last day and then started to discuss the presence of PC Sergeant, who had taken over from the police constable at 3 o’clock that afternoon. No one could make any sense of it at all. Completely out of the blue Audrey shouted, “Cars. Cars, coming towards me, spraying me with water. They came very close. I was so frightened. A car came up behind me and knocked me off my bike and then I think it turned around and headed straight for me,” Audrey was almost hysterical at this point, her voice getting higher and higher with each word.

“Mum, I don’t think it was heading for you, you haven’t ridden a bike for years and the visibility in the lanes was really bad last night,” Greg said, a little patronisingly.

“He’s right Audrey; you were probably disorientated and just fell off your bike. It happens,” Ned chirped in.

“Sorry to be the bearer of bad news, but it isn’t quite as simple as that.” said DS Sergeant as he strolled into the room holding a piece of pink plastic in his hand. “We found this on the road and the bicycle has been recovered from a field just up the lane from the incident, it’s completely smashed, it looks as though a car has run over it, not just once but several times.” The young PC followed closely behind him taking an electronic notebook out of his top pocket. He stood in the far corner of the room eyes flitting between each occupant, scanning the room as though he was making a mental note of everyone’s reactions.

The family sat looking over at the police officer who had made the statement, open-mouthed they stared at him in disbelief.

Audrey was the first one to speak. She looked at the officer with a light of recognition in her eyes, "Bob Sergeant, is that you, goodness, I haven't seen you in about 25 years. You were in the same class as June weren't you? I heard rumours that you got married and were transferred to Manchester?"

DS Sergeant smiled at Audrey. "Well, well, I really didn't think you'd recognise me Mrs Knight; you certainly do have a good memory. Yes, yes and yes, I was in the same class as the lovely Vicar. I was transferred to Manchester, I did get married and had a boy," he waved a hand towards his son standing in the corner. "I'm very happily divorced and back here permanently now, just waiting for retirement. So that's the short version of the last twenty five years. When this is all over we'll have a catch-up. However in the meantime, I need to ask you a few questions. Hope you don't mind," he said looking at Audrey's visitors, whose jaws were still dropped, making them look like the village idiots.

"No. No. No. No." all four visitors said in unison.

"Perhaps you could just wait outside for a couple of minutes?" Bob looked at the family members.

"I think one of us should stay with mum," Greg said.

"No problem at all Mr Knight, I presume it's Mr Knight. You have your mother's look about you. Perhaps Mr Knight Snr would like to make himself comfortable and sit in?" Bob replied.

Bob Sergeant asked all the normal questions in a very casual way, enemies, upset anyone, any arguments etc.

Audrey replied to the officer's questions. "Well no, not really, I can't think of anyone who would want to harm me. Patricia and Roger Swinger have it in their heads that he's related to the Duke whose family owned Rookery Castle for many years. Julie Tattershall has been suspended, she's not too happy about that, but it was nothing to do with me. Oh and there's Mrs Gahir." Audrey smiled.

"Mrs Gahir?" Ned said with a puzzled look on his face.

"Sorry it was a joke. Mrs Gahir said her husband fancied me, but I don't think she'd go as far as to try to get rid of me," Audrey laughed and Ned joined in; the thought was so unbelievable they both found it very amusing.

"Mr Knight, were all your family at home with you when the accident happened?"

"Yes Sergeant, we were all together at the dinner table and then we went into the sitting room until around 9 o'clock. Theo and the girls went upstairs and then everyone started to drift to their rooms after that. I stayed up to wait for Audrey and dozed off for an hour. Obviously I was a little concerned when she hadn't returned home by 11 o'clock. It was then that I called The Gatehouse and spoke to April, when she said Audrey wasn't there I got the family up, the sisters joined us and we started the search."

"So everyone was in the castle between 9 and 9.30?" DS Sergeant asked.

"Yes everyone was getting ready to retire from 9 o'clock but we were all saying goodnight to each other and getting drinks from the kitchen for quite a time. I think the last to leave the sitting room was probably Bobby - he went up at about 9.45. We were talking about football until then. It was after he left that I had forty winks."

"Ok we'll leave it there for now," he said and looked over at the constable who closed his notepad. "You must be tired Mrs Knight. I believe you may be out tomorrow, so we'll make some enquiries in the village. Let's see if anyone noticed a speeding car or anything suspicious. If you can remember anything about the car or if you can add anything to your statement, please get in touch." He passed Audrey and Ned cards with his name and mobile number on. "I'm not too sure what's going on, but I'm certain we'll get to the bottom of it eventually. It could just have been a drunk driver that didn't like bicycles, particularly very pink ones," he smiled and headed towards the door. "I'll be calling in at the castle sometime tomorrow and I'll be speaking to the Belle sisters as well. Robin will take statements from everyone. I'll be a lot happier when you're at home and surrounded by your family Mrs Knight but until that happens I'll make sure that the hospital staff are aware of the circumstances and I'll get the patrols to keep their eyes open, maybe even pop in during the night."

"No need for that Bob," Ned said, "We'll make sure someone is with Audrey all the time. There's enough of us to do shifts until she's home. Perhaps you could have a word with the staff so we don't encounter any objections?"

"Certainly, I will do that Mr Knight, I'm sure there's nothing to worry about, but better safe than sorry."

"Please call me Ned, officer."

"And do call me Audrey, when anyone calls me Mrs Knight I always think of Ned's mother," Audrey smiled and shuddered at the thought.

"Ok Ned, Audrey, please continue to call me Bob, but if I'm with anyone other than Robin, perhaps you could revert to Sergeant. Some of the hierarchy are of the old school; they don't like us to be too familiar with families when we're investigating. They prefer doing the silly handshakes," Bob said, much to the amusement of everyone, particularly the three boys who were listening at the door.

Robin Sergeant opened the door and all three boys came tumbling in though the doorway, tripping over each other as they attempted to look nonchalant.

Both the police officers had grins on their faces as they nodded to both Ned and Audrey and they left the room.

"Unfortunate name to have if you join the police force, Sergeant." said Bobby.

"Sure is, Detective Sergeant Sergeant, it's a wonder he didn't call his son Constable, Police Constable Constable Sergeant," said Pete laughing.

The boys then spent a few minutes thinking of inappropriate names to be lumbered with if you joined the police force, they were laughing uncontrollably when Audrey spoke.

"I don't think they're telling us the whole story Ned," said Audrey with a slightly shaky voice.

"Yes dear, I get that impression as well, they seem to be a bit over the top but at least we know you're safe and sound," Ned grinned.

Greg reached into his pocket for his mobile phone; he started to text the rest of the family and included the Belle sisters, "I'll start organising the rota."

"How did you know about the rota Greg, you were outside the room when we were discussing it." Ned commented still grinning.

Greg looked a little sheepish before Pete came to his rescue. "Greg has inherited some of Mum's mystic powers, he's telepathic."

Everyone's eyes shot to the ceiling in mock disbelief at the statement. Pete looked proudly around the room at his ingenuity.

A couple of hours later, Louisa, Liz and Holly arrived, "Mum's getting your tea ready Ned, it's one of your favourites, liver and bacon with onion gravy and mash." said Louisa handing Audrey a clean nighty and a container with homemade chocolate chip cookies in it.

"I'm off then, can't be late. Celia's a demon when her food gets cold." Ned bent down and gave Audrey a quick peck on the lips, before heading towards the door.

Liz grabbed a cookie after giving her nana a hug, getting her purse out she said, "I'm going downstairs to get some drinks from the café. Anyone want anything?"

They gave Liz their drinks orders and she disappeared through the door.

"Oh Nana, I'm so sorry, I think all this could be my fault." sobbed Holly.

Louisa sighed, "She's got it in her head, that the accident could be something to do with school."

"School?" Audrey questioned.

“Well if you remember, a few weeks ago a couple of bullies tried to beat her up. Holly being Holly she floored both the girls and gave them a few bruises to take home,” Louisa stopped to take a breath and shove a handkerchief in the hands of her youngest daughter.

Audrey nodded, she did remember, both girls had been suspended because a teacher saw the whole thing from a classroom window.

Louisa continued, “Well one of the girls had been in trouble many times before and was expelled. Her parents weren’t happy. The girl played on the fact that we’d come into money, saying that Holly had been given preferential treatment because she was rich. We did get a solicitor's letter at the time, threatening to sue for compensation but our solicitor replied, basically saying go ahead, it’s your money you’ll be wasting.”

Audrey frowned, “I wonder if that’s what the police are worried about?”

“I wouldn’t be surprised. The Royle family are notorious in the area they live in and most of them have been in and out of prison for most of their lives. If my memory serves me well the whole family are bad uns,” Louisa’s eyebrows raised and she nodded her head several times.

“But why me, surely they’d be taking it out on Holly, or you, or Greg?”

“Because it was my pink bike you were riding Nan,” shouted Holly before blowing her nose. “It’s my fault Nana; if you had died I would have been to blame. I shouldn’t have flattened them after they tried to beat me up. Ohhhhh I feel awful, I feel soooooooooo guilty.”

“OK Holly you can drop the theatrics. Playing the drama queen isn’t appropriate at this time and there’s no one around to see what a superb actress you are,” Louisa said a little impatiently.

With that, Holly lowered the handkerchief from her face, pouted like a little girl and flounced out of the room, throwing herself sulkily onto the chair in the corridor all signs of tears gone.

Louisa and Audrey chuckled for several minutes before agreeing that Holly would make a terrific actress and perhaps they should pursue that possibility.

"I think I'll mention all that to the police when I next see them. It may be that they already know and that's why they seem to be a little over-zealous. Really if it is them, I think it's disgusting that they would try to run down a little girl," said Audrey taking a bite out of a biscuit, her face changing into a look of sublime ecstasy as it melted in her mouth.

"Don't let Holly hear you calling her a little girl Audrey, she would really throw a strop. She thinks she's all grown up now," Louisa said whilst peering through the doorway to look at her daughter who was concentrating on her mobile phone, no doubt commenting on Facebook as to the unfairness of the situation.

Liz came back with four steaming hot Lattes and they sat very contentedly dunking chocolate biscuits in their drinks and talking about this, that and really nothing at all until Pete, Bobby and Celia arrived.

It took several minutes for the handover and Audrey couldn't believe that Celia had brought in a cake tin full of carrot and walnut muffins. "I'm going to look like a house end when I leave this place," she laughed.

"No chance of that with these two lads, I'm sure they'll help you out," Celia said extracting a muffin from the tin.

"Ok you've twisted my arm Celia. Not sure I could face more than one after that huge dinner though, but if I must, I must," smiled Pete.

"Well I can't let the side down, I think I could squeeze a couple in," said Bobby grabbing two muffins, one in each hand."

"See what I mean, I've only made a dozen and I'm sure the nurses will want some. Ned and Greg will want a couple later. I'm staying with you until 11 o'clock and the boys are here until the early hours. Ned will come then and Greg will be here early in the morning. The staff are bringing a cot into the room so whoever is staying can have a doze," Celia bit into her muffin and smiled with satisfaction. "I'm not sure there'll be enough for you Audrey.

Perhaps I should have brought two dozen," Celia looked around when no one spoke. It was obvious why they hadn't made any comments - their mouths were full of carrot and walnut muffins.

Audrey finished her last mouthful and said, "Very efficient Celia, can I hazard a guess as to who has organised the rota?"

"I don't think there's doubt in anybody's mind Audrey, your son and my son-in-law is in his element. Bobby had to prize the crayons out of his hand - he was going to do a colour chart." They all laughed and nodded their heads, that was Greg alright.

The night went without incident, Audrey slept peacefully after the medications trolley came around. She wasn't left on her own at all and in the morning Ned went home and Greg enjoyed a cup of coffee and a slice of toast bought to him by the staff.

By midday, the doctors had signed Audrey off with a bag full of medication and she was driven home by her son.

CHAPTER 8

Romeo and Juliet.

“Hello Grumpsy, I’m here again, is Nana Audrey dead?”

“No Jack she isn’t dead, she’s doing fine and she’ll probably be out of hospital later today. Why did you think she was dead?”

“Cos mum and dad were saying that they hoped you’d both mention them in your will, and I thought you only had wills if you was dead, and mum said if you left her some money, she would be able to give up work. So are you going to leave her some money Grumpsy?”

Celia came into the kitchen at this point, and hearing just part of the conversation had a look of sheer horror on her face. She went over to the cupboard and started to pick out some of Jack’s favourite biscuits. “I think you may have misunderstood Jack. You shouldn’t be listening to conversations that don’t concern you,” she said.

“But I’d never get to know nuffin if I didn’t listen, specially when they think I’m asleep,” Jack whined. Sitting on the stool, legs tucked up underneath him, he leaned over towards Ned and whispered in a secretive manner: “When it was dark and I was supposed to be asleep, I crept downstairs. I think Daddy was tickling mummy because she was making funny noises, sort of laughing and crying and she kept calling daddy’s name. Don’t know why, cos he was right there in front of her.” Jack said getting down from the table, he moved over to where Celia was standing and on tiptoe tried to see into the biscuit barrel.

“I think it’s time to feed the ducks Jack,” Celia said grabbing hold of Jack's hand, guiding him forcefully towards the door.

Just as he was approaching the doorway, Jack pulled his arm away from Celia and turned towards Ned. “Well Grumpsy are you going to leave mummy some money in your will? She was talking to Aunty Louisa the other day and said she was really peed off with work. What does peed off mean Grumpsy?”

Celia managed to grab his arm again and pulled him through the doorway, pretending she hadn't heard him. "The ducks are waiting for us Jack; you don't want to disappoint them do you? Let's hurry, I'll race you."

Jack squealed with delight, and bolted through the door, running as fast as his little legs could carry him towards the moat at the side of the castle.

Celia looked back at Ned with an apologetic smile; Ned's face was contorted into a disapproving grimace. Celia beat a hasty retreat and ran after Jack, calling his name as she ran, hands full of biscuits and bread.

Ned's face melted into a smile. "Audrey would have loved that one," he said aloud, chuckling before lowering his face and continuing to study his crossword. It had only been a few days but he missed her so much.

Just before lunch, Audrey arrived home and the family, apart from Theo and Holly who were both at school, surrounded her. Liz had managed to get the afternoon off, with a promise to her boss she would work extra hours tomorrow and Saturday, to make up the shortfall. Celia was just starting to prepare a prawn salad, Audrey's favourite, when the doorbell rang. Bobby got up to answer it and ushered PC Sergeant in.

"Hope you folks don't mind, I've arranged to meet DS Sergeant here and I'm a little early. Thought I'd wait in here if it's alright with you." He smiled and looked around the room. His eyes wandered around, taking in the scene of all the people sitting around the kitchen table.

Liz looked at the handsome young police officer, and wanting to get his attention said. "Why don't you just call him Dad, it seems silly calling your Dad, DS Sergeant," she pouted, as she sat up straight in her chair and thrust her chest out. She was wearing a very tight short-sleeved T-shirt with a low scoop neck. She knew she looked good, and the light green colour suited her dark complexion. Her dark brown hair was gathered on top of her head, and secured with a green sparkling clip. It made her brown eyes look even bigger and emphasised her high cheekbones.

He stopped as if mesmerised as soon as he laid eyes on Liz and his heart started to thud in his chest. There was definitely something about her – her intense brown eyes, her slightly crooked smile – it made coherent speech almost impossible.

"Hello earth to plod, Romeo, Romeo, could you take your eyes of Juliet for a second, do you want a cuppa?" Pete said standing by the kettle.

After a short delay, the young policeman dragged his eyes away from Liz, and just nodded his head.

"Oh give me strength, love's young dream, coffee ok? Sugar and milk?" Pete enquired.

Robin cleared his throat putting on his best, I'm here on official business face, and said "Yes both please, just one spoon of sugar I'm watching my figure." He blushed realising what he'd said, but rather than dig himself a deeper hole, he decided to pretend he hadn't said it.

They all moved around the table to make room for the young man and Pete put a cup of coffee in front of him. The cup was decorated with a huge pair of lips blowing a kiss. Everyone but Liz and Robin noticed the choice of cup, smiles and nods went around the table.

Liz sat for a few minutes looking at Robin and batting her eyelashes. She felt her heart leap in her chest as his deep brown eyes met hers. She ran a hand up the back of her head making sure the clip was straight and her hair still secure, and then tugged on her fringe and smiled, flashing a set of bright white and perfect teeth which seemed to glow against her dusky olive skin.

Robin smiled across the table at Liz, his eyes shining with mischief. He'd stopped blushing now, and some of his youthful confidence had returned. He ran his fingers through his short thick black hair, took a sip of his coffee and put the cup down, still not noticing the ruby red lips painted on the side. "I'm really sorry, but I have to take statements from you all. I've seen the three ladies at the Gatehouse and now it's your turn, is there somewhere I could use to conduct a private conversation?"

"What if we said no," Greg said growling at Robin, and throwing withering looks at his eldest daughter.

"That would be fine Sir, you could come along to the station, and we could take your statements there, but DS Sergeant, he looked over at Liz and grinned, sorry Dad, thought it might be less stressful and time consuming for you all if we did it here."

"humph!" said Greg, and continued to dunk a custard cream into his coffee.

"Of course Robin no problem at all, we aren't short of space in our home as you can see," Ned laughed and stood up.

"The library might be a good place Ned. It's got a couple of chairs in there and a desk," Audrey said.

"That sounds perfect Madam. Please lead the way Sir. Feel free to come in to see me in any order. I'll only keep each person five or maybe ten minutes, no longer for the initial statements. What time do the children get back from school? About half past three is it?"

"I'm picking them up at three o'clock, so it's probably going to be half past, when we get back here." Pete was still smiling at his choice of mug for the constable.

"That sounds tailor-made, just perfect," Robin said as he stood up, winking at Liz. He slid his chair back under the table, and then followed Ned out of the room, along the corridor and into the library.

"I've already dropped Jack off, and I'm halfway through the prawn salad. I'll go first then I can get back to finish it off. Lunch is at one thirty," Celia said washing her hands and drying them on her blue checked apron, as she headed towards the library.

Greg, true to form, quickly wrote out a list of names and approximate times and pinned it on the notice board in the kitchen. He'd put himself last and so went into the cloakroom picking up a couple of balls and whistling the dogs; he went outside and headed towards the fields at the back of the castle. The dogs herded him and each other as they went through the back courtyard, weaving in and out, as they headed towards the drystone wall, which had once separated the castle from the tenanted farms. The dogs easily jumped the three foot border, and Greg climbed over the stile, which was set in the wall. The fields behind the castle had once had several tenant farmers working smallholdings, the farmers' families lived in tied cottages almost out of sight of the castle, but all that was a long time ago, the cottages had long since been abandoned and were now in disrepair.

At half past one it was Louisa's turn to be interviewed and when she entered the library she was carrying a tray. On it was a plate with a large prawn sandwich and some crisps, a glass of iced water and a coffee, milk and only one sugar, for Robin. He munched thankfully into his lunch while he was taking her statement. She told him about the family in the next village, and how they'd reacted to their daughter's expulsion from Holly's school. Once he had written everything down, they sat for a few minutes just chatting about his transfer from Manchester to the small village. She decided she really liked this young man and smiled at him as she was leaving saying "Don't mind Greg, he's a pussycat really. He's just very protective of the children. It's a family trait."

"That's the way it should be Mrs Knight, if you can't look out for your family, who will take care of them?" His smile was genuine but behind it, he was thinking of how his mother had betrayed him when she left.

DS Bob Sergeant arrived shortly before the children arrived back from school. He followed Audrey into the sitting room and they had a short chat. He started the conversation, "So it's going to be difficult trying to catch up on all the gossip for the last 25 years. Let's start with the Belle sisters. What are they doing? Are they all married?" He seemed to be very interested in June and confessed he'd had quite a crush on her at school. "I've always liked a well-rounded woman, is she still well-rounded?" he said with a twinkle in his eye.

"I suggest you see for yourself Bob. Will you be attending the family service on Sunday? I'm sure you'll be very welcome. It will give you an opportunity to get to know more people in the community," Audrey said looking over at the door as Theo and Holly walked in followed a few seconds later by Ned bringing Bob a cup of coffee and a slice of lemon drizzle cake.

Uncle Pete said we had to come in here, cos you wanted to talk to us," said Theo taking off his blazer and throwing it at the back of a chair, it missed and slid down onto the floor in a heap.

Holly curled up in one corner of the sofa, hugging a cushion and managed to look very bored, which she had perfected to a fine art.

Bob took official statements from Theo and Holly individually, using their grandparents as responsible adults due to their age. Both of them answered all the questions that were put to them and after they'd finished, Audrey told them to go into the kitchen and get a drink and a slice of cake. The evening meal would be around half past six as normal.

"Oh great, cake, I love cake," said Theo "Is it chocolate cake, Nan?"

"It could be Theo, you will have to wait and see. Go on now hun, we need to give our statements to Bob so he can be on his way," Audrey stood up and opened the door looking over at Holly.

"I don't want cake. My best jeans are getting too tight. Liz says I'm starting to look like one of the Roly Polys." Holly blew out her cheeks and pushed her arms out as though she had a football under each armpit.

"Well get yourself a piece of fruit then Holly, that's much healthier," Audrey said still holding onto the door handle with one hand and pointing into the reception room with her other hand.

Holly dragged herself off the sofa and stomped towards the door as if each leg weighed a ton.

"Perhaps if you took the dogs for a walk occasionally, you'd find your waist would miraculously decrease in size," commented Ned.

"Oh great thanks for that, it's made me feel so much better. I felt bad before but I feel like slitting my wrists now. It's what I love about you Grandpapa - your humanitarianism." Holly replied sarcastically.

"No need to thank me Holly, that's what I was put on this earth for, to nurture Roly Polys," said Ned as he screwed up his face in a fake smile.

"Oh really Ned, honestly you have no compassion whatsoever," Audrey scolded.

"Mmmm you're right, but at least I admit my little idiosyncrasies Darling."

Bob cleared his throat, trying not to laugh, "I think I should take your statements now before world war three breaks out. Are you ready?"

"Yep fire away officer. I promise to tell the truth, the whole truth and nothing but the truth," he leaned forward on his seat and said in a lowered tone "But I can't vouch for her over there. I've always suspected she had homicidal tendencies."

"Well I think I should stay well away from that comment Ned," Bob said as he flicked his finger over the page on the tablet, and wrote Ned's name down with the date. OK Ned take it from the top,

"I'll just go and get us a drink while you're interrogating him Bob, I don't want to be witness to any torture but please feel free to record his pain, so I can put it on continuous loop on my phone. It will help me sleep at night." said Audrey as she disappeared through the door.

Both men looked at each other and laughed before they continued on a more sober note.

When Audrey came back into the room ten minutes later, with two glasses of freshly squeezed orange juice, Ned left so that Bob could take her statement in privacy. She told Bob what she could remember and about the family that had tried to cause trouble for Holly at school. He said he couldn't go into too much detail, but their names had come up during his enquiries, as it generally did if anything went wrong within a twenty mile radius of the notorious family's home.

Bob's son Robin was true to his word and only took about ten minutes to take each statement from the family. Liz's statement obviously took a little longer and when she came out she had a big smile on her face. She met Holly in the passageway and they ran into the kitchen, chattering like two over-excited chimpanzees, jumping up and down, until they bumped into their father who was on his way to the library to be interviewed. They fell suddenly silent and Greg said, "We'll talk later Liz." The girls grimaced and were very quiet until he was out of earshot and then they continued their frenzied conversation.

Everyone made their way to the kitchen, including the two police officers, where they all had refreshments. The family had managed to take a half hour break to have a delicious lunch, all at different times, due to the interviews. Almost all the prawn salad had been eaten. Audrey was feeling very tired and excused herself to go upstairs and have a little nap. It had been a long and tiring day.

"I think we have everything we need at the moment, don't we Robin?" Bob said just draining the dregs from his coffee cup.

"Yes everything is done and dusted. I just have to get these statements on the system," Robin replied.

"Are we any nearer finding out what actually happened on the road on Monday evening Bob?" Ned questioned.

"We do have a few leads and we're making some progress but without witnesses it's always a little hit and miss, if you'll pardon the pun, but don't worry we'll get to the bottom of it."

Bobby stepped forward. "So does that mean you don't have a clue?"

Ned shot him a disapproving look, "Bobby, don't be rude. I'm sure they're doing everything they can."

"Just to put your mind at rest, yes we do have a clue; we have several clues which we are following up. The reason I was a little late today is that we have pulled someone in for questioning, I really can't say any more than that at the moment. We'd better let you get on, I'm sure you're all very busy. Good afternoon. We'll see ourselves out."

The two police officers disappeared through the back door taking the long way around to their cars, which were parked at the front of the building. As soon as they'd gone, the room erupted in conversation; they all felt a lot better knowing that there was someone in police custody, even if they didn't know who it was.

"I think we should have a family meeting this evening and see what we're going to do about the hidden rooms; Mum's accident has put us off the scent a little bit." Greg said standing up and scraping his chair back.

"Good idea, I'd forgotten about that," Bobby leaned back in his chair stretching. "I didn't sleep well last night; I think I'll have a powernap."

"Ok we'll wake you up in time for dinner," Louisa said "I think it calls for a takeaway tonight, we're all a little weary. How about pizza everyone?"

They all nodded in agreement and went their separate ways.

The pizza was delivered at 7 o'clock, just a little while after everyone appeared, as if by teleportation in the kitchen. Plates were out and cans and bottles had been hastily pulled out of the fridge and then they all sat down to eat.

"Goodness I didn't realise how hungry I was," Audrey muttered through a mouthful of pepperoni pizza, "I don't usually manage three slices."

"You could always join me in the Roly Poly club," Holly said devouring her fourth slice and helping herself to some fries.

"When I'm feeling better I'm going on a healthy eating plan and perhaps take some exercise classes. Who fancies joining me?" Audrey asked.

The question seemed to divide the family. Half were enthusiastic, half just looked at her as if she'd just asked them to walk the full length of the Great Wall of China.

"Well I'll leave it up to you. I'm going to start in a few days and look for some classes in the area, or maybe if there's enough of us we could get someone in. But it is going to happen; I'm determined to grow old healthily not like an aging Buddha." Audrey continued to talk to everyone about the secret rooms and decided it was time to come clean and tell them about her adventure with the Belle sisters.

"Oh Audrey, I can't believe you put yourself in danger like that and why keep it a secret?" Ned growled at her very disapprovingly.

"I came to the decision because you've always been sceptical about my intuition and when you're around it makes me jumpy. I can't get a feel for things. You and Greg take the micky at the drop of a hat and it does nothing for my confidence," Audrey stood and took her plate to the sink head lowered, shoulders sagging. She had a look of deflation about her.

"I know I've always appeared to be doubtful, but I really do think both you and May have an uncanny intuition. I'm not sure what it is, but when you are together I do feel a little uneasy. That's why I come out with all the wisecracks. It's because I don't know what to say or do when you two are doing your sixth sense thing," Ned said as he walked over to Audrey and put his arms around her. "I'm sorry, I'm just not very good at all the emotional stuff, and when I'm out of my depth I resort to sarcasm. I promise I'll try not to do it in future. However, I do think we should explore this castle as a family. Please don't feel you are on your own: we're all behind you. Aren't we guys?" Ned turned towards the family who were still seated at the table.

"Yes we are mum and I'm sorry as well. I find anything even a little bit spooky very daunting. Perhaps I'm a little too much like Dad. I really will try to be more open-minded and supportive," Greg said as he looked over at his mum and dad.

Everyone agreed that they should do the searches as a family but include the Belle sisters in their plans.

"I think now that Tom has put electricity in the first part, we should investigate and take some battery operated lanterns to place around the areas that aren't wired yet." Pete said.

"Good idea bro, I'll go and get those lanterns and torches we left in the old coach house. Do we fancy doing a little exploration this evening?" Bobby asked as he headed towards the back door.

"I'll call the Gatehouse and ask the sisters to join us," said Audrey.

They all agreed and Greg put a plan together. "Theo, Liz, and Holly will stop by the wardrobe doors. Louisa and Celia can stay by the door in the first room. All the rest of us will go and open that door again. Mum don't forget all the keys. We'll take the tags Celia and Louisa used when they started opening the rooms in the main areas. Is everyone ok with that?"

"Sounds like a plan to me" said Pete.

"Lead the way Greg, you go first and if a giant sword comes hurtling towards me I can hide behind you," said Bobby and dived behind his brother in mock fright.

Everyone laughed but Greg, "You are so infantile Bobby, it's about time you grew up."

"Don't want to grow up, can't make me," smiled Bobby.

"There's no reply at the Gatehouse so I've left a message on the answering machine," said Audrey as she joined Ned and Celia at the doors of the lift.

Everyone else climbed the stairs and they met in Ned's room a few moments later.

CHAPTER 9

Ya Don't Mess With This Nana.

The family followed Greg's plan and all looked at their watches. The children were left in Ned's room. They were told to stay put and not to wander off, much to their disappointment. Liz telephoned Bobby's mobile and they both put the phones on loudspeaker. Theo connected with his Dad's phone; Holly connected with Pete's phone and did the same thing. Greg turned to the children and said, "If we aren't back in this room in one hour, call the Gatehouse and get May over here. If they still aren't in, call Bob Sergeant. In the meantime, we'll all be able to listen in on what's happening." Audrey had just connected with Louisa's mobile as they started down the corridor.

Theo, Holly and Liz remained where they were, as the rest of the family moved along the now well-lit corridor. Celia and Louisa stayed in the four-poster bedroom; they had come armed with a bucket with a small amount of soapy water in it, a couple of sponges, some dusters and polish. They were determined to give the room a bit of a spruce up, Louisa started to do a search taking out drawers and looking behind them. Celia began to strip the bed and look under the mattress, even crawling under the bed to see if anything was hidden there.

The remainder of the family went down the stairs; Greg was the first one to reach the bottom step. Ned started across the door that had formed a bridge over the last few steps.

"What was that noise? It sounded like a very quiet moan," Ned said after he'd stepped on the door.

"Yes we heard that last time," Greg replied.

"April heard it when we came down," Audrey whispered, remembering the last time she was here and becoming a little agitated at the thought.

They all entered the dormitory and Greg showed his mother where he'd found the books.

“I will try to do a little more delving into those books later. I get the feeling they hold the key to everything that’s happened in the castle,” said Audrey getting the big brass key out of her pocket. She held it in her hand for a couple of minutes to see if she could get any sensations from it, there was nothing. She hadn’t felt anything when May was with her, so it was unlikely she’d get any insights when she was on her own.

They stood in front of the door to the sitting room that Audrey and the Belle sisters had discovered. Pete took the key from Audrey, he pulled out a small oil can from a haversack he was carrying, squirting some oil on to the key and into the lock, the key turned easily when it was inserted.

“Well done Pete, never thought to bring an oil can with me. You got anything else of interest in that bag you’re carrying,” Ned smiled proudly at his middle son.

“That would be telling dad, but I can say that this bag is a bit like mum’s shopping bag, it’s got everything in it, including the kitchen sink.”

Audrey went into the room first; it was exactly as she had remembered it, cold and uninviting. Bobby placed a lantern on the table next to the cups and saucers; he jumped back as a mouse dived down behind the table and disappeared through a hole in the floorboards. “Jesus Christ” he said clutching his chest, “good job I haven’t got a week heart.”

“Language Bobby, no blaspheming. You don’t know who you’ll upset,” Audrey’s lips twitching as she tried not to smile.

Bobby looked around furtively, his eyes screwed up as he peered around the room, waiting for the shadows thrown by the lantern to come alive.

“Theo is everything ok with you?” Greg spoke into his mobile phone but there was no reply.

“Louisa are you alright?” Audrey looked at her phone in the shadowy light, she held it up in the air, but there wasn’t a sound. They all examined the displays on their mobiles but none of them had a signal.

“I think we’ll try some walkie-talkies next time, we may be able to communicate a little better with them. Ok we will just give it another twenty minutes before we turn back, otherwise they’ll be sending for reinforcements.” Greg continued to explore the room.

“How about me and Bobby going back just to put their minds at rest, that will give you a little more time,” Pete said.

“Good idea Pete. I think thirty minutes will be enough, my nerves won’t take much more,” Ned grinned as he looked at his boys. “When we do start back? No jumping out and trying to frighten me to death. I’m more valuable to you alive. I’ve already cut you out of my will. The money’s going to the Dogs Trust.”

Greg, Ned and Audrey opened the door at the far end of the room. Greg had brought Pete’s oil can with him. He oiled the hinges before proceeding down the steps. It was a long way down with many twists, turns and a couple of small landings. Audrey counted 40 steps; she didn’t know how far they’d travelled but it would have to be at least two floors. The narrow staircase opening out into a large room at the bottom. They shone their torches into the room as they walked further in. Movement seemed to be all around them, scurrying creatures disappearing in every direction as the light bounced off the walls, ceiling and floor.

“The old kitchens! Look over there it’s the original black stove,” said Audrey looking around in amazement.

The pots and pans were still hanging from hooks and standing stacked on shelving. A door stood ajar. It had quite obviously been the pantry - old tins, bottles and jars still adorned the rustic shelves. A very small window frame was set in the back wall. There was no glass. Ivy was coming through it and had rooted itself to the wooden shelving and the walls.

“That must be the back door,” said Greg going over and trying to open a large stable type door split into two sections. It had two handles and large rusty bolts at the top and bottom; he squirted them with oil but still couldn’t budge them. “I can’t remember seeing this when we inspected the outside walls.”

Ned joined his son in trying to unbolt the door. “It’s probably covered completely with ivy on the outside. We will have to estimate where this room is and start cutting the ivy away. I should imagine it’s going to be quite a job. I have to say this is an amazing room, steeped in history. What do you think Audrey?”

Audrey stood in the middle of the kitchen and said, “I think we need to get back. I’m getting a very funny feeling. Let’s go Ned.”

Greg took several photos of the room and continued clicking his mobile camera as they went up the stairs; they travelled slowly through each room, allowing Greg to take pictures and videos as they headed towards the bedchamber they’d first discovered. Pete and Bobby were waiting for them and it was reassuring to see the electric lighting Tom had installed. It made everywhere less intimidating when the area was well lit.

Louisa and Celia had gone to reassure the children. They had left Pete and Bobby to wait for the rest of the family to return.

“I’ve got loads of photos. I’ll attach the mobile to the telly and we can all have a good look later" Greg said enthusiastically.

Audrey’s phone had been silent for quite a while but suddenly it burst into life and they all heard Louisa’s voice shouting, but couldn’t hear what was being said. There was definitely anguish in her voice. Greg, Pete and Bobby went running up the corridor and through the wardrobe followed by Ned and Audrey. They headed towards the sound of the hysterical voices and breathlessly passed out of Ned’s room and along the hallway. Turning right they ended up in front of the lift. Louisa was there; as soon as she saw Greg she flew into his arms and broke down in tears. “They’re stuck in the lift, mum and the children. They can’t get out and they say the lift keeps shaking. There are some awful noises coming from the shaft.”

Pete reached into his rucksack and pulled out a small jemmy wrench. He put the end of it in the middle of the sliding door and he and Greg pushed with all their strength until the doors finally opened. The lift compartment was halfway between floors; they could just see the children and Celia through a gap in the roof. They were crouched on the floor, obviously absolutely terrified. The cage started to shake and the four occupants screamed frantically.

May, April and June came bounding up the stairs breathless and anxious.

"I felt there was something wrong even before we got your message. We all ran here as quickly as we could," said May.

The lift stopped shaking and jerked down another couple of feet. The children screamed even louder and everyone stood rooted to the spot for a few seconds.

Audrey's face changed from horror to rage. Her head moved from side to side, her eyes darting around as if she were looking for something. May reached over and held her hand; Audrey took a big deep breath in and screamed in a powerful voice.

"Leave my family alone or face my wrath.

Ashes to ashes.

Dust to dust.

May the wind blow you, wandering ghost and clear the world of the living,

Turn you to where you belong.

May you disappear without a trace to hell and damnation."

The lights in the hallway flickered and a cold wind blew, whipping around everyone standing in front of the lift. It raged so fiercely it looked as though they were in a wind tunnel, making them stagger as they leaned against the walls to try to steady themselves. They all stood, muscles tensed, eyes darting from side to side trying to see if they could catch a glimpse of what had starting this sudden tempest. The wind subsided as quickly as it had started and there was a strange and eerie stillness filling the space. Without any warning, the lift quietly ascended and stopped in front of the shocked family. The doors were already open and the occupants crept silently out as if they were trying to escape unnoticed. Once on firm ground everyone hugged whilst both laughing and crying uncontrollably at the same time.

The family slowly and uneasily descended the stairs; no one spoke, the children holding onto their parents still letting out the occasional sob. Celia just kept looking straight ahead; Pete and Bobby stood either side of her, holding her hands to help her balance as she unsteadily and gradually took one nervous step at a time. Once down the stairs they all headed towards the kitchen, while Ned went into the wine store wheeling out a drinks trolley containing several bottles of spirits. Everyone still in shock took their regular seats at the table, the Belle sisters retrieving some folding chairs from the cloakroom store. Bobby and Pete brought glasses to the table; Ned waved his hand towards the trolley for everyone to help themselves. Hardly a word was spoken as everyone, including the children, helped themselves to whisky and brandy, gulping the first one down and quickly filling up again. Ned poured Celia a large single malt and put it in front of her but she didn't seem to notice it was there.

"I think one is enough Theo," said his Dad, but by the time Greg had finished the sentence, Theo had poured himself another large tipple and drunk it straight down. His face was an expressionless mask, until he realized what he was drinking and started to cough and splutter. Greg patted him on his back, "got bones in it had it son?" he chuckled and everyone broke out into laughter, brought on, no doubt, by relief.

Once Theo had stopped choking and everyone had calmed down, he said, "Don't think that ghost knows ya don't mess with my Nana."

Everyone looked in Audrey's direction, their faces a picture of confusion and realisation as it started dawning on them what had just happened.

"Before you all start, can I say....DON'T, I've only had a couple of whiskies and I think this is definitely a several whisky situation," Audrey said as she went to the freezer and got out a large packet of ice, opened it and emptied it into an ice bucket. She placed it front of her, putting several lumps into her glass and then topping it up with the whisky. She sat down rather heavily and unsteadily on her chair at the head of the table.

"Ummm errrr aren't you on antibiotics Audrey?" May said reluctantly.

"Only for five days and I can drink with them, I checked," snapped Audrey.

Even May and June had partaken of a small libation. May put her glass down after emptying it and got herself a large glass of water with ice and lemon. April poured herself another brandy and June put the kettle on.

"You've got to talk sometime you know; none of us has a clue what just happened and I think we deserve an explanation," said Bobby his face serious for once.

"Ok I'll start while I'm still able to speak. When I was looking at that first journal that Greg found I managed to make out a few words, but nothing that I found was really interesting. However, when I put the book down the pages turned by themselves and the name Edith suddenly appeared on the cover, then disappeared just as quickly. I heard someone in the room snuffle, as if they had a cold or were crying and everything went silent. I realized that we must have at least a couple of spirits because the one that wrote Edith felt young and uncertain. The other one that we encountered didn't feel dangerous just mischievous but when he took form for a few seconds, I got the impression he was quite elderly. So, to cut a long story short, I looked up incantations on how to exorcise a ghost, when I realized the children were in danger it sort of....kind of.......just came out of my mouth," slurred Audrey in a very matter of fact tone.

"That corresponds with my findings," said April, "there have been several deaths on the land and in the castle. The Duke disappeared and no one ever found out what happened to him, I went to the Old Manor Nursing Home with June and spoke to some of the older residents. We met a very interesting gentleman called George; he's going to be an unbelievable 103 next month."

"Get on with it April I'm losing the will to live," Ned held his head in his hands with a forlorn look on his face.

Greg was writing furiously on a notepad he'd snatched from the kitchen work surface, it had the face of a border collie on the top of each page; he had to turn over several pages of shopping ingredients before he got to a one he could actually write on.

"I was Ned. Don't interrupt me again or I'll lose the thread," April looked puzzled then closed her eyes, "Oh yes I remember now. That means he was born in 1914, he said he lived in one of the tied cottages and when he was eight or nine years old, his older brother went to work in the stables. He rambled for a long time about his brother who loved horses but kept sneezing whenever he was grooming them. The Master of the house disappeared and there was a lot of talk between his mother and the neighbours, about him running off with one of the dance hall girls."

Ned took a deep breath in ready to interrupt again.

"**S H U T U P** Ned. Believe it or not I am keeping it short. The old dear went on for hours. This is the shortened version."

"God help us if you decided to tell the full length version. It would probably be in competition with Lord of the Rings the full trilogy with the outtakes," muttered Ned.

May and June took orders for coffee, while Audrey and Celia poured themselves another large glass of whisky and everyone settled down again to hear more of April's story.

"Are you sure this 'oldie' can be trusted to tell us the truth?" Greg looked at April with an expression of doubt on his face.

"George can't remember what day it is. He asked me who I was at least twenty times, but according to the nurses he can tell you in great detail what happened seventy years ago. He's a bit sketchy after 1999 and sometimes thinks he's seventeen again, which he demonstrated by pinching everyone's bottom when they got within grasping distance. He tried to get out of his wheelchair several times because he'd forgotten he couldn't walk. Now son of Ned may I continue?"

Greg was just opening a can of beer and handing cans out to his brothers, when he looked over at April and said, "Oh please do, I'm riveted."

"Mmmmm you should be. OK where was I?...Ohhhh yes. After the Duke disappeared one of the maids, who George's brother Albert was sweet on, went to live at the vicarage in Stafford. Albert was upset and took to drink.

George can remember when he was about fourteen or fifteen the Dukes son, who was a right queer bloke according to George, had an accident. He can't remember too much about it, fell down the stairs or something and died. His mother lived for a few years after, but all the money was gone, all the servants were let go and she went stark raving mad ending up in Stallington Hall.

The castle remained empty for years but George can't remember too much, only what his Mum wrote in her letters. He'd joined the army and was serving in India, so he didn't get back to the village until 1947 after WW2 had ended. When he did return home, the castle had been taken over by the Army as a convalescent hospital for the recovery of injured soldiers. That's as far as I've got which takes us up to 1948. I have the feeling that the ghost could be the wayward son, whose name was Albert Edward but everyone called him Teddy. I've just started looking through newspapers and land deeds, so I'll probably be able to gather more information a little quicker as we get nearer the present time."

Everyone joined in with words of congratulations. "What an incredible story, I'm sure we could spend some time with George. If we can get past Patricia the Rottweiler, maybe we could have a few words with Victoria, she was born around 1923 and her mother was Edith. It can't be a coincidence it must be the same Edith that wrote the journals. I think whilst April is trawling through the internet, June and May could be trying to speak to some more of the older villagers, like Tom and people at the nursing home. We could bribe them with homemade scones, that usually goes down well and I'll try to decipher more of the journals" Audrey looked over at Celia who was still staring blankly in front of her.

"Perhaps Celia and the children will feel a little better after a good night's sleep," Audrey lifted her glass and emptied the last dregs into her mouth. Peering into the empty tumbler, one eye closed, not believing it was empty again, she turned it upside down and shook it. She reached for the whisky bottle to fill the vessel up again, but much to her disgust the bottle was empty and no matter how much she shook it, there was no way she was getting anymore of the golden nectar out of the bottle. She leaned over and swopped her glass for the full one which was in still front of Celia.

“I think I’m tooooo traumatized to go into school tomorrow. I’m worried I may faint after my ordeal,” said Holly touching her forehead with the back of her hand, feigning a swoon.

“Well if she’s not going, I’m not going either. I won’t be able to sleep tonight anyway. I think I have post-traumatic stress disorder - the room keeps going out of focus,” said Theo looking a little green around the gills.

“That’s more likely the alcohol Theo, but I suppose a day off won’t hurt,” Greg said helping his son to his feet.

“Perhaps just this once the children can sleep with us Greg, we can drag a few mattresses into our room. Louisa looked pleadingly at her husband.

He nodded in resignation and the three children all smiled.

“Sleepover, how lovely, do you think we should call the police and tell them what’s happened?” said Liz suddenly seeming to wake up.

No came the reply from everyone except Audrey, whose eyes had become slits as she slithered out of her chair, disappearing under the table. By the time Ned had walked around to where she’d been sitting, faint snuffles and snores could be heard from under the table. Audrey was curled in a ball her head resting on a disgruntled Sky, the oldest of the dogs, who was cranky at the best of times; she was still holding a half-empty glass of whisky. Everyone seemed to be very impressed that she hadn’t spilt a drop whilst gracefully sliding into her present sleeping position.

CHAPTER 10

Weeping Pussy Willow.

"Hi Ned, where's Audrey?" May said cheerily as she and June breezed in just before lunchtime.

"She's in the library, taken her coffee and toast with her, she's looking through those journals. I'm surprised she can see this morning, but after a shower and a coffee she's back to normal. Great resilience my wife, outstanding," came Ned's reply.

The sisters went directly to the library and stood by the desk, where Audrey was scribbling furiously in a notebook that was placed right next to the open journal.

"Hi girls, you ok?" Audrey smiled at the sisters and took another gulp of coffee and a bite of her toast.

"We're fine hun, must say you've made a remarkable recovery," May said pinching a slice of toast off the plate.

"I've had a lot of practice May. These journals are absolutely fascinating, but I can only find five and I know there were six. The one that was in the best condition is missing; I can't imagine what's happened to it." Audrey said while still scanning the pages of the battered and half-eaten journal in front of her. "This girl is very unhappy; she's been put into service by her family because her father died in a farm accident. Just imagine 14 years old and all her money is given to her mum to try to keep the family fed. She's got a couple of sisters and a brother I think, all younger than her."

"Unfortunately that was typical of what happened in the old days. What year is it Aud? I can't remember if you've told me," June gave into temptation and pinched the last piece of toast from the plate. "Is there an indication on what year the journals start and finish?"

"Well that's a good question and I think the mice might know more than I do. I could only make out 192 the rest was chewed, so it doesn't take a genius to work out it was somewhere between 1920 and 1929," Audrey reached out and absentmindedly started feeling around the empty plate whilst still looking at the journal. Her eyes darted over to where she thought the toast would be. She had puzzled look on her face until she looked up to see May and June chewing merrily on her breakfast. She gave them a look and June, realising what the grouchy look was all about said, "I umm think I'll head for the kitchen and get some more toast, does anyone want any?"

Audrey said, "More toast? I think I would like **some** toast please June."

"None for me sis, I've already had two slices," May said completely oblivious to the fact that Audrey's breakfast had disappeared before she could help herself to a second slice. "It was delicious though, golden and crunchy, smothered in butter. Oh go on then you've twisted my arm. Just one more slice please."

The doorbell rang a few minutes later as June was returning with a plateful of golden buttered toast. She opened the door to Mrs Gahir and Patricia, "Oh hello ladies, Audrey and May are in the library. Patricia barged past her, Mrs Gahir gave June one of her 'I'm so sorry smiles' as she tiptoed past, following the dragon lady into the library.

"Hello Ladies so nice to see you, is it your day to sort out the library? I think I must have lost track of time." Audrey lifted her head for just a few seconds and then went back to looking through a very large magnifying glass at a page in the journal.

"We seem to be a little higgledy-piggledy with the rota. I'll get working on it. Julie is still sulking and we've hardly seen her since she had her temper tantrum. The chemist is still shut. Well come on Mrs Gahir let's get working. Are you lot going to be in here all day getting under our feet. The room isn't big enough for five of us?" Patricia had an accusing look on her face as she stared at each of the women in the room. She bent over pinching a piece of toast from the plate sitting next to Audrey and popped it into her mouth tearing it ferociously in two.

"We're going to the nursing home to visit some residents," May said very nonchalantly giving a little smile and a wink at Audrey.

"I'm here all day, got things to do, hope you don't mind Patricia but it is my home. Thought I'd just remind you in case you'd forgotten." Audrey gave Patricia a smile that definitely didn't reach her eyes as she leaned over to pick up a piece of toast, before returning to her magnifying glass.

"Umph, well I suppose I can't grumble. Come on Mrs Gahir we'll make a start then." Patricia moved the steps out of the way and Mrs Gahir took out her laptop.

"Bye then sees you later," June said heading towards the door with her sister.

Audrey reached out for a piece of toast only to find the plate empty, she looked up to see June vanishing through the door with a piece of toast in her hand, Mrs Gahir was chomping away at a slice and Patricia was popping the last triangle in her mouth. Giving up with the toast Audrey started to look forward to lunch, which was only an hour or two away, she continued to investigate the pages she was lovingly and gently turning.

Patricia kept looking over at Audrey furtively whilst bringing down a handful of books at a time. She got quite cross when she noticed that Mrs Gahir wasn't keeping up with her; in fact she was about six books behind. "What is wrong with you, you're miles behind, keep your mind on the job in hand dear or we'll never finish."

Mrs Gahir looked up her eyes full of tears, "I'm so sorry I can't concentrate. I'm just too upset."

"Oh Goodness, I'm sorry, I was so engrossed with this journal that I didn't notice how distressed you were. Whatever is the matter? Is there anything I can do?" Audrey got up from her chair and put her arm around the weeping woman.

Patricia just frowned in disgust and flopped down on a spare chair, not even trying to disguise her annoyance.

"I think him indoors is having an affair," Mrs Gahir said in-between sobs, shaking off Audrey's arm from her shoulder. "I just don't know what to do."

“So what makes you think he’s playing away and with whom?” Patricia said leaning forward as though she was an interrogator in the SS.

“He keeps disappearing for an hour at a time, making excuses as to where he’s going. When I walk in the room and he’s on the phone he clears his throat and says “sorry wrong number.” We can’t possibly be receiving several wrong numbers every week.”

“Is it the landline or the mobile he’s using? Patricia continued her questioning and leaned further forward towards the distressed Mrs Gahir.

“His mobile, and yes I’ve checked it but he's deleted most of the calls.”

“Most of the calls,” Patricia’s eyes were bulging out of their sockets and she leaned even further forward in her chair; her generous bottom was resting precariously on the edge of the seat. She had leaned a little too far and the chair tipped, toppling over with a clatter, she only just managed to grab hold of the table to stop herself from falling on her ample derriere. Quickly recovering she picked the chair up and stood leaning on the back of it. “Most of the calls?” she repeated.

“Yes he’s made calls to the castle, to your pub and to the Vicar's mobile. So Audrey is it you or one of the other loose women living in this viper's den. I can’t believe it’s you Patricia, my husband isn’t that desperate, but it could be Sarah, she goes about almost naked most of the time and as for the Vicar, I really don’t know. I can’t blame any woman for falling for his charms. He’s such a handsome man, it would be so difficult to say no to him,” Mrs Gahir’s eyes rested on Audrey for a few seconds before she sighed and then started sobbing into her handkerchief.

Audrey was looking particularly guilty as she left the room to go and fetch some coffee and biscuits. She came back a few minutes later balancing a very heavy tray full of coffee and a huge pile of biscuits. She was completely composed considering she’d just been accused of having an affair with her friend’s husband, but on entering the room she stared inquisitively at Patricia, who was balancing unsteadily on the ladder, leaning over perilously trying to reach some books that were just out of her grasp.

"The tray was ready, Celia had made it up and was ready to bring it in, what are you doing up there Patricia, can I help you?"

"No. No. No," Patricia came down the steps looking very flustered, "I just thought I'd be getting on with the cataloguing while Mrs Gahir was composing herself." She quickly changed the subject; "I notice you aren't denying the accusation, Audrey. Could there be some truth in it?"

"Certainly not, good grief, I'm way too old to be taking part in those sorts of shenanigans. Even if I wasn't too old I definitely wouldn't be tempted by Mr Gahir, not that he isn't a lovely man. I'm sure some ladies find him very appealing, sort of, not me of course I'm happily married, but you know," her voice trailed off as she tried to backtrack, then decided the best way forward was to distract the four accusing eyes boring into her. "Coffee and biscuits anyone? They're homemade ginger biscuits, very nice, they're still warm," she pushed the tray forward trying to tempt them but to no avail. Mrs Gahir was too upset to eat and Patricia said she couldn't possibly eat another morsel while her friend was so unhappy.

The two visitors continued to stare at her for several seconds before heading for the door, noses in the air. Neither of them spoke. Patricia reached over as she passed Audrey helping herself to a handful of biscuits.

"Oh err well, I'll see you ladies soon I hope," Audrey said in quite a high-pitched and strained voice and then she returned to the kitchen with the tray minus most of the biscuits.

Theo and Holly had been turfed out of bed at 9am. Just because they had a day off school didn't mean they could laze in bed. Celia and Louisa set them on in the kitchen helping to prepare lunch. Theo had laid the table and Holly was stirring the soup when everyone arrived and took their places. Right in the middle of the table was a huge plate of crusty bread and on either side a bowl of grated cheese. Holly used the largest ladle they had to spoon the onion soup into bowls and Theo carried them over to the hungry diners. Everyone sniffed the air and smiled, but they waited until all the place settings had a bowl of the steaming liquid on them and Theo and Holly had sat down before they all started to tuck in.

It was only about fifteen minutes later when all the bowls had been emptied that the two younger children cleared the table and loaded everything in the dishwasher.

Celia cleared her throat. "If I could have your attention please, I would like to ask a favour of you all."

They looked at Celia in anticipation willing her to hurry so that they could get back to their work.

"Jack and Janet have had a bit of a flood in their home," noises of sympathy came from the attentive family. "They were wondering if I could look after Jack Jnr for a few extra hours a day so they can clear and clean up without having to keep watching him. You know what a handful he is. Obviously I wouldn't say yes until I'd cleared it with you. If it is a problem, I could always take him out, but it would be so much easier if you would agree to let me look after him here?" She looked around the table with a pleading look in her eyes.

Louisa stood up, "Well it's up to Audrey and Ned, but could I make a suggestion?"

Ned and Audrey looked over at Louisa and Celia, Audrey smiling and Ned grimacing as usual. "Go on Louisa, we're all ears," said Ned with a hint of resignation in his voice. He knew if the three ladies came up with a plan, none of the men would want to argue with them, but it did mean that the male contingent would earn brownie points; it was always a good bargaining tool to have up your sleeve in case of emergencies.

"Well, the children are off school today and over the weekend, if they can look after Jack for a few hours and me and mum look after him the rest of the time, he could stay here in Mum's room just for a couple of nights. If Greg, Pete and Bobby would go over to Jack and Janet's house to help, it would be cleared and finished a lot sooner. What do you think guys?"

The boys looked at each other and thought that if they could spend a day or so helping the unfortunate couple that would mean less time being annoyed by Jack Jnr. The three boys nodded their heads in approval and Greg started writing a list of the things they needed to take with them.

“Could we hire a couple of industrial dehumidifiers and put it on the castle's account?” Greg said looking over at his father.

“Good idea, I’ll do that and bring them over to you. Celia do you want to come with me and then we can pick Jack up on the way back,” Ned said scrambling to get up - he loved a challenge.

“Oh that would be wonderful Ned, thank you so much, I’ll telephone and ask them to pack an overnight bag for Jack. I’ll make an apple crumble for dinner tonight, your favourite Ned.” Celia and Audrey almost always finished off any food menu with the words ‘your favourite’, even if it wasn’t. It seemed to make people feel more special and, more importantly, made them more pliable when asking for a favour.

Theo and Holly were still in shock at having to look after Jack, but they knew any protest was futile. Liz joined Louisa and Audrey at the table as they listed few games they could play with Jack to keep him occupied.

Ned arrived back with Celia and Jack in the late afternoon. Jack was pulling a roll-along suitcase in the shape of a train. Louisa unpacked for her nephew and they came back downstairs with the train. He spent a very happy half an hour sitting on the train and scooting up and down the hallway making all the normal train noises that small boys make.

Audrey couldn’t help looking back at the happy times when her boys were his age; they had done exactly the same thing in the small hallway of their home, only it was a homemade train. Ned had attached four small wheels to a basket, the engine was a cardboard box, the funnel on top had been a couple of toilet roll tubes stuck together and he’d painted all of it red. Greg had played on it for months and so when the other two boys had reached four years old Ned had made them each one as well, joyful memories. She sighed and put the fish pie in the oven to cook.

Because lunch was late so was dinner. They didn’t finish until 7.30pm and Jack was starting to yawn - it had been a full and adventurous day for the young lad. "We'll go to bed soon Jack." Celia ruffled her grandson's hair as he fought to try to stifle a yawn.

"Just a few more minutes Nana p a l e a s e," he said making his eyes as big as he could, trying to pretend he wasn't tired at all.

"Ok Jack, just this once we'll stay up until 8 o'clock, then we'll both go to my room, I'll read you a story then we'll call your mum to say goodnight and see how they're getting on." Celia joined the rest of the family and plonked down on the sofa in the sitting room. Jack had acquired a second wind and was running around the room arms outstretched making aeroplane noises. Everyone looked around at him and made a shhhh noise to try to quieten him. He stood still like a statue making a funny face.

"Perhaps I should go out and play on the front steps."

"Excellent idea Jack but don't wander off. We'll come out and make sure you're alright in a couple of minutes," Louisa didn't sound too enthusiastic but it was only going to be a few minutes and the property was very secure. What trouble could he get into in that time? She thought about that statement and then turned to Theo, "Can you go and keep an eye on him darling, I'm completely bushed?"

Theo was just shuffling towards the door with a look that said you owe me one, when Jack came running back in.

"Yippee is tonight the witchy thing when we go trick and treating?"

"No that's months away Jack, come on let's go outside. I'll play aeroplanes with you," Theo said grabbing the small boy's hand.

"Why do you think its Halloween Jack, what's made you say that?" Bobby said slumping even further down the sofa resting his head on the back cushion and looking up at the ceiling.

"Because somebody has already started to dress the tree outside, like dad does with spooky things," he replied.

They all straightened up sensing that there was something wrong.

"What do you mean spooky things Jack?" Liz said unfolding her legs from underneath her and placing her feet firmly on the floor, leaning forward to better hear his reply.

"Like the black cat hanging from the tree and all the blood," Jack replied innocently.

They all darted towards the front door and stood at the top of the few steps leading down to the front courtyard. Jack was right; a black cat was dangling on the end of a noose from the tree that stood proudly in the centre of the front lawn. Either side of the tree stood two Victorian fountains and the water gushing out of them was blood red.

A realisation seemed to hit them all at once, a few screams escaped their lips and the boys ran over to the tree while the ladies ushered the children inside the house, Jack still unaware that anything was wrong.

"Come on Jack we'll go upstairs and read that story," Celia said trying to persuade Jack to go up the stairs.

"But it isn't 8 o'clock yet Nana," he bleated, his bottom lip dropping and starting to tremble.

"Come on Jack I'll give you a piggy back. Get a move on Holly you can help me," Theo said bending down so Jack could climb on his back.

"We'll stay with Jack Mum; let us know what's happening as soon as you know. Holly said racing up the stairs behind her brother and a giggling Jack as he enjoyed his piggyback ride.

Pete as usual was equipped for any occasion and he pulled out a penknife from his pocket, cutting through the rope that secured Cinders to the tree. They carefully carried her into the cloakroom, she was as stiff as a board and they laid her down in the basket by the backdoor. The dogs sniffed at her before whining and crying at the loss of their friend. Pete stroked her and all four men brushed tears away as they covered her with a blanket. Greg picked up the basket and took it to the wine closet. It was cool in there, best place for her until they could decide what to do.

Jack cleaned his teeth and Holly helped him into his pj's. Theo read him a story but he was sound asleep before the end. They set the mobile child alarm that Jack's parents had packed in his overnight case. Both the children wanted to go downstairs to see what was happening, but dreading their fears might be right and that the Halloween decoration really wasn't a decoration. Walking down the grand staircase, still unable to get into the lift after their fright the other day, they hardly spoke, both realising that if it had been a sick joke, someone would have told them. They walked into the kitchen to see sombre faces and a few red eyes. Holly immediately choked back a sob. Theo who was usually full of things to say, most of them quite annoying, was uncharacteristically quiet.

Greg had just finished speaking on his mobile phone as they found a place to sit at the table, "I've spoken to Bob Sergeant, he said there's nothing they can do at the moment but he's concerned, too much of a coincidence with the accident happening only a few days ago. He's treating it as suspicious and wants us to get Cinders to a vet for a post mortem, to get a clearer picture of what might have happened. In the meantime, don't go near the area until he can get someone over to look around."

"It can't be anything to do with the accident can it? I really can't believe I've done anything that would justify someone trying to injure me or kill poor Cinders. She may have been a pain in the bum at times but it's like losing a member of our family. Does anyone have any suggestions?" Audrey was very upset and somewhat shocked. All the family tried to persuade her to go and lie down but she declined and instead Ned bought out the drinks' trolley again.

"Not so much this evening old girl. Greg can't continue to carry you upstairs every night," He said handing Audrey a small glass.

"Why not, I carried him upstairs when he fell asleep for years," Audrey sipped a whiskey and smiled trying to make light of a very sad situation.

"Perhaps when I fall asleep you could carry me upstairs like you used to?" Greg helped himself to a small beer from the fridge.

"With the help of a block and tackle I think she may be able to do that," Bobby let out a false laugh, not wanting to joke but afraid to dwell on the incident with Cinders just in case he broke down.

Greg was on the mobile again to the vet in the next village. "Ok. Ok. Thank you for that, it would be a great help. We'll see you soon." He ended the call and turned to the family, he's on call, just delivered a foal at Blake Hall Farm, he's just going to finish up there and call in on his way back home. Pete, is the main gate still open?"

"No, I lock up before dinner about 6pm when I'm taking the dogs for a walk; the only way into the grounds is over the fields or through the gatehouse. Shall I telephone the sisters to see if they saw anything?"

"Good idea mate, but could you call into the gatehouse and ask them rather than phone, you could open the gates to let the vet in while you're there." Greg said squeezing Theo's shoulder; he knew his son wouldn't want to cry but he wanted to show him some comfort.

"Consider it done." Pete threw on a jacket and picked up a torch whistling the dogs to follow him as he opened the back door.

Greg pulled out a writing pad and pen from the kitchen cupboard. "Ok let's look at who we think it could be. Everyone, take a few minutes to think about it then give me your answers." He wrote a few names on the pad and then asked everyone individually who they thought could have done it and for what reason.

Who	Why	Votes
Patricia	Has delusions of grandeur, wants to be married to a Duke and move into the castle, she's a vindictive nasty piece of work.	7
Royle Family	They have a vendetta against Holly because the girl was expelled; they're all criminals and are known to be violent.	6
Mrs Gahir	Audrey may be having an affair with her husband.	4
Julie	Could blame Audrey, For reporting and having her suspended	4
Roger	Could just want to make his wife happy or they	3

Swinger	could be doing it between them, giving each other an alibi.	
Belle sisters	They want to be the only witches in town.	1
A total stranger	No ideas why, could be something to do with the castle's past. If Audrey leaves everyone else goes with her and the castle is empty again.	9

They could hear the dogs barking as they came in the back door to the cloakroom. Pete's voice could be heard telling them to lie down. Everyone turned towards the door as Pete strode in followed closely by a small slim man in his late 30's. He paused in the doorway; his complexion was ruddy due to years of the outdoor life. He took off his cap revealing short fair hair and a pixie like face.

He introduced himself in a thick Irish accent, "Larry O'Leary at your service. Mr Knight?" he scanned the room eyes resting on each of the men.

"Well that will be all of us, but I'm Greg the person you spoke to on the telephone." Greg held out his hand and it was clasped in a vice like grip by the man.

Everyone introduced themselves and then Ned took Mr O'Leary to the wine store and handed over the basket containing Cinders, still wrapped affectionately in her favourite blanket. He then directed him out of the front door so as not to upset the family any further.

When Ned got back, Pete was studying the suspect list and after a few seconds decided it was either the Royle family or a total stranger.

"I can't see any of the others doing anything so evil, not even Patricia. We've known them all for years, to think that we didn't spot homicidal tendencies in them before now is just unbelievable," Pete waved the piece of paper around as he spoke.

"Maybe we should show this to the police when they call round. It might be of no use at all but you never know," Audrey got up and said goodnight as she slowly went through the door. Her head hung down and her shoulders slumped, she seemed to have aged 10 years in the last few days.

CHAPTER 11

Sweet Caroline.

There was a solemn atmosphere at breakfast, the conversation was quite forced and seemed unnatural compared to the normal humdrum around the kitchen table.

"Any plans for today guys?" Audrey started to load the dishwasher as she spoke.

"Nana said we could take the dogs for a walk and have a picnic today, but only if I'm a really good boy," Jack was shovelling chocolate coco pops into his mouth at an alarming rate.

"I think we should go over to Janet and Jack's house to help them again, many hands make light work and all that," Ned took his empty plate and cup over to Audrey to dispose of.

"Good idea, Dad, I don't fancy hanging around here today, I need to keep busy," Pete went into the cloakroom to feed the hungry dogs, they greeted him with happy whimpering knowing that after food there was always a walk.

"Theo, do you want to help us or go with Jack?" Greg said whilst flicking through his 'things to do book'.

"Help you, Dad," Theo tried to ignore Jack's pouting face, obviously disappointed. Repenting he added "But when we get back I'm playing pool in the games room with Jack, no one else just me and my mate. Boys only."

Jack's grin spread from ear to ear, Theo had called him mate, this really was going to be the best visit ever. A piggyback, a story and playing pool with Theo, things just couldn't get better, he never ever wanted to go home.

Liz went off to work taking her sister with her; Holly had a Saturday job in the cafe opposite the hairdressing salon so they travelled together.

A couple of hours later Celia and Louisa had loaded Jack and the dogs into

Pete's jeep, it was the only car apart from the large people carrier that could hold all three dogs comfortably. A small icebox full of sandwiches, cakes and juice sat next to Jack on the back seat, the little boy was clutching a precious bag of doggie treats in his hand. He sat on his booster seat eyes sparkling with excitement at the thought of his adventure.

"Are you going to be ok on your own Audrey, you could come with us, I'm really not comfortable leaving you on your own," Louisa sat next to Audrey in the kitchen showing concern on her face.

"I'll be fine Louisa; honestly, I've got the sisters coming around for brunch. We're having mushroom risotto May's been foraging again. They'll be here around 11 o'clock, I'll only be on my own for an hour, just long enough to take another look at those journals," Audrey smiled and patted her daughter in laws hand before rising and heading towards the library. "Go on with you now, Jack and the dogs will burst with excitement if you don't start out soon."

Louisa laughed and waved as she went out of the back door and got into the car, "Everyone ready," she said as she started the engine.

"Yeeeeessssss," Jack shouted jumping up and down, the dogs started barking and whining as they drove off in the direction of Manifold Valley.

Audrey was sitting in the library looking through the last few pages of the first journal, when she heard the sisters calling her name as they walked through the reception room.

"In here ladies." Audrey continued looking through the magnifying glass at the last page.

"I've left the mushrooms in the kitchen, Audrey," May said looking over Audrey's shoulder. "Any luck with those journals?"

"Its hard work they're so worn, perhaps I'll have better luck with the next one. I still haven't found the final journal yet, it's really bugging me. I'm sure I counted six and there are only five here. Greg can remember that last one being in a lot better condition than the other books. This first one is the worst and they get progressively better, but the last one was in really good nick," Audrey put her magnifying glass down and April picked up the jotter with all of Audrey's notes.

"Only 14 and working six and half days a week, probably for a pittance, this cook seems to be a bit of a tyrant, not exactly a fairy godmother type," April squinted trying to decipher Audrey's writing. "Do you know, between these journals and the information we've got from the residents of the old folks home, I'm sure we could write an historical novel."

"What a good idea April, it will give us all something to do in those dark winter nights we dislike so much," June was gazing up at all the books which still seemed to be in no particular order. "How are Patricia, Julia and Mrs Gahir doing at cataloguing this lot?"

"I'm afraid they aren't doing that well, Mrs Gahir is so upset about Mr Gahir's fidelity and Julie is hiding away, not speaking to any of us. I'm afraid all cataloguing work has come to an abrupt end. Perhaps that could be another project for the winter months." Audrey put everything in neat piles while they all chatted as they looked through the books on the table.

"I'm so sorry about Cinders Aud; she was a grumpy old girl but a real character, any idea who could have done such a thing dear?" June was standing next to Audrey and rubbing her arm in a sympathetic manner.

Audrey shook her head and her eyes filled with tears as she remembered the trauma of last night, it bought back the grief she felt at the loss of the little black bundle of fur.

The other two sisters gave their condolences as they all started back through the reception area towards the kitchen.

The doorbell rang just as they passed between the front door and the staircase making them all jump. Audrey unbolted the door and opened it, the sisters peering over her shoulder to see who the visitor was. A small and very pretty oriental girl was standing in front of them; her straight black hair that was cut in a bob framed her face beautifully.

"Can I help you young lady," Audrey smiled at the stranger.

"I'm really not sure, I'm the replacement pharmacist and I've been trying to get into the shop in the village since 8 o'clock this morning, the back and front doors are bolted and no one's answering." The young lady said in a questioning voice.

"Perhaps Julie's gone out somewhere?" April chirped from behind Audrey.

"I know someone's in there because I saw the curtains move upstairs, later I saw a shadow moving in the shop." The young woman retorted.

"I've just called her mobile whilst you were talking and its gone straight through to voicemail." May looked suspiciously over Audrey's shoulder at the stranger, who was still standing on the steps in front of the door.

The tone of the visitor's voice suggested she was frustrated as she continued. "The postmistress said she didn't know what was happening, she ushered me out of the door before slamming it shut and putting the closed sign up, even though it was only twenty past ten. I saw a young woman cleaning the front door of the pub and I asked for her help, she said the proprietor was busy in the cellar and his wife was upstairs looking after her sick mother in law. However, she did suggest I speak to the Belle sisters and gave me directions, but there's no reply at the Gatehouse and then I noticed the gate was open to the castle, so I decided to enquire here. I suppose you don't have any idea where I can find the sisters or how I can get into the shop do you?" She looked at her watch. "I can't believe the time, the official hours are 8.30 to 12.15 so we close the shop in thirty minutes anyway and I haven't even managed to open it yet." The young woman looked at Audrey in desperation.

"Come on in dear, one mystery solved, these three ladies standing behind me are the Belle sisters. We're just going to have a cuppa and a spot of lunch, you can join us and we'll fill you in with what we know." Audrey introduced the Belle sisters as she walked through the grand entrance.

"Oh I'm very pleased to meet you all, I'm Caroline," said the smiling girl as she followed the four ladies through the reception room down the corridor and into the kitchen.

The sisters entertained Caroline at the kitchen table while Audrey prepared the risotto. She looked pleased that most of the mushrooms had been chopped up as she added oil, red onion and garlic to the fry pan, after a few minutes she stirred in the rice and added more olive oil to the mixture. Pouring a healthy measure of white wine into the pan she then took the half empty bottle to the table to have with the meal. Joining in with most of the conversation in the kitchen, she added vegetable stock bit by bit, stirring until the rice was tender and most of the liquid had disappeared, she then added some of the chopped mushrooms along with parsley, butter, salt and pepper. May had already put five bowls, cutlery and napkins on the table; Audrey bought the large frying pan to the table for everyone to help themselves. April poured a small amount of wine in each glass and sniffed the air in gastronomic appreciation. Audrey went to the fridge and pulled out a bowl of parmesan cheese and as she was placing it on the table said to May.

"Thank you for chopping the mushrooms it made such a difference; it took much less time to do the lunch."

"I didn't," May looked confused.

"The chopped mushrooms were on the work surface, so own up and take the praise, she said to the other two sisters," Audrey's brow furrowed.

April shook her head as she took a sip of her wine, June shook her head as she put a forkful of the food into her mouth.

"Stop," Audrey ran to the other side of the table and thumped June on the back, making her spit the mixture out onto the full plate in front of her.

"What was that all about, you've ruined a perfectly good plate of food," June said with disgust.

Caroline looked bemused as she reached for her glass of water.

"Before we go any further ladies can you all confirm you didn't chop those mushrooms?" They all responded negatively to the question. "May, can you just come and take a look at the mushrooms that are left over?" Audrey made her way with May to the kitchen work surface.

May rooted through the mushrooms, picking out several pieces that looked hazel-brown. "It's difficult to say with any accuracy because they've been chopped and mixed up with my mushrooms, but I think these pieces I've pulled out here aren't mushrooms at all, maybe some sort of bulb?" She said inquisitively as she continued to look through the uncooked mushrooms, pulling out a few more pieces. May had been foraging for over fifty years, she'd learnt from her Aunty Dorothy who used to take her walking when she a young child. There was no way she'd made a mistake and picked something that wasn't edible.

Caroline came over and looked at the few bits that had been segregated from the rest. "If you can put them in a container I may be able to get a report on them, a lot of bulbs are poisonous and can produce some very unpleasant symptoms. Mostly they just cause an upset stomach, but some are known to cause fatalities. What on earth have you ladies been up to?"

"It's a very long story, Hun, if you've got a few hours to spare we'll tell you all about it." Audrey said still a little shocked at the discovery. "In the meantime I'll do cheese on toast, April can you put the kettle on again please? I think a strong coffee is required."

Audrey emptied the risotto into a container and wrote on it, 'do not eat gone off' and whilst she and April were busy May and June bought Caroline up to date with the happenings in the Village.

"Goodness, I thought this was just a sleepy little village not Midsomer," she joked as a big pile of cheese on toast was put in the centre of the table with a pot of coffee and several pieces of carrot and walnut cake.

After a very belated brunch, the sisters cleared the table and Audrey took Caroline to the Library to show her the journals.

"How amazing that these have been uncovered after all this time, it's a miracle that the journals survived at all." Caroline looked admiringly at the old documents.

The other ladies came in a few minutes later after starting the dishwasher and tidying the kitchen.

"Oh do you have another cat Audrey?" Caroline enquired.

"No darling, we only had Cinders, what makes you say that."

"I thought I saw a black shadow going under the desk over there," Caroline looked confused as she walked over and bent down to peep behind and underneath the desk.

"Oh goodness, I hope it's not a rat or something," June started to back away as the other ladies looked around the room, moving chairs to try to find the mysterious shadow.

"Sorry, I must have been mistaken; probably just a shadow being thrown from the ivy outside, it is quite windy out there." Caroline continued to look around the room.

They all agreed it was an easy error; the ivy climbing up the walls of the castle had started to infiltrate the windows, causing shapes and shadows to flit around the room. The clouds had started to form outside and the room went particularly dark and cold, the grandfather clock in the reception room chimed 2o'clock. "Goodness I didn't realise it was so late," Audrey said checking her watch.

All the guests started heading towards the door, May gave Caroline a plastic zip bag containing the pieces she had pulled out of the mushrooms and then threw the rest away. They were just heading out of the back door when the people carrier pulled up and the men got out, Audrey had just finished introducing her family to Caroline when the jeep came to a halt by the side of them and Louisa and Celia alighted.

After the introductions were over a little voice shouted. "Are you going to undo my belt, I need a poo poo."

"Oh goodness Jack, I forgot all about you," Celia unstrapped him and ran at full pelt to the toilet underneath the reception staircase with Jack under her arm.

Louisa laughed, "I think a few too many cakes, we've already stopped once on the way back and it's only a thirty minute drive"

Pete opened the back of the jeep and the dogs jumped down, immediately going over to sniff the stranger. Sky let out a deep and long growl, bearing her teeth. "That's enough Sky, sorry about that Caroline, she doesn't take kindly to strangers.

Caroline smiled and sidestepped a few paces putting herself right by the side of Bobby, who was standing by the car trying to look disinterested.

"So you're Chinese then, where do you work at the take-away in the town? How about kung foo do you do all the kicking stuff, throwing your arms and legs all over the place?" Bobby crouched down trying to look like a Ninja warrior and failing miserably.

"I do several martial arts Bobby, I find it very useful when men try to take advantage of a poor little shop girl," Caroline responded, a slightly amused smile spreading over her sharp intelligent face, her arms folded in front of her.

"Does this mean we're ok for a discount on our takeaway then," Bobby tried to smile but it looked more like as a grimace, it was very difficult to look debonair and manly when Sheppie was trying to sniff at his crouch and Duke had his nose firmly nestled in-between the cheeks of his bum.

Caroline just looked at him shaking her head in disbelief; waving at everyone she said, "bye bye see you all again soon, I have to rush to put my pinny on now." She turned and walked with the sisters down the path to their home. Her car was parked in the driveway to the Gatehouse and as she got in to start the drive home the sisters assured her they would try their best to sort out her problem with the shop.

Audrey looked at Bobby, "I wonder what it is about you that incites female hostility?"

"I think he takes after me. He has natural charm," Ned smiled at Audrey, eyes sparkling.

"What! What have I done now?" Bobby looked around with genuine puzzlement, shrugging his shoulders, hands raised palms up and fingers splayed.

"The young lady was our replacement pharmacist. If you have a prescription for anything at all, may I suggest you take it to another Chemist!" Audrey tutted and returned to the kitchen to get a cuppa.

Theo and Jack spent a couple of hours in the games room while Audrey started the tea. Ned was doing his crossword in a comfortable old chair he had placed in a corner of the kitchen. It had a lamp positioned behind it that shone a bright light just above his shoulder, illuminating the pages of his newspaper. He liked sitting there, he said it was 'to keep the ladies company', but everyone knew it was so that he could eavesdrop on conversations when people had forgotten he was around.

Liz and Holly had returned from work joining Celia and Louisa at the kitchen table, neither of them were happy. They started talking about opening a salon so they could all work together, making it a family affair.

"That's an excellent name for your salon girls, 'Family Affair' another nice project for autumn," Audrey commented. "With some planning and hard work you could easily be open for the Christmas and New Year rush, depending on whether you buy an existing salon or open a new one."

"Oh that would be wonderful, I never thought I'd miss working but I think I am a little too young to retire." Louisa picked out a spoon from the cutlery drawer and scooped up a spoonful of the delicious dark gravy Audrey had just made "Mmmm delish," she sniffed the air like the old Bisto adverts, "Is there sausages, mash and peas to go with that onion gravy Audrey?"

Audrey smiled and nodded her head. "You know, if you three are going to be working I really do think we should get some help, We can afford it and I hate housework it seems a relentless chore, you clean, it gets dirty, you clean, it gets dirty etc., etc., etc.," she said lowering her head and shoulders a couple of inches with each etc.

"Can we have a slick dolly bird in a micro mini, please?" Everyone jumped and turned towards the corner, they'd forgotten Ned was there. "Just a suggestion, but if we are going to have a family vote, my choice is for a young good looking cleaner one with legs up to her bottom."

“If she can clean, wash, iron and slap old men into shape, I’m all for that.” Audrey threw Ned a look which said, ‘Be afraid, very afraid’, “Remember Ned, you have to sleep sometime.” She let out a witchy cackle.

Most of the seats at the kitchen table where full when Ned put the plate of thick plump sausages in the middle, in-between the bowl of peas and the smooth creamy mashed potato. Greg was the last to sit down and so he picked up the two steaming jugs of onion gravy from the counter and put one in front of his mother and the other by the side of his father’s plate. Just then his mobile phone rang out. His ring tone was 'Tain't What You Do It's the Way That You Do It’, he looked at the screen his face changing from annoyance to concern.

“It’s the vet,” he pressed the answer button and said “Yes, Mr O’Leary, what news do you have for us?” he listened quietly for a moment and then looked over to his mother and then his father “Do we want to have Cinders cremated or would you prefer it if she came home?”

Both Audrey and Ned said they would prefer to have her at home.

“Thank you for your time Mr O’Leary; we do appreciate the speedy response. I will pass that information onto the family.” He put the mobile back into the top pocket of his shirt and took a few deep breaths before continuing. “As far as he can ascertain she died of natural causes, her heart gave out, she wasn’t strung up until several hours after she died.”

“Oh dear, I’m not sure how to react to that. I suppose we have to look on the positive side and thank the Lord that she died peacefully. However, who on earth would do that to her, it really does beggar belief. I hope they rot in hell.” Ned said with great emotion.

“If I see Cinders swinging from the tree again will that mean its Halloween and I get to see fireworks?” Jack’s eyes were wide and bright; he was swinging a very large sausage on the end of his fork from side to side, his mouth open and his head going from left to right following the banger.

Everyone chuckled, trust Jack to be so matter of fact in his innocence, no one answered his question but he didn’t seem to mind, his mouth was full of sausage and mashed potatoes, the onion gravy was dripping from his chin, slithering down and forming a brown stain on his superman t-shirt.

Jack had a serious dilemma; he'd been told by Nana Celia that he was going home after he'd eaten. This had been playing on his mind for the last couple of hours. If he was very quiet, he mentally zipped his lips together; maybe they wouldn't notice he was there. Did Theo know he was supposed to go home? If he didn't, perhaps he could sneak into the games room with his best mate, they would forget about him and it would be too late to go home, Nana didn't like to drive in the dark. If he stayed over, he may be able to pinch another sausage and play with Theo. That would be the best thing ever, there may even be fireworks, nobody had said there wouldn't be. But, but, but it's Sunday tomorrow and they would make him go to Church with them and then he would have to be very quiet and very, very still for hours. His concentration was broken by Nana Audrey's voice "Jack would you like another sausage honey."

"My tummy is starting to hurt, I don't think I can," he whined.

"Oh never mind I'll save you one for your supper," Audrey took the leftovers to the fridge; Jack's eyes were glued to her.

"Super, am I stopping over again?" he said hopefully

"Yes Jack, you can go back tomorrow afternoon after dinner," Celia was sitting opposite him with a coffee cradled in her hands.

"Do I have to go to church?" he bleated picking up his chocolate shake and talking a big gulp, smacking his lips as he put the glass down.

"Yes Jack you do," Celia sighed, she knew this was the start of a thousand questions.

"I don't have my Sunday best with me," he got down off his stool.

"Your mum and dad are going to drop them off later; they're going to the Raven Arms for a meal."

“Am I going with them for a meal?” he stood looking over at his Nana, his back arched and stomach sticking out, hands on hips he definitely looked like a chubby gnome.

“Theo, Holly, Liz can you take Jack to the games room please? I’ll pay you,” Celia looked at the three children with pleading eyes.

“What’s it worth?” Theo could see a bribery situation arising.

“Five pounds each,” Celia was still sipping her coffee and wondering if it would be a wise move to put a brandy in it so early in the evening.

“Make it ten pounds and it’s a deal Nana,” The teenager had his bargaining face on.

“Children take Jack to the games room……NOW,” Louisa had spoken; they grabbed Jack and headed towards the games room. Theo, stomping off as though he’d suffered a terrible injustice. “I’ll bring you drinks and Chocolate chip biscuits, I’ve got a chocolate dipping sauce as well,” Louisa was on top form, she really knew how to manipulate.

CHAPTER 12

Dem Bones, Dem Bones, Dem Dry Bones.

The family awoke to a stormy and wet Sunday morning, the sky was dark and the clouds where full of even more rain.

“Well that’s scuppered our plans to cut back that ivy on the East Wall Greg, I don’t think it’s wise to be taking an electric strimmer out in this weather.” Ned looked over at the turbulent sky through the kitchen window.

“True Dad, you with an electric strimmer isn’t exactly a match made in heaven, without throwing water into the deadly combination.” Greg was looking at his to do list as he spoke. “Where’s Mum this morning?”

“I think everything has caught up with her son, she was so tired she could hardly lift her head off the pillow. I’ve been telling her since she was released from hospital that she should take it easy, but you know your mother, stubborn woman.” Ned picked up the morning paper and turned the pages until he found his crossword. “I don’t like the Sunday paper it’s full of adverts, weighs a ton. There’s at least three trees been chopped down for this one paper it’s a waste, I only want to do the crossword and look at the sports pages.”

Bobby had entered the kitchen as his father was speaking, “Have you thought of looking at the paper online? You could pick and choose what you looked at then and it wouldn’t involve any trees at all, unless you printed off the crossword and Sudoku, but that would only mean one A4 sheet, much better for the conservation efforts.”

Greg and Ned turned to Bobby. Ned grunted and looked at him in disgust.

“Why do you keep trying to annoy him like that Bobby, he’s only just mastered that ten year old mobile phone, he doesn’t even know how to turn the computer on,” Greg snapped at Bobby knowing that his dad would be in a bad mood for most of the day after being shown up as a dinosaur.

Bobby smiled, eyebrows raised. “I’m going over to see some mates after church; I won’t be back until late this evening.”

Greg looked at his brother as the truth then dawned on him, so that was why he'd annoyed Dad; he won't be around to face the consequences. He strode quickly towards the stairs to get himself changed, he'd definitely think of some way to pay Bobby back, something unimaginably evil.

Jack looked so incredibly cute in his blazer and long trousers when they all met in the reception room, he was standing tall, nose in the air, holding onto Theo's hand as they all went through the big double doors and started down the steps to the driveway. The family produced and opened several large umbrellas as they continued walking along the drive, which was now glistening with the rain. It had been tipping down for several hours. They continued through the large gates which Ned locked behind them, before following the family along the towpath to the church.

Jack had a secret, which he only shared with Theo, his bestest mate in the whole wide world. He'd found Grumpsy's' stash of liquorish Pontefract cakes and put a handful in each of his blazer pockets. Theo laughed but promised not to tell anybody.

They all trooped into the church taking their seats in the pew at the front. As the service began Jack pulled out one of the round liquorice discs and started to munch merrily away. During the service, nobody noticed the dark sludge running from the corners of his mouth and down the clean white shirt he was wearing. He crammed pieces of liquorice in his mouth, looking around furtively between mouthfuls of the black goo to make sure no one noticed. He occasionally smiled at his best mate and sneaked the odd piece into Theo's hand, Jack couldn't understand why Theo kept putting them into his inside pocket and wasn't eating any of them. He looked at him quizzically; perhaps he was saving them for later he thought, popping another one in his mouth, chewing furiously.

The service ended and the family started to queue up to leave the church. They were all saying goodbye and thank you to the vicar, the men shaking June's hand and the women giving her a hug and a peck on the cheek, when it was Jack's turn he smiled at June showing a set of black teeth. Celia looked at him not really believing how he could have possibly got himself into that state in an hour and with nobody noticing. When they got back home Jack was given a mug of juice and then whisked upstairs to get changed and clean his teeth. He was then loaded complete with case and toys into Celia's car and returned to his parents.

Audrey was feeling much better after a lazy morning, but her headache was still lingering despite the painkillers she'd taken. "What are we doing for lunch guys; have you anything in mind Louisa?"

"I think you ladies have done enough cooking and cleaning this week, I'm going to treat us all, I've booked a table at the Raven Arms we'll just wait for Celia to get back then we'll take a drive down. "Anyone volunteering to drive?" Ned looked around at the boys to see which one of them put their hands up. To his surprise, both Greg and Pete raised their hands and laughed at the same time.

"Great minds think alike," Pete said, "I don't mind driving, I only drink coke anyway so it makes no difference to me."

"Well done son, is the people carrier ready?"

"Yes it is, I took it to the carwash and filled up with petrol." Greg answered his father's question while searching the biscuit barrel for a custard cream. "Bobby isn't going to be very happy at missing out on the Sunday treat."

"Perhaps we should ask the pub to do a takeaway for him," Louisa shoved her husband out of the way while she put the kettle on. "I don't think eating biscuits is good at this time, it'll ruin your appetite."

Greg bit into his custard cream, holding the remaining half of the biscuit up at eye level inspecting it. "Ohhh I don't think so," he said very slowly "I'm sure he'll have eaten already, he said he was going to be late." Greg smiled remembering the conversation he'd had with his brother earlier in the day.

Celia returned and was delighted to be going out, they all got into the large people carrier and arrived at the pub at 2pm.

"Just enough time for a little drinky poo," Audrey said eyes shining at the thought of not having to clear tables and wash dishes, this really was a luxury she thought to herself.

Patricia was sitting on a stool at the corner of the bar talking to Sarah as the family came into the lounge bar, Ned, Greg and Pete ordered the drinks from Sarah and Audrey stood chatting to Patricia.

“So anything new Patricia?” Audrey said reaching over for a glass of dry white Chardonnay the barmaid had placed beside her.

“Roger is at the hospital with his mum, we think she’s had another little stroke, we found her wandering around upstairs in the middle of the night. She was very confused and kept asking where her mum was. Roger was really upset, he came back early this morning to collect her medication, they wanted to see it at the hospital. After a quick sandwich he went back, I haven’t heard from him since. I know she can be a royal pain in the bum but I will miss her if she goes,” Patricia was uncharacteristically emotional as she looked over at Audrey, tears in her eyes.

“Well she's reached a good old age Patricia, I think you have to prepare yourself for the worst news and if she comes back home treat it as a bonus.” Audrey patted her hand and for once Patricia didn’t tut or bristle, she just seemed to sink further down into the stool, looking despairingly into her cup before draining the last dregs of coffee.

Audrey wanted to quiz her about the birth certificate she’d found, but realised it wasn’t the right time. “Have you seen anything of Julie?”

Patricia looked at her before taking on board what she’d just said, “Oh no, Sarah said the new pharmacist was trying to get in and couldn’t, I believe she told her to look up the Belle sisters to see if they’d got a spare key. Now you’ve bought up the subject I do believe we hold a key, I’ll try to find it a little later.”

The waitress came through and showed them to their table, everyone had already decided on what they wanted while Audrey and Patricia were nattering. Audrey took a quick look at the menu and immediately decided on Beef and Yorkshire Puds, the waitress took their orders and came back a few minutes later. “Your meal will be about half an hour. Would you like wine and could I get you some nibbles to keep you going?”

Ned ordered a bottle of white and a bottle of red from the wine list and the young woman immediately returned with the bottles and glasses, along with a plate full of olives, a bowl of dipping oil and a stack of crusty garlic bread. Greg and Pete both reached over the moment the plates touched the table. "You boys are eager, have you been saving yourself for this feast," the girl smiled and looked over at Holly. "Hi Holly how are you doing, have you got anything planned for the summer break?"

"Think I'll be put to work in the castle probably Jemima, but I'm still waiting on at the café on a Saturday. Mum is thinking of going back to work so I'm sure she'll have something to keep me out of mischief." Both girls laughed as Jemima walked away.

"Do you know her from school Holly?" Louisa asked her daughter.

"Yep, she's in a couple of my classes, she's a really nice girl, I think they have some money issues at home, her clothes are sometimes a bit worn and when we used to go on day trips and outings she never joined in."

The family looked over at Jemima as she was scribbling in a notepad on the bar. She was quite petite, her dark skin seemed to emphasis the whiteness of her shirt, her dark Afro-Caribbean hair was perched on top of her head, held in place with clips.

The food was delicious and everyone but Audrey and Louisa ordered dessert. "Nothing you fancy on the dessert menu Louisa," Greg looked at his wife in surprise.

"No, I only like cheesecake and tiramisu, they don't have any on the menu today and I'm absolutely stuffed anyway."

"Always room for pudding" May called out. May and April walked through the door with their dad, Tom.

Everyone laughed and the Belle family came over to chat, pulling up chairs as Ned, Greg and Pete shuffled around to make room for them.

"We're not eating; we just came in for a drink." April said before shouting over to the bar, "mine's a gin and tonic, a sparkling water for May and a pint of old ale for Dad."

Jemima walked in to clear plates and make room for desserts when Tom stood up, caught hold of her hand and swung her round. He pointed at her and broke into song.

"My my my Jemima,
Why why why Jemima,
I could see, that girl was no good for me
But I was lost like a slave that no man could free

La La La La La La La Da Da Da"

Everyone was crying with laughter as Jemima managed to slide away, but you could still hear her laughing as she disappeared into the kitchen. Even Patricia was holding her stomach as she slipped off the bar stool and made her way over to the table. There was no one else in the restaurant, everyone had left earlier, so the boys bought over another table and a few more chairs. Sarah, Jemima and the chef bought over trays of desserts and a couple of bottles of wine, dragging over chairs and sitting down with Patricia and their customers.

"Mmmm I feel a party coming on," Ted said before starting to sing again.

"We are family;
I got all my friends with me.
We are family,
Get up ev'rybody and sing.
We are family,
I got all my friends with me.
We are family,
Get up ev'rybody and sing."

May and April joined in and within minutes, everyone was up dancing and singing. The party broke up a few of hours later, the staff from the pub started the evening service, April, May and Tom ran to the car and drove at some speed along the lanes to get ready for June's evening prayers.

The Knight family were just leaving when a smiling Patricia came over and hugged all of them in turn, "I can't tell you just how much better I feel, I can't remember the last time I really let my hair down and had such a good time. Thank you all."

Everyone was stunned and muttered likewise and some other polite responses. They were shocked at Patricia showing her human side, it quite took them aback. They hastily got into the car and Pete drove them back.

As soon as they returned, Greg gathered his dad, Pete, and Theo and went upstairs, he wanted to move the door that had fallen on top of the armour on the stairs. He said it was about time they tidied up the area and got Tom in again to put some more lighting in the new areas that had been uncovered.

They made their way to the steps and wrestled with the heavy door for a few minutes without success.

"Perhaps a car jack may get it high enough for us to manoeuvre, have you got one in your Mary Poppins bag Pete?" Greg leaned against the stone wall panting, Theo was sprawled out over the doorstep and Ned was looking on ready to give some advice.

"No, but I know where I can get one, give me ten minutes and I'll be back." Pete ran up the steps and through the door, leaving the other three to look around yet again. They went down to the old kitchen and started pulling ivy through the small window in the pantry.

"If we can't clear the ivy from the outside today, maybe we can start clearing it from the inside." Ned started pulling with all his strength and got quite a lot of it through the window. "We could do with some clippers and garden sacks."

Theo looked at his mobile phone, "Hey, I've got a signal when I stand by the back door. Shall I call Mum and ask her to get sacks and clippers for you Grumpsy?"

"Don't call me Grumpsy or I really will get grumpsy with a backhand across your earhole. Yes, tell her there's no hurry, I suppose it could all wait until tomorrow, but if she's doing nothing."

"Mum says Holly and Liz aren't doing anything she'll send them down."

A couple of minutes later there was an almighty bang. They jumped looking up at the ceiling, the noise sounded as though it emanated from there.

"What the dickens was that?" Ned leaned on a table which stood in the middle of the floor, "it seems sturdy enough," he pulled out an old stool from underneath and then stepped up onto the table, which enabled him to reach up and touch the ceiling. "I can feel a faint vibration. Oh it's gone now. Wonder what it was? I suppose we'd better get back to the steps Pete should be there soon."

They all met up a few second later on the steps, Ned took the bags and clippers off the girls and went into the dormitory to watch what the boys were doing, the girls stood at the top of the steps looking on with curiosity at Greg and Pete at work.

"There, it's starting to rise up at this end, Dad, Theo, you stand with your feet pressed up against the bottom of the door to make sure it doesn't slip, brace yourselves against the wall. As soon as we get it high enough this side we'll push it up to a standing position, then you two can move into the dormitory out of the way. We'll try to walk it towards the wall Pete, we can lean it there for a while until we can decide what to do with it." Greg was in charge again and they all felt better. If anything went wrong they could always blame him.

Everything was going smoothly, the car jack did its job and as soon as it had lifted the door around eighteen inches the boys pushed it up until it was standing, Ned and Theo moved into the dormitory and Greg and Pete walked the door backwards until it was resting against the wall.

"Perfect" Ned said, everyone was congratulating themselves, until Holly let out a little scream.

"Scared Holly, you seen an incy wincy spider?" Theo said laughing.

"No, but I can see a hand sticking out of that suit of armour," Holly's voice was trembling as she started to back into the old bedroom, reversing into Liz and standing on her toe as she started to beat a hasty retreat.

"Owwww, that hurt! You stood on my toe stupid. A hand? Really, Holly what an imagination you've got."

"As much as I really don't want it to be true, I think Holly is right, what do you think Greg?" Pete leaned forward as he spoke, gently shoving the armour with his foot; the breastplate slid away revealing a ribcage, as they all jumped back the whole suit slid down the steps coming to a rest at the bottom. The helmet rocked from side to side a few times and then bounced down the last couple of steps coming to rest by Theo's feet. The boy moved back, his eyes bulging and mouth open when he realised the helmet had split open revealing a human skull.

They stood paralysed for a moment or two before Ned composed himself again "I think we should move very slowly, don't disturb anything. We'll leave the bags and clippers here, move around the mmmm errrrrr skeleton, being very careful not to touch anything, Pete you go first."

Pete managed to stride up two steps putting his hands on the walls to steady himself. He stopped a couple of steps up and Theo wriggled around the skull putting his foot on the third step and Pete took his hand pulling him clear. Ned did the same thing and Greg's long powerful legs made short work of the exercise.

They all stood at the top of the steps looking down at the remains.

"So what do we do now, Dad?" Liz asked whilst standing on tiptoe to look over Theo's shoulder.

Before Greg could speak, Ned said, "I think we should call your friend the policeman Liz."

"Oh Goodie" she smiled and clapped her hands as they all made their way into the main area of the castle and down into the kitchen.

CHAPTER 13

Revenge is so sweet.

It was just after 8pm when the doorbell rang. Liz and Holly rushed to answer the door, much to Liz's delight it was Robin and his father Bob standing on the doorstep. They were soaking wet, even though the walk from their car to the door was only a few yards, their hair was plastered to their heads and water was running down the faces of the officers, they couldn't have been any wetter if they'd just got out of the moat. Holly ran to the kitchen to tell the family they'd arrived and Liz chose to demurely lead the way.

Theo took the visitors soaked raincoats and hung them on coat hangers in the cloakroom by the side of the radiator. He looked over to where Cinders should have been, he missed her so much; choking back a sob he turned and came back into the kitchen. Audrey handed the two men large towels to dry themselves, whilst piping hot coffee and chocolate digestive biscuits were hastily served. Greg and Ned bought the officers up to date. Pete was towel drying the dogs, they looked like drowned rats after their short early evening walk.

"Well there seems to be an event a day in this place since you people moved in," Bob shook his head in disbelief, his face stern. "Could you take me to this skeleton please gentlemen? Constable stay here and take a group statement, just so we've got something down on record," he smiled at his son and as he got up he winked at Liz, who blushed and dipped her head in a shy pose.

Half an hour later there had been a lot of smiling and whispering going on between Robin and Liz, as the young constable was trying to piece together what had happened that day.

"It sounded like a good party at the Raven Arms. Next time you're there you'll have to give me a call and I can join in the fun. After this case is over of course, can't mix business and pleasure," Robin drained his coffee cup and was just putting his electronic notebook away when Bob came back. He looked enquiringly at his dad, who was also his superior officer, a fact that he couldn't forget, not even for a moment, or he would get the rough edge of DS Sergeant's tongue.

"Well it's definitely a skeleton, no doubt about that at all, I've called forensics, they'll be here as soon as they can. In the meantime, I think it goes without saying; you will all have to avoid that part of the house. Unfortunately, because it's an unexplained death, it's probably going to be taken out of my hands. I'll more than likely be doing most of the leg work and it depends on what the enquiry reveals as to what happens from here on," Bob slumped down on one of the kitchen chairs looking very weary. "This is typical; I retire in a few weeks. I thought this posting would be a nice cushy number, but sods law it's proving to be anything but. In the last week or so since I got here, there's been Audrey's accident, a dead cat, red fountains and now a skeleton has turned up, unbelievably all those incidents revolve around this one family." His eyebrows rose making the furrows on his forehead more prominent; his weathered face looked older than his 50 years. He lifted his hand and wiped imaginary sweat off his forehead, sighing and looking pensive.

"You forgot the poisoned mushrooms Sir," Theo said going into the fridge to get out another can of Zero Coke.

"What poisoned mushrooms?" The young constable said standing up and taking his notepad out.

Audrey sighed and threw a threatening look at her grandson; she wondered which door he'd been listening at to discover that information.

"We don't know they were poisoned Theo," Audrey turned to look at Bob and Robin. "The Belle sisters came around for a spot of lunch; there was some doubt as to who actually chopped the mushrooms that May had foraged. None of us had chopping them and when we looked into the bowl there was something grated into the mixture; Caroline and May thought it looked like a bulb of some sort so we decided to leave well alone."

"Ok. Ok. Ok. Just back up there," Bob looked even more exasperated than he had before. "Where is this bowl now and who is Caroline?"

"The bowl has been washed up; I put some of the contents in a plastic container in the freezer. The rest I gave to Caroline, she said she could probably find out what the mystery ingredient was. Caroline, by the way is the new pharmacist sent from Cornwallis chemists, she's temporarily replacing Julie who is suspended. The poor girl was trying to gain entry to the shop, we think Julie was there but wouldn't answer the door, she tried to use her keys, but both doors were bolted on the inside. Sarah at the pub pointed her in the direction of the Belle sisters; I think she was just trying to pass the buck personally, but whatever. There was no reply at the gatehouse and our gate was open so she came here to see if I knew where the sisters were, obviously they were here, because we were going to have a mushroom risotto. Caroline joined us for lunch, which ended up being cheese on toast. That's the truth the whole truth and nothing but the truth Ma Lord," Audrey went over to put the kettle on and then decided this was going to be at least a two whisky moment, so she asked Ned to get the drinks trolley.

"So the pharmacist just wandered through the unopened gate and knocked on your door, you let a complete stranger in despite the unusual goings on. How do you know she came straight to your front door, could she have gone around the back first and chopped up the mushrooms depositing the foreign substance before she came around to the front?" Robin said his eyes widening in disbelief at the irresponsible behaviour.

Audrey's brow furrowed and she shrugged her shoulders apologetically, "I'd never thought of that, how silly of me. She's a pharmacist and would know all about poisons, she is a pharmacist isn't she? Oh goodness, it was Julie's replacement wasn't it?"

"Well I'll leave the boss here to explain all about that." Robin stood in the corner out of the way.

"Now I know this seems unbelievable, but I think I'm getting the picture," Smiling as he rocked back on the chair.

Everyone looked at him in disbelief. Only Robin showed a glimmer of understanding.

"I took a call at the station on Saturday afternoon from the Head Office of the Cornwallis Pharmacy Group. They asked for a couple of the boys to meet a Ms Chen at the shop in the village at 8.30 on Monday morning to gain entry. Apparently, a solicitor is going to be there with all the documentation to force entry if required, they have requested a senior officer because of the amount of controlled drugs on the premises. Therefore, the visit you had on Saturday by Ms Chen confirms what you've just told me. However, that doesn't rule her out of the incidents that have befallen the family over the last few days. I'll have to make some enquiries about her."

"She seemed such a lovely girl, I can't imagine she's got anything to do with all this," Audrey looked bemused as she looked over to the door, which had just opened.

Ned came in with the drinks trolley and offered the officers a little tipple.

Bob glanced over at Robin and then looked at his watch; "I was off duty an hour ago, you're driving son. A Guinness or a Murphy's would be great, thanks Ned."

Ned put a pint glass of Guinness in front of Bob, "Any news on the car that mangled Audrey's bike or what happened to the cat?"

"I've been meaning to come over and bring you up to date, but you know what it's like, not enough hours in the day."

Ned smiled at Bob nodding his head, he remembered when he was working the time just seemed to disappear.

Bob continued, "The cat I'm afraid is a bit of a lost cause, we've received the report from Mr O'Leary and unless someone confesses it is unlikely we'll get to the bottom of it, but it will still going to be an open case for a while. I get the feeling that all these incidents are linked, so when we solve one, we'll solve them all. The red fountains were created with beetroot, simple but effective.

Audrey's accident is another matter. We've had six people in for questioning, all from the same family. All of them have been charged with burglary, apparently the spate of break-ins in the area recently are attributed to the Royle family. They've coughed to breaking and entering and taking property without permission, but deny anything to do with the bike incident, several of them did make some very negative comments regarding the Knight family though, so we can't completely rule them out, they're a very large family with a lot of dubious acquaintances. Unfortunately, CCTV does place them at the scene of the crimes ten miles away at the time, so now we're a bit stumped, but I'm pursuing another couple of leads and I'll let you know what I find.

The incident with the mushrooms worries me though, that would lead me to believe that they weren't just targeting Audrey, but the Belle sisters too. Have you any idea if the container of mushrooms was interfered with here or at their house?" He looked over at Audrey and then took a long slow gulp of his beer, smacking his lips in appreciation before returning the glass to the table.

"The mushrooms were in a plastic bowl with a lid on; I presumed it had been interfered with in this kitchen, because it was on the work surface for around an hour whilst we were all in the library and talking to Caroline at the front door. The back door was open and the main gate was open as well, so I just jumped to the conclusion it was here. Now I come to think about it the container wasn't see through, so you couldn't actually see the contents clearly, it could have been done at the gatehouse and May bought it over here unwittingly," Audrey picked up her empty glass and raised it in front of Ned's nose.

"Another one, Audrey? Are you sure?" Ned looked at his wife reproachfully.

"Do bears poo in the woods Ned?" Audrey said tipping her glass upside down and shaking it.

Ned poured Audrey a small measure and filled the glass with ice sneaking a measure of water in the glass while Audrey was distracted.

"Water Ned, you've put water in this very fine single malt, what were you thinking, that's sacrilege," Audrey turned on Ned anger in her eyes.

"Ohhhh Grumpsy fancy putting a bit of water in Nana's glass, shame on you," Holly said sarcastically.

"It can't be a bit of water Holly it's a drop of water, a bit is solid, a drop is liquid, a bit of water is an ice cube, which is a necessary element to scotch on the rocks." Audrey said with some exasperation in her voice, whilst reaching for the single malt and putting a very large drop in her glass.

Holly pulled a face and stomped out of the kitchen slamming the door behind her.

Pete and Greg started talking about the skeleton in the suit of armour; everyone joined in and were all talking over each other when Louisa stood up and very quietly went over to the door where Holly had made her stage exit. She put her hand on the handle and motioned everyone to carry on talking, with one swift movement she turned the handle and threw the door wide open. Holly fell into the room and did a lengthy running fall, trying and failing to keep her balance she ended up at the other end of the kitchen sprawled on the floor.

She stood up very gracefully, looked at her mother and said, "I suppose you think that's funny."

Not only Louisa but everyone in the room thought it was funny, the howls of laughter continued for quite a time before one by one they all composed themselves. Holly sat making a most peculiar face as she tried her best not to smile at her unceremonious entrance.

"How far have you got with the journals Audrey," Louisa said pouring herself a small glass of dry white wine.

"I'm working through them with great difficulty, I can only pick out an occasional word, but there is more talk of Albert the stable boy. She really likes him and she says he has a soft spot for her, I think he's George's brother. I'm having a meeting with the sisters tomorrow, they've got more info from the nursing home," Audrey looked at the whisky bottle and thought better of it, she got a glass of sparkling water from the fridge and put a slice of lemon in it. "There's more mention of Mrs Shufflebotham and

I get a sneaky suspicion that the cook is seeing one of the other servants but I can't make out who it is."

"If she's a Mrs that's a bit dicey under your own roof unless she's a widow?," Ned was putting the kettle on and filling up the plate of biscuits, "anyone for cheese and biscuits, I thought I'd get some snacks out for when our visitors arrive, its 10 o'clock so they should be here soon."

"I'm for that Dad" Greg said opening cupboards looking for crisps and nuts.

After some thought Audrey replied to Ned's question about the cook, "in those days the cook was always called Mrs regardless of her status, she could have been unmarried or a widow it wouldn't have made any difference, they were all called Mrs and sometimes the servants would be called by a name that the aristocracy chose for them. They could have called all the cooks the same name over the years, the same for maids and butlers etc; it saved them trying to remember new names. Crazy but true, according to my internet research," Audrey opened a jar of olives and pickled onions, adding them to the crisps Greg had found, putting them next to the cheese and biscuits Ned had placed on the table.

They were all tucking into the snack when the doorbell rang again; Theo made a dash to the door to let the forensic team in, there were two of them, a lady, who Audrey knew vaguely as Sukie Ryan, she was engaged to an old friend, the local doctor Donald Scott. Dr Ryan was accompanied by an unfamiliar stranger, they carried four large cases and had white suits in plastic bags shoved under their arms. Bob and Robin lead them upstairs.

"No need for the white suits for a while, I suggest you put them on when you get to the master bedroom," he started up the stairs when Ned came into the reception room.

"You might want to put your cases in the lift, it's quite small so I suggest one of you takes the lift up with the equipment and the rest of you walk, it's only a couple of floors."

"Thanks for that mate, this stuff is really heavy, will we need to bring the floodlights in?" The man said.

"I don't think so, the steps and some of the rooms are quite well lit, I'd see what you think when you get there, you can always come down again." Bob said as he started climbing the staircase to the second floor.

Everyone met in the hallway leading to Ned's room. They stopped at the door and asked Robin to cordon the area off while they worked.

Audrey told them there was food downstairs when they'd finished and asked if they would like to take a drink with them.

"Thank you for that but we'll be ok, we come equipped with most things but thank you for the offer. It's likely we're going to be here for a few hours, so if anyone wants to retire please feel free, unless you sleep in this bedroom that is," Sukie said as she disappeared into the wardrobe.

"Ok everyone, let's leave them to it, no sneaking back up Theo, we'll be watching both you and Holly," Greg herded the children down the staircase and as soon as they arrived back in the kitchen, minus Bob and Robin, everyone started hoovering up the food on the table.

"I'm taking the dogs out, anyone want to join me?" Pete was just about to go through to the cloakroom when it suddenly dawned on Ned what had happened earlier in the day.

"When we were in the old kitchen downstairs did anyone hear a big bang?" Ned imitated a bang by dropping an empty tray on the floor.

"Goodness Ned, you made me jump you old fool," Audrey took a swing at his arm with a tea towel, which much to her satisfaction landed with a noise a little like Indiana Jones's whip. "Pete frightened us all earlier when he dropped those damned car jacks on this stone floor."

Greg went over to the alcove, which housed a full size fridge and two freezers; he bent down and felt the stone floor just in front of them. Looking up at his dad smiling he said "The floors vibrating slightly, looks as if the old kitchen is right underneath the new one Dad."

"So if my sense of direction isn't misleading me, the door to the old kitchen is situated just around the corner and right by the start of the moat, alongside the orangery. We'll do some investigating when the weather has cleared up and we've got rid of our visitors," Ned helped himself to a large piece of Edam looking very pleased with himself.

"That could be why Cinders was always trying to dig up the tiles under the sink." Audrey took the last piece of Edam much to Ned's dismay.

"She could probably smell the mice or rats," Pete opened the door and the dogs came running out, looking as if they'd been imprisoned for days.

"Rats. Rats. We have RATS," Liz screeched.

"Of course we have rats Liz; we have a moat and probably another floor of rooms down below. The ivy and the bushes are overgrown, it's an ideal breeding ground for vermin, we'll have a look at it and see if we can open any more rooms soon, but just for the moment I think we should all get some sleep," Louisa yawned and headed towards the door, kissing her husband as she passed him. "Come on children, its school tomorrow and I've a feeling it's going to be a busy day."

Pete took the dogs out, Greg and Ned agreed that they would take it in turns to have a nap in the sitting room, until all there visitors had left and they could lock up. Ned opened a very nice bottle of port; Greg helped himself to a bottle of old English cider before getting his pad and pen out and writing a list of things to do tomorrow. He gave his dad a piece of paper and pen, asking him to try to estimate how big that kitchen was and where he thought it might start and end.

Pete returned with the dogs; they tiptoed around the area where Cinders used to sleep as though she were still there. He fed the hungry animals before joining his father and brother. "Anyone for coffee?" he said finishing off the crisps on the side as he waited for the kettle to boil.

"No ta, you've been down in the kitchen Pete. Do you think it's this shape and size?" His dad a piece of paper towards him. Pete picked it up and turned it around and around with a puzzled look on his face.

"Not sure, I think it was bigger than that, but I can't see how that door can be where you say it is. I've been looking outside and if it is there it would come out in the moat or under the Orangery, it's all very disorientating," he didn't have time to say anything else as the dogs started barking furiously and in walked a very wet and disgruntled Bobby.

"I must have left my mobile and my gate key somewhere, I could have sworn I'd put them in my jacket pocket. I've just had to walk down the lanes and come overland where we found Mum, it's taken me ages, I couldn't get in through the side door because it was bolted, thank God you're still up, I'd have been outside until the morning if the back door hadn't been open. What's with the van and police car outside, what's happened?" Bobby was peeling his wet jacket off his shivering body.

"You could have tried to get through the dog flap Bobby, I do remember you attempting to get through a very small kitchen window, when you didn't want to disturb Mater and Pater at two o'clock in the morning," Greg started chuckling, giving himself an imaginary pat on the back for locking the entrance gates and bolting the front door.

"Who locked the gates and bolted the side door?" Bobby looked at all three of them hoping to spot the guilty party.

"I did, I thought you'd have your keys with you, just trying to keep us all safe bro," Greg said with a self-satisfied grin on his face. "We've had a bit of excitement while you've been out I'm sure Pete will update you. I'm going to have a nap in the sitting room for an hour. Greg swaggered out of the room, very pleased with himself, that'll teach Bobby to put dad in a bad mood he laughed to himself.

It was in the early hours of Monday morning when the forensic team left. The two police officers escorted Ned to his room to pick up a few essentials and he moved them into Audrey's room, she must have been exhausted because she never stirred while he stacked a few shirts, trousers, his pyjamas with some underwear on the chair in the corner. Bob and Robin put police tape on both Ned's door and the adjoining door, which led to Audrey's room.

Everyone was extremely tired, including the two officers, even though they had both been fed and had drunk numerous cups of coffee, they still looked as though they needed a good night's sleep. They walked down the steps to the police car, waving and agreeing to be back early the next morning. Greg followed the car down to the main gate; he had already opened it earlier to let out the people in the white van. The dogs followed him as he locked everything up again.

By three am, all the visitors had disappeared and the family decided to try to get a couple of hours well deserved shut eye. Once upstairs the boys disappeared to their rooms and Ned slipped silently into Audrey's room. She lay peacefully, breathing evenly with an occasional snuffle; he undressed and slipped into bed beside her.

Audrey awoke and turned over to face him, "Everyone gone?" she yawned and stretched.

"Yes they have dear, go back to sleep we've got a big day tomorrow," Ned pulled the covers up covering his wife's shoulders and within seconds they were both in the land of nod.

CHAPTER 14

Rookery Castle Enterprises; a Family Affair.

Audrey gathered some clothes and crept into her bathroom, had a quick shower and dressed as silently as she could; Ned was still sound asleep, snoring and grunting away. It was just after six am and the skies had cleared after yesterday's torrential rain, the sun was rising above the trees at the far side of the estate, lighting up the fields and old farmers cottages in the distance. It was starting to look like a beautiful day.

Downstairs she let the dogs out and again they avoided the cushion where Cinders always lay, looking over at the cat basket. She thought she saw a black shape; it was early in the morning so she rubbed her eyes. It was still there, just a shadowy shape. Reaching inside her cardigan pocket and pulling out a bright blue spectacle case, she opened it and put on her glasses. Normally she wouldn't wear them unless it was absolutely necessary, vanity was a terrible thing but as the cloakroom was still in shadows and no one was about to witness just how bad her eyesight was, she felt justified. In the corner of the cloakroom, what looked like a small dark cloud was hovering just above Cinders basket. She crept forward and put her hand into the smoky ball, it went straight through and the cloud parted, she took her hand away and it closed up again. "Is that you Cinders?" Audrey said a little nervously. What looked like two green gems shone out of the middle of the cloud making her jump, it moved from the basket and started winding in and out of her legs. Audrey laughed "Oh I'm so pleased to see you Cinders, it's lovely to have you back girl, but please don't show yourself to anyone else just yet, let it be our secret."

The shape disappeared and Audrey continued to make a pot of coffee. A few minutes later she was sitting at the table with a mug of the sweet dark liquid, looking out of the window at the new day. She smiled as she felt a familiar tickle on her ankles as if fur was brushing against them.

By seven am Louisa and Celia had risen followed a little later by Theo and the girls. Ned was still fast asleep and the boys stayed in bed for an hour or so after everyone else had gathered in the kitchen. Eventually, they walked in, having followed the smell of bacon and eggs cooking. Like zombies, they followed their noses down the stairs, into the hallway and eventually sat themselves one by one in their chairs at the table.

"Coffee's in the pot, juice is on the table, bacon eggs and mushrooms are in the hot holding trays, make you own toast," Audrey was particularly cheery having had a good nights restful sleep.

Liz started to gather her siblings to drop them off at school. "Come on you guys, we'll be late, get a move on, you aren't even dressed yet."

Theo and Holly glared at her they explained it was half term.

"Oh goodness I'd forgotten," Liz said with an apologetic smile.

"You're not the only one, so had I, I wouldn't have dragged you out of bed so early if I'd known it was a holiday," Louisa said, "but, it's good to get up early, more of the day to enjoy."

The two teenagers dragged their bodies through the kitchen and sat back down; Holly looked at her mother with a sorrowful expression on her face. Theo rested his head on the table and pretended to snore.

Breakfast was hastily eaten and all the dishes cleared away when the doorbell rang. This time Audrey went speedily to open the front door, she found it was the Detective Sergeant and alongside him a particularly attractive female police officer. Good morning Mrs Knight I've bought someone to meet you all. Audrey led the way to the back of the castle and into the kitchen.

Pete and Bobby had taken the dogs out for a walk, but everyone else was discussing the events of yesterday as Bob and the young lady entered the room. Bob cleared his throat and everyone looked around, eyes resting on the woman by his side, she was quite tall and her uniform seemed a little too tight for her, she removed her hat to reveal short fair hair and as she smiled dimples appeared in both sides of her full cheeks.

"This is Community Support Officer Mandy Riley. Officer Riley you have in front of you just some of the infamous Knight family, who just happen to be old friends of mine, so we go back more than a few years, I am trusting them into your care. Do not let me down," he spoke the last few words very slowly as he held her in his gaze.

Louisa broke the tension "Do we call you Officer Riley or Mandy."

"I recognise you from the hospital don't I? You sat in the corridor for hours," Audrey smiled as she recognised one of her hospital bodyguards.

"Yes guilty as charged Mrs Knight, but please call me Mandy, officer seems so official and according to DS Sergeant here, we're going to be spending quite a lot of time together," she said her grey-blue eyes sparkling with kindness.

I'm going to leave an officer with you around the clock for a couple of days, until I can get a little further with the case. The officers will patrol the grounds and they will be calling in at The Gatehouse several times a day as well. I am presuming that is ok with you all?" Bob Sergeant said in his best official voice and the family all nodded in agreement.

"Sergeant Sergeant, would you like a coffee and some toast?" Audrey said trying her very best not to giggle.

"No thank you Mrs Knight I have a chemist to open, PC Sergeant is there at the moment with Ms Chen, Julie just isn't co-operating." Bob, or DS Sergeant as he had to be called in front of junior officers, took his leave.

"Come on Mandy sit yourself down. What would you like to drink?" Audrey pulled out the mug with the kissing lips from the cupboard, thought better of it and replaced it with a large pink cup that had a smiley face on it, an herb of some sort sticking out of the side of it's mouth.

"Coffee please, Mrs Knight. White with two sugars," Mandy replied.

"Oh call me Audrey and this is Louisa."

Everyone introduced themselves while Mandy sipped her coffee, also helping herself to a piece of toast from the plate that had been placed in front of her. "How is your head Audrey, I believe you had a nasty fall?"

"Well thank you for asking. Not many people have enquired after the first couple of days," Audrey looked around the room with a frown on her face. "I still get an occasional headache, but the blurred vision has disappeared, I've mastered the comb over with the help of Louisa, she's a hairdresser," Audrey nodded over to her daughter in law. "I'm due back at the hospital soon; they want to take another x-ray to make sure the fracture is healing alright."

Mandy smiled and nodded her head in sympathy. She heard a noise and stood up, turning quickly to come face to face with Ned.

"Owd on there duck, I'm a good guy, no handcuffs unless it's in the bedroom," Ned laughed, putting his arms out offering her the opportunity to handcuff him.

"Mandy, this is my husband Ned, you can let him pass, you have to feel sorry for him he thinks he's funny. Ned this is CSO Mandy Riley she's going to be stationed here for a while. DS Sergeant thinks it would be better if we had a police presence for a few days. Now sit down I'll get you coffee and a bacon butty, try your very best not to embarrass yourself."

Ned smiled and shook hands with Mandy, "Very pleased to meet you dear, there's a whole brood of us living here, you'll get used to us eventually and we're not a bad lot." He winked and settled himself at the table picking up yesterday's crossword while he waited for his breakfast.

One by one, the family congregated in the kitchen, everyone introducing themselves to their guest and taking their places at the table. Almost immediately, they started to discuss what they were going to do that day.

"Louisa, have you thought anymore about opening a hair and beauty salon, Honey?" Celia looked over at her daughter.

"You must be a mind reader mum, I was just thinking about that. I've had a chat with Liz and we've decided to go into partnership; Liz took a beauty course at college when she studied hairdressing. I've got a couple of old friends I've worked with in the past and we're thinking about asking them if they would like to rent a chair."

Ned took a deep breath in but Audrey put her hand up in a stop motion, he relaxed and screwed his face up in resignation. Everyone at the table grinned, Audrey new her husband so well, he was about to make a remark about renting a chair. Louisa wasn't a confident person and Audrey wanted her to be heard without interruption. Louisa continued, "I'm not sure where to open it though, I don't think Liz's boss would be very happy if we opened one in the same town. Liz gets the impression she's not ready to retire yet, so there's no chance of buying her out. It will probably cost a lot of money and I only have a couple of thousand saved."

Ned took a breath in, but this time Audrey didn't stop him. "I think it's a great idea, you and Liz going in partnership and don't worry about the money, I'm sure we can back you, in fact we could be sleeping partners."

Liz ran around the table and stood behind Ned her arms wrapped around his neck, "Oh thank you, thank you, thank you, Grandad. You won't regret it, we'll be a huge success, I promise."

Mandy excused herself, "I'm just going to take little walk over to see the Belle sisters, then I'll take a stroll around the grounds if that's ok?"

"If you come back here after you've visited the three witches of Heathbrook, I'll show you around the estate, the dogs are ready for another walk anyway. Is about half an hour ok?" Pete said as he helped himself to another coffee.

"Perfect Pete thank you, I'll see you back here." Mandy said as she went towards the back door.

As soon as she was out of earshot, they all turned their attention to Pete.

"Just being friendly, don't want her to think we're a family of weirdo's," Pete said downing his coffee.

"Could I have everyone's attention for a few minutes please," Audrey stood up and waited for them to finish their conversations before she began. "I know we're all busy investigating the castle, cleaning tidying etc., but I do think we should be looking to the future, originally when I had the idea of us all moving in together I thought you would all take twelve months off work to concentrate on our home, but Louisa has given me an idea. Even though we've quite a substantial amount of money in the bank and we've invested quite a bit as well, it won't last us all forever. We have to think about keeping ourselves occupied and bring some money in. I've been thinking of a couple of ideas and I'd like everyone to consider them seriously." She paused making sure they were all paying attention, "The first one is the old tied cottages, they've gone to rack and ruin and for no good reason, they obviously at some time or another had electricity, water and sewage installed in them. I think we should invest some money and do them up ourselves, we could either rent them out to locals or hire them out has holiday cottages." Everyone nodded in agreement to her idea.

"The second one is Louisa and Liz want to open a salon, why don't we go the whole hog and open a Spa, either in the grounds or in the castle. We have far too much room, a lot of the space just isn't being utilised properly. We've discovered the old kitchens, if there's one room, I'm sure there will be a whole floor to work with. Greg has always wanted to be a gym instructor or personal trainer; he's been harping on about it for years. We could have a nice little gym, a sauna, steam room, a small swimming pool. Perhaps even a café bar, I'm sure we could make cakes and biscuits for afternoon teas." Audrey paused for a moment or two to let the idea sink in.

"Idea number three, is buying a few marquees and holding craft fares."

"Wedding fares are all the rage now Nana and we could offer a bridal package," Liz was getting really excited.

"If you have a coffee bar I could wait on the tables, I'm quite experienced now." Holly said almost jumping up and down in her seat.

"I'm sure I could clear tables and fill the dishwasher, I'm the best dishwasher stacker in the world. Nana Celia says so," Theo thought again about his statement and started to backtrack. "Obviously I couldn't do lots of hours because of school, basketball and Rugby practice but I could definitely do a Saturday morning and work during school holidays."

"Couldn't we hold weddings, we have a great little church at the end of the drive, the bride and groom could have the reception in the marquee. Me and Pete could get a licence and set up a bar, in fact there'd be no harm in us having a small bar area in the café. Wine and cake birthday or hen parties," Bobby said enthusiastically thinking with hen parties there would be many attractive young women; it was his idea of heaven.

"We have the four turrets that are completely empty, in fact we've only been in one of them so far, if we can't find the keys to the other three I'm sure we could break in. We could turn them into accommodation for the bride and groom," Pete joined in.

Everyone stopped talking and looked around at each other as their brains raced nineteen to the dozen.

"Well I think all of those ideas are feasible, it will take some hard work and capital, but we don't have to do it all at once, we could just start with the salon and then build it up from there," Ned said looking very pleased with the plan. "If it was a little later in the day I would raise a glass, but at the moment we only have coffee and juice so, raise your cups ladies and gentlemen to Rookery Castle Enterprises."

They all raised their cups clanking them together and repeating Ned's words 'Rookery Castle Enterprises', they said before draining their drinks.

Louisa waited for a few seconds before saying, "Rookery Castle Enterprises; a Family Affair," she smiled head high, all of a sudden the quiet shy wife and mother, looked every inch a budding entrepreneur.

A little knock came at the back door and they saw Mandy standing outside waving through the glass a big cheery smile lighting up her face. "Ready when you are Pete," she shouted.

Pete got the dogs and joined her outside; they walked away from the castle up the hill, he was going to have a look around the cottages and report back, as to what he thought needed doing to make them habitable.

Bobby and Greg got the large bunch of keys that were hanging on a hook in the cloakroom, heading to the turrets to see if any of the keys fitted he doors. Greg had his notebook with him and some labels, to make sure, if any of the keys opened the doors they could easily find them again. Bobby was armed with Pete's spray oil and a long thin leaver they had used on the door in the hidden room a few days earlier.

The rest of the family disappeared, leaving Ned and Audrey alone.

"Well done Audrey, you handled that superbly, I don't think they realised it was a prepared speech. Louisa is a budding talent, I can see where Holly gets her acting talent from," Ned laughed, a look of approval on his face.

"Well when we agreed that the boys were just ambling along and nothing really constructive was happening, it seemed the best way to get them enthusiastic again. We all need something to do and look forward to, I think what we've suggested will keep them occupied for the next few years. Keep them out of mischief," Audrey said as she finished clearing the dishes away and placing some of the uneaten toast from breakfast in bag. "Looks like bread and butter pudding for dessert this evening."

Ned went over to Audrey and turned her towards him, he placed both his hands on her shoulders and said, "I am so incredibly proud of you darling, you are an amazing woman and I don't think I tell you often enough just how much I love you."

Audrey looked up at Ned putting her cupped hands either side of his face. "Oh Ned that is a lovely thing to say, I know you love me and I hope you know how much a love you, neither of us are particularly lovey-dovey types but it doesn't mean we don't care."

Their moment was shattered by the Belle sisters marching in. "So Aud, what do you think of this armed guard we've got, she doesn't seem particularly ferocious to me," June threw herself onto a chair.

"I don't know June, I wouldn't arm wrestle her for a quid," Ned said pulling away from Audrey, feeling a little embarrassed at being caught in a tender moment.

"I think she's lovely. Pete seems to be getting on well with her, I've just seen them walking back from the cottages, chatting away quite amicably, which is very unusual for him, he's generally quite nervous when in female company," May commented sitting next to her sister at the table.

“She’s quite a buxom wench, perhaps he’s more comfortable with a more rounded person,” April put the kettle on “Coffee anyone?”

Ned picked up his paper and sat in the corner away from the women as they sat discussing Pete’s lack of a love life.

“What’s happening with Julie, do you know if Caroline has managed to take charge of the shop yet?” Audrey sat sipping a glass of cold water.

“Not sure, but luckily for all parties the flat has a separate entrance, it can be completely segregated from the shop, so the owners can rest assured that Julie can’t get in the shop and can’t be accused of any wrong doing as far as the stock etc., is concerned,” April said looking around.

“I can’t imagine Julie doing anything illegal, can you?” June said whilst pulling open the cupboard doors looking for the biscuit tin.

“I think Julie has a lot of psychological problems and all drink related unfortunately, it would be so good if we could convince her to get some help. She was such a lovely lady before drink took over,” Audrey stopped talking as she took her mobile phone out of her pocket, “Sorry ladies I have to take this call,” she said as she was walking out of the kitchen and into the cloakroom, hoping to get a bit more privacy. “Hello Mr Gahir.”

The ladies continued talking about how to help the pharmacist get over her alcohol problem; June had found the biscuits and helped herself to a few.

“The problem being that she doesn’t realise she has a problem, you can’t help anyone unless they want to be helped. We’ll have to wait until she’s ready.” June said.

Eventually Audrey came back into the kitchen; the sisters looked at Audrey expectantly. “Is there a problem at the post office Audrey?” April asked.

“No. everything is fine,” Audrey responded, looking over at Ned who was chuckling to himself, lifting his newspaper to hide his amusement.

“Mrs Gahir isn’t correct in her accusations with regard to you and her husband is she?” April said questioningly.

“I’m surprised you can even suggest that April Belle,” Audrey responded.

“But you haven’t denied it have you Audrey,” April looked over with a holier than though look on her face.

May looked out of the window and exclaimed, “Oh look Pete’s coming back with the dogs, the officer isn’t with him, I wonder where she’s gone?” She got up and opened the cloakroom door. “Where is your police friend Pete, you haven’t lost her have you?”

“Pete was just hanging the dog leads up and refreshing the their water bowl, “No she’s taking another look around the front, then she’s going to be handing over to someone else,” he went into the treat cupboard in the cloakroom and gave each dog a chewy bone to eat.

“She seems like a nice girl,” Ned said from the corner having now put his crossword down.

“She’s ok, loves dogs and does a lot of running. She’s completed the Potters Arf Marathon every year for the last 10 years,” Pete said looking impressed.

“Well done her, perhaps you could do something like that next year Pete,” Ned said walking over to stroke the dogs.

Pete didn’t reply, he just ambled out of the back door. “Think I’ll go and join Greg and Bobby, see what they’re up to.”

“I’m going over to the Coach House; I think there’s a really good spot by the side to dig out an allotment, lots of sun and a bit of shelter from the elements from that clump of trees up there. If we dig it out this year it will be ready for planting next year,” Ned grabbed his jacket from the cloakroom and put on his boots.

“If you hurry you may be able to get some late potatoes and green beans in, it is only the end May, but you will have to be quick,” Audrey was reaching for her coat as she spoke.

“Good idea Audrey, I’ll consider that, rather than digging it out ourselves perhaps we could hire a little digger, it’d be done in no time. I’ll need a shed and a greenhouse, there's electricity in the Coach House so it would be the ideal place." Ned whistled the dogs as he walked out of the cloakroom. Even though they'd just been for a walk, another outing was just too good an opportunity to miss.

"I'm going down to the shop to try to speak to Julie, I don't care if she's fallen out with us, I think we have a duty as members of the WI to try to help her, even if she doesn't want to be helped. Anyone want to join me?"

All the women agreed they should try and they all trooped out. Audrey left a note for her family and then locked the back door as they left.

On the way down the drive they bumped into Mandy, who had just completed her inspection of the front of the property. She was going to hand over to another officer in around half an hour so she walked down the drive to the gates with them.

"Will you be over again tomorrow Mandy?" Audrey asked.

"Yes I'll probably be with you around seven in the morning to three in the afternoon tomorrow Audrey, the boss is trying to make sure you get the same officers at the same times each day so you aren't disrupted too much," Mandy closed the gate. "I think we need to keep this magnificent gate locked twenty-four seven, is there any way we could get a key so we can enter and leave without disturbing you?

"Oh yes of course. Bobby got locked out the other day so I've asked Greg to fit a key safe to the side. I'll make sure you get the code, but you can always get into the estate through the Gatehouse as long as the sisters are in," Audrey locked the gate and handed the officer the key. "I've got a key to the gatehouse so if need be I can get in through there. I'll call Greg and remind him about the key safe. I'm sure he'll be able to fit it today he's always very efficient."

Mandy waited for her replacement, he was due any minute and the women continued with their journey to the village to see Julie.

CHAPTER 15

What a tangled web we weave when first we practice to deceive!

Julie Tattershall was standing at the window of her flat, which was situated over the top of the chemist shop. She always thought of it as her shop because she'd been running it and worked in it alone for over 20 years. This stopped unexpectedly and unreasonably when some busy body reported her for being drunk whilst dispensing controlled drugs. Utter nonsense of course. Ok she liked a little tipple, but mostly it was medicinal for her arthritis. The alcohol seemed to make her antidepressants and nerve tablets work a little better.

Most of last night had been taken up contemplating what to do for the best, the very best thing she could do to be reinstated. The shop was her life. When she was making up peoples prescriptions, she felt important, as though people depended on her, not quite so alone. After much soul searching and some Oramorph and Diazepam, all absolutely necessary for her health and wellbeing, she had made the decision to let the temporary replacement into the shop and try to get on with them. That way, when she was proven innocent and put back in charge, the girl would have to report that she had been co-operative.

Looking down the road that ran through the village, she saw the oriental girl standing with that idiot of a constable from the local station. A car pulled up and she saw Bob Sergeant get out. "Well, well" she said to the empty room "look who it isn't, the great detective Robert Sergeant returns." She took another drink of the ice-cold vodka and walked into the bathroom to gargle with peppermint mouthwash. Checking in the full-length mirror in the hallway, to make sure she looked smart and efficient, she started down the stairs. There were two doors leading off the small hallway at the bottom. The door in front of her had a glass panel in the top half with a wrought iron grid covering the opaque glass; this led to the yard outside where her silver Nissan Note was parked. Before she reached the door, she turned to the left and went through the solid wood door leading into the shop. Walking towards the front door she saw the three figures looking through the reinforced glass door at her. Julie pulled herself up to her full height and put on a great big smile as she unbolted the door.

"Hello there," she said in a singingly cheery voice. "You must be Caroline Chen. I'm Julie Tattershall and I am very pleased to meet you," she said extending her arm and shaking the young girl's hand.

Caroline looked at her suspiciously. Julie turned towards the two men, "Hello Bob, I was told you were in the village again. Good to see you've returned to the fold. We must get together and talk over old times, Detective Sergeant? Well done, very impressive."

Bob looked at her and smiled. He wasn't fooled for a moment. He knew this lady from years ago; she had been a devious child and teenager. He had no reason to believe she'd changed at all, but he thought he'd go along with the deception to see what she was up to.

"I'll look forward to that Julie. Ms Chen tried to get in on Saturday to no avail, what was the problem?"

Julie smiled as though butter wouldn't melt in her mouth, "I didn't get much sleep on Friday night so I took a sleeping tablet at around 4am I must have slept right through, sorry for any inconvenience." She looked at Caroline and giggled, "I hope you won't hold that against me my dear, I get the feeling we're going to be good friends. Hopefully you won't have to work in this dreary backwater for long, once the panel has reinstated me."

Caroline looked at her, smiled and took her time to reply, choosing her words carefully. "Well it's all water under the bridge Ms Tattershall. Perhaps if we could come in and I can familiarise myself with the shop before I open to the public."

"Shall I stop with you and give you a hand?" Julie said enthusiastically, eyes wide, almost popping out of her head.

Caroline continued to smile, saying, "No that's alright Ms Tattershall I won't inconvenience you. I always think finding your own way around a shop helps you to familiarise yourself. I've been a locum for a few years and it has been a very successful way of working. Perhaps I could trouble you for your keys to the cupboards and store room I seem to have left mine at the office," Caroline's arm stretched out in front of her, palm up.

Julie slowly pulled out the keys from her pocket and jiggled them up and down in front of Caroline's face, begrudgingly slapping them with force into the outstretched hand. She was proud of her acting ability. She'd fooled them; she wasn't bothered about giving the whippersnapper, the viper in her den, the shop keys. She'd got a spare set upstairs. Thinking to herself just how clever she was, she turned towards the door and the stairs that led to her flat, her sanctuary, saying, "Bye, bye, see you later," she waved and disappeared through the door and up the stairs.

As soon as Caroline heard the footsteps getting further and further away and the door to the flat banging shut, she quickly bolted the adjoining door and put the keys in her bag, pulling out the master keys she'd been given by head office. She unlocked all the drawers and cupboards and then pulled out a large sheaf of papers held together by a binding comb from her briefcase. She laid the heavy documents on the counter along with several different coloured pens and turned to the officers who were still standing in the doorway.

"Thank you for your help, I really do appreciate it, but I think I can take it from here. If I have any trouble from Ms Tattershall upstairs I will call the station, I've a feeling I shall probably have you on speed dial before too long," She laughed as she opened the door for the two men.

Bob turned as she was shutting the door, "Watch that one Ms Chen, she can be a nasty piece of work."

"Oh I certainly will Sir, but I don't think she'll bother me too much, I'm not fooled by her one iota. If she resorts to violence, I have a black belt in several martial arts, I've taken down bigger and better than that lady," She laughed as she closed and locked the door behind them. It was 9.30 and the shop opened at 10am so she had a little time to look around before she started to work properly.

It was a couple of hours and several drinks later when Julie was again looking out of the window of her flat. She saw the evil witches she thought had ganged up on her and made her life a misery. She needed some more medication for her nerves so she reached for a bottle that was sitting amongst many others in a cupboard in the bathroom. She looked at the pills in her hand and reached for a glass of water, but decided against it and she swilled them down with a very large vodka and tonic.

Swaying slightly she saw the women enter the shop below, "How shall I deal with this situation now?" she said speaking aloud to her reflection in the mirror. I want to know which one of those interfering old bags lied and reported me to head office. It hit her like a ton of bricks. Of course, get close to them again. If she was friendly one of them may just own up, or could let slip the name of the person who had betrayed her. She had a wash and combed her hair, putting a nice bright summer dress on and a pair of white sandals. She finished off her drink and poured herself another one. "Just one for the road," she said aloud. After filling her glass and adding a dribble of tonic, she threw the empty vodka bottle in the bin; it clattered when it hit the other bottles that had been put there over the last few days. "Must empty that later," she said as she checked to make sure there was another bottle ready for when she got back. Opening the cupboard she saw four bottles remained, she lifted them to make sure they were all full and then wrote on her shopping list 'more vodka'.

As she was walking very unsteadily down the stairs, she heard her enemies laughing with her replacement and cringed at the thought of having to be nice to them. Still it wouldn't be for long. One of them would slip up and then she would know, at last, who had deceived her. Maybe it was all of them, that would be a little more difficult to deal with but she'd find a way.

The four women had entered the shop to find Caroline behind the counter; she was ticking a list as she took stock of items on the shelving behind her.

"Oh how lovely to see you ladies again." Carolyn cooed as she turned away from the shelving to face them. "Audrey, I was going to call you later, I did several tests at home yesterday on the mystery ingredients you gave me, I even looked at them closely through a microscope, but because they were chopped up so finely it was virtually impossible to ascertain what they were. I could go further and send them to a forensic lab if you wanted me to? It would cost money though, they charge a fortune."

Audrey looked at the pharmacist at length, before deciding she was much too nice a person to want to do anyone any harm, but she would keep an eye on her just in case. "It's alright Caroline. I don't really think it matters just at this moment in time. The police have a sample. I don't know if they want to pursue it or not, but I don't think it is anything I want to delve into too closely. I have enough on my plate at the moment. The mysteries are coming in thick and fast." Audrey put her elbows on the counter and leaned forward so her face was immediately in front of the petite young woman, "We've found a skeleton inside a suit of armour!"

Caroline at that moment looked a little like a goldfish gasping for breath "Never, really, how bizarre, you are kidding me aren't you? This is a joke, come on ladies give me the punch line."

All four women shook their heads so vigorously they looked a little like Jim Cary when he was starring in the film The Mask. May's long fair hair was tied up in a ponytail, which swung around and hit June in the face as her head shook from side to side.

They filled Caroline in on the events of the last day or so since they'd last met. Caroline was shocked, "Well what are they going to do about it? Who is it, any ideas?"

"The Police are investigating. I would presume it will be a difficult job. God knows how long it's been there. It could be months or years, or decades, maybe even a century or so," Audrey shrugged her shoulders and laughed, "I keep telling Ned if he doesn't behave, they'll be retrieving his skeleton in a few year's time, but not in a Knight's armour." They all smiled knowing Audrey's sense of humour and guessing at Ned's sarcastic reply.

Caroline came from behind the counter to join them. In a very serious voice she said "I didn't do all my training for nothing. I can tell you when buried six feet down, without a coffin, in ordinary soil, if a body hasn't been embalmed; an adult normally takes eight to twelve years to decompose to a skeleton. However if placed in a coffin the body can take many years longer, depending on what type of materials are used. For example, a solid oak coffin will hugely slow down the process. Whether decomposition would be slower or faster inside a suit of armour, also in the cold damp atmosphere you described it is difficult to calculate, but I would say you have to be looking at 20 years plus."

They all stood looking at her aghast at her knowledge. Audrey and the Belle sisters continued to talk about who they thought it might be, particularly April who had been researching on the internet. May and June had taken some notes when they visited the occupants of the nursing home. They all had a couple of theories but nothing definite.

Julie tried the internal door and realised it was bolted from the inside, so she cursed and proceeded out of the back door and around to the front of the building. As she passed the back of the empty lock up and then the post office, she saw Mrs Gahir washing dishes in the small kitchen at the back of the shop. "Good morning. Fine day isn't it?" she shouted cheerily as she waved at the postmistress. Mrs Gahir looked at her, raised her hand in a half-hearted wave and broke into a nervous smile, which looked more like a baby who had wind. Julie hadn't been seen nor had she spoken to anyone in quite a few days, so Mrs Gahir was understandably shocked at her neighbour's friendly behaviour. Perhaps its Julie that him indoors was cavorting with behind her back, she wrestled with the idea for a few moments, unable to decide, but she thought it was definitely worth pondering over for a while longer. She poured herself a large glass of almond milk and helped herself to a slice of Gulab Jamun Cake. She'd made it the day before to console herself. She always felt better when she'd had a slice of cake.

There were three shops in the row, all of them having been converted several years ago from six small two terraced cottages. There were just two upstairs flats, both of them stretching over the lock up shop below, which was situated in between the post office and the chemist shop. Julie walked along the narrow alleyway that separated the shops from the rear of some terraced houses. Turning the corner she passed in front of the post office. Julie waved and blew a kiss at Mr Gahir. His wife was watching from the kitchen door, she'd just taken a bite of the cake when she saw Julie's blatant flirtatiousness and immediately started to choke. Her husband was totally mystified by Julie's unusual behaviour, to even wave and smile was completely out of character and he couldn't understand why on earth she'd done it. It was only when he looked over and saw his wife's face that he realised Julie had just done it to cause trouble and cause trouble she had, judging by the fury in his wife's eyes. He was in deep trouble. Julie had succeeded in her malicious quest.

Audrey was continuing to bring Caroline up to date when the front door opened causing the bell, which was perched on top of the doorframe, to ring out. They all turned around to see Julie standing in the doorway, all smiles and full of confidence. She greeted them all and started talking about the castle library, asking how they were getting on.

They all spluttered their replies and asked Julie if she was feeling ok.

"I'm just wonderful thank you, perfectly wonderful. Whoever reported me deserves a medal. It made me realise just how much I was drinking. Obviously that was no good for my health. I was becoming so dehydrated my skin was starting to look like leather. I've started a beauty regime now, cleanse, tone and moisturise twice a day. Just feel my skin; it's so soft, just like a baby's bottom." She leaned forward pointing her cheek in their direction so each one of them could gently stroke it.

"Oh yes very nice Julie," June said and continued to ask her what products she was using.

All the women were taken aback by Julie's friendliness. But they had come to the shop to try to help her and so all of them in turn, heaped praise on their fellow WI member, laughing and joking with her about the happenings over at the castle and generally keeping her informed on what was happening in the WI.

After a tortuous twenty minutes the doorbell rang again and Tom stepped through the door, whistling 'Oh what a beautiful morning'. "Hi Dad. Have you brought your prescription in?" April said thrusting her arm into his so she was linking him as he approached the counter. He smiled at his eldest daughter and handed over the prescription, "Who is this lovely young lady I see before me," Tom said with a kind and friendly look on his face.

"I'm Caroline Chen," she looked down at the prescription before finishing her sentence. "Mr Belle and I'm very pleased to meet you, I'll be here for the next few weeks, so don't hesitate to call in if you need anything," Caroline stretched her child like arm over the counter and smiled at Tom. He took the outstretched hand and turning it palm down, bent over and kissed it lightly before letting it go. "And I'm pleased to meet you too. It's nice to have a pretty girl behind the counter instead of old crow face."

"Dad!" May said reproachfully.

"Oh sorry Julie, didn't see you there love, still standing at mid-day that can't be bad," he said with mischief in his eyes.

His daughters groaned, as he'd got older he seemed to be getting more and more outspoken. They wondered what he was going to say next.

"Only joking Julie, just thought I'd have a big of fun ma dear," he said winking at her.

"I'll get this ready for you now Mr Belle. It will be about ten minutes, would you like to wait?" Caroline put the prescription on her clipboard and started towards the stockroom.

The Belle sisters shouted "Noooooooo," in unison.

"No need to wait Dad. You get off home and I'll bring it with me when I get your lunch. I'll be over in half an hour or so!" June looked at him imploringly hoping he would take her up on her offer.

"Ok darlings. See you in a little while," Tom opened the door and smiled before starting to sing.

"Sweet Caroline da da da
Good times never seemed so good
I'd be inclined da da da
To believe they never would
la la la."

The next verse was lost as the door closed and he walked down the road, his shoulders jiggling up and down in rhythm to the song he was now whistling, because he couldn't remember the words.

Everyone in the shop started to talk at once, anxious to break the stony silence that Tom's comment had left.

Caroline returned from the storeroom with Tom's prescription and handed it over to June. After a little chitchat, they all agreed to meet at the Castle Library the following evening at around 5.30, to resume sorting the books. June said she would go along to the post office and invite Mrs Gahir to join them. They all agreed that she was the best person under the circumstances to reach out to the postmistress.

"I'm doing nothing tomorrow evening, would you mind if I joined you? I love books; it would be a real treat for me." Caroline said hopefully with a pleading look in her eyes.

"Oh that would be lovely Caroline, wouldn't it ladies? Help you fit in with the community; you really would be very welcome. We could walk up to the castle together, or I could drive you over there. It's a few minutes walk, it takes longer to drive. I'll leave it up to you. Whatever you decide is ok with me," Julie said with a gushing smile, "I'll nip over to the pub and ask Patricia to join us. It would be absolutely wonderful if we had a full complement. I'll make sure she's going to be there, I can be very persuasive when I want to be."

"Are you sure Julie, it's not putting you to too much trouble is it?" Audrey asked.

"No, No, dear in fact it would be my pleasure. Can't wait to see you all again. I'm so excited I could burst," Julie opened the shop door, humming a tune she started to totter over to the pub. It had opened a few minutes before for the lunchtime trade.

"I'll come with you Julie; I'm not doing anything at the moment. It'll be nice to socialise for an hour." Audrey followed Julie and much to her surprise, April and May joined them.

The women could not believe Julie's personality change. They were more than a little sceptical, but willing to give her the benefit of the doubt.

"I'll just nip home and give Dad his medication. I'll do him a sandwich while I'm there then join you in a few minutes," June started to speed walk towards her dad's cottage which was just across the road. She quickly unpacked his medication, made him a cuppa and put together a cheese and onion sandwich, laying a packet of plain crisps by the side of the plate, along with a lemon fairy cake. "It's here on the kitchen table Dad, when you're ready," there was no reply. She went into the living room to see her dad sitting on the reclining chair fast asleep. "Bye Dad, sees ya later," she said very quietly, closing the front door gently as she went out. She headed towards the 'Raven Arms', hoping she hadn't missed any of the fireworks. She was sure there were going to be fireworks at some time. Something was most definitely brewing and she didn't want to miss out.

CHAPTER 16

OL' GITS CORNER.

The Raven Arms was quiet. It had only just opened and Sarah was giving the shelving a quick wipe down while she had nothing else to do.

"I'll have a lime and soda please Sarah," Audrey was the first one to order. "Same for me please" May said, her eyes wondering over to the corner table where three elderly men were just sitting down.

"Hi Archie. Nice to see you out and about. How's the back now?" Sarah said as she poured the soda and lime drinks.

"Oh same as usual Sarah, I've got some help around the house now. Everything is getting a bit too much for me." the old man said as he sat in between his other two friends at the table.

Sarah looked sympathetically at the three amigos in the corner then turned to face her other customers, "What's yours April, Gin and Tonic with ice and a slice?"

"That's frighteningly accurate young lady, are you psychic?" laughed April.

Sarah smiled at April and looked across at Julie, ready to take her order.

"Is Patricia in?" Julie said leaning to one side, trying to look past Sarah into the kitchen behind to see if she could catch a glimpse of the landlady.

"She's upstairs Miss Tattershall, but she'll be down in a minute or two. We're a bit short staffed. The kitchen porter's off with the trots, so Jemima's in the kitchen most of the time."

"Ok, hum, I'll have a coffee please Sarah," In a very quiet voice she added, "put me a large brandy in there my dear, my tummy's a little off today."

"Aww, sorry to hear that. Maybe it's a bug going around." Sarah said, discretely putting a large measure of brandy in the cup, only leaving enough room for very small amount of coffee. "Would you like a mug rather than a cup?"

Julie shook her head and sat on a stool by the bar. Sarah put the cup of coffee in front of her with a small jug of cream by the side. She ignored the cream and took a gulp of the dark beverage before she looked over at her friends seated at the table a few feet away. She lifted her coffee cup in the air and said, "Cheers ladies."

"Aren't you joining us dear?" April said twirling her lemon and ice around the glass with a yellow cocktail stirrer.

"My back is none too good darling. If I sit on those chairs I'll probably never get up again. I'm fine on this stool thank you. I can still join in the conversation."

Nicely done, Julie thought to herself. If I get to close to them they'll smell the brandy, can't have that, they'll think I'm a drunkard.

Jemima ran through the front doors, her olive skin glistening with sweat, her dark curly hair tied up in a ribbon on top of her head. "So sorry I'm late, has chef noticed?" she said to Sarah as she scurried towards the kitchen door.

Before Sarah could answer the chef bellowed "Jemima, get your bum in here, the Beresford Walkers are due in and the salad isn't prepped yet."

Jemima quickly took off her short denim patchwork jacket, throwing it on a coat hook on the wall in-between the stairs to the flat and the kitchen door. There was a babble of voices in the porch leading to the bar as Sarah delivered three pints of beer to the men in the corner. The door opened and Ned walked in, followed by his three sons and Theo. Audrey waved and they all came over. Pete moved a small table from an alcove and Bobby brought some chairs over. They sat down and joined the women.

"Well this is a pleasant surprise. What are you boys doing here?" Audrey said sipping her drink

"I could say the same thing to you, but considering you're all well-known alcoholics I won't bother. Hi Julie, you come out of hiding. Almost didn't recognise you it's been so long." Ned wondered to the bar and ordered a pint of Guinness and four cokes.

Julie shuffled herself around trying to move the cup away from Ned, hoping his sense of smell wasn't good. "Not been feeling good Ned. I'm taking a few days off to recuperate" she slurred.

"More water with it dear. That's your problem; need to take more water with it." Ned turned towards the table as he waited for his drinks, "I'll let Greg explain what we're doing here. Don't be frightened Greg lad speak up." Ned chuckled as he saw the look on his wife's face.

"We've been surveying and taking notes on different parts of the estate so Dad thought it would be good to bring all the information together. Get something sketched out on paper so we can get a clearer picture. He suggested he might like a Guinness so here we are," Greg said.

Theo helped his grandad bring the drinks to the table from the bar. They all sat down and Ned ripped open three packets of crisps and a big bag of peanuts placing them in the middle of the table.

"Is this lunch then?" Bobby said as he took a huge handful of crisps.

"Let's look at it as an aperitif." Pete said helping himself to some peanuts.

"Can I have chips please? I'm starving." Theo pulled out a nutty health bar from his pocket and bit it in half.

"I've just messaged the rest of the family, I thought they might like to join us for some sandwiches and a plate of chips," Audrey said, seriously considering if crisps and nuts were a healthy option for lunch. She started to reach over towards the crisps and then withdrew her hand, deciding to wait and have a sandwich and salad. Since her accident she hadn't thought very much about her fitness regime, but as she was passing the post office earlier, she saw a notice that said Pilates classes starting in the church hall. Perhaps that would be a good idea. A little more gentle than riding a bike up and down country lanes and definitely less dangerous.

Jemima came out of the kitchen and ordered herself an energy drink from the bar. As she was waiting she saw the family gathering and waved.

"Hi Jemima," April spluttered through a mouthful of crisps.

"Hello Jemima," Audrey said, thankful for the interruption. The crisps where looking ever more tempting. "You haven't met the youngest of our terrible trio have you? Jemima, this is Bobby. Bobby this is Jemima. She's just started as a waitress here in her spare time. She knows our Holly."

"Hi Bobby," the young waitress said raising her hand in a quick greeting.

"Jemima. That's an unusual name. Is your last name Puddle-Duck?" Bobby laughed thinking it was a huge joke.

"I can honestly say that no one has ever said that to me before Bobby. It's so nice to meet someone who has such original thoughts." Jemima looked at him with a sarcastic smile on her face before picking up her drink from the bar and disappeared into the kitchen.

"A chip off the old block," Ned said grinning from ear to ear.

Everyone shook his or her head in disbelief at Bobby's sense of humour.

"What? What have I said now? I don't believe you lot. You've all had a humour bypass," Bobby took a drink of his coke and finished off the nuts.

Sarah had just put the telephone down and was nervously holding a piece of paper. She definitely didn't look happy. Audrey put in an order for a big platter of assorted sandwiches, some salad and six bowls of chips.

Sarah smiled and sighed with relief, "You must be a mind reader Audrey, the Beresford walkers have just telephoned to say they're running an hour late, and there's only eight of them not twelve which was their original booking. Chef would have been furious if you hadn't saved the day. He hates having his food standing around. He says it spoils the flavours if it isn't fresh. Anyone would think he was preparing a Michelin star meal instead of a plate of sarnies," Sarah took the order, along with the message from the walkers into the kitchen.

Only a few minutes later the rest of the Knight family burst through the doors accompanied by June. "Hi guys," they said as Greg pulled another table over and Theo picked up a few stools from another part of the bar so they could all sit down.

Jess and Holly went to the bar to order drinks. While they were waiting, a tall overweight man in his early sixties came through the front door.

"Oh hello Roger, so sorry to hear about your mums illness, how is she?" Audrey stood up as she spoke.

"Hi Audrey, she's not too good actually, unconscious at the moment. I don't like leaving her but I felt I needed a break, so I've left a couple of my cousins sitting with her."

The man strode over to the three men in the corner and sat down, before rudely clicking his fingers at Sarah and pointing towards the table to indicate he wanted a drink. Sarah took over a very large brandy; whilst nimbly avoiding his wondering hands. He chatted to the men at the table until Liz and Holly walked towards him to go to the toilets.

"Weellll heeellloooo, I sayyyyy, who do we have here, a bevy of beauties I do declare," he said standing up and blocking the doorway to the toilets.

Holly viewed him with distaste and Liz looked as though she had a nasty stench under her nose. A smell of cigarettes and spirits drifted in the air.

"Could we pass please, we're on our way to the bathroom," Liz said curtly.

Roger moved to one side to allow the girls through, but he gave Liz's bottom a little pat as she passed. She let out a tiny yelp and jumped forward trying to avoid any further contact.

"Pervo," Holly shrieked.

"Hey, that's my sister your touching up you old dirty old man," Theo was on his way to the gents and so was only a matter of a few feet behind the girls, he bravely jumped to the defence of his sibling.

"Sorry, sorry, sorry just a little accident. I didn't mean any harm, just a slight mishap." He sneered as he held his hands up in the air in mock surrender. He turned his head and eyed the two girls up and down, the old men Roger was sitting with cackled, giving him the thumbs up in approval. He turned back to the old men in the corner and chuckled.

Theo took his opportunity. Standing sideways on one leg he raised the other leg and gave Roger a swift, but gentle tap behind the unsuspecting proprietor's knee with the heel of his foot. Roger's knee gave way; he fell to the floor and into a kneeling position in front of the girls.

"No need to get down on your knees and beg Mr Landlord. We're a very forgiving family," Holly said putting on her best sarcastic voice.

The man still on his knees turned his head. His eyes had narrowed into slits and his face was a shade in-between purple and red. The look he was giving the young boy was pure evil.

Theo held his hands up, adopting the same stance that Roger Swinger had assumed a few seconds before. "Sorry, sorry, sorry Mr Swinger just a little accident. I didn't mean any harm, just a slight mishap."

Everyone in the bar clapped their hands and cheered, screaming with laughter. Even Patricia who had come downstairs to help stood behind the bar with her tongue in her cheek to stop herself laughing.

Julie had Patricia in her sights and seemed to be completely oblivious to what was going on in the room.

Roger slowly got to his feet, clearing his throat he pointed to Theo, "I'll have you. Call the police Patricia I want this rogue charged with assault.

"I think that would be a very bad move on your part Mr Swinger," Greg stood face to face with the obnoxious man. "I'm sure if you were to do that, particularly with Theo only being thirteen year old you would be a laughing stock. Also we could counter sue with sexual assault, in front of several people you admitted to touching a young girl's bottom. Not a very good advert for the pub, wouldn't you say Sir?" Greg emphasised the Sir.

The atmosphere in the room went from jovial to extremely tense; in fact, you could cut through the air with a knife. Pete and Bobby had moved from the table where the rest of the family were sitting and stood either side of Theo. Even the most secure person would have felt intimidated as the four members of the Knight family drew themselves up to their full height and stood in between the landlord and the two young girls.

Roger muttered under his breath and headed towards the stairs to his flat. The three men who had been sitting with him and had encouraged his antics decided to beat a hasty retreat. Well, as hastily as the Octogenarians could move.

As they vacated their seats in the corner, Theo read aloud from a plaque, which was on the wall just above where the old men and Roger had been sitting. "Ol Gits Corner," he said grinning.

"Very apt," Liz said as she disappeared into the toilet with her sister.

Sarah and Jemima bought out the platters of sandwiches, dishes of colourful rainbow salad and bowls of chunky handmade chips.

Patricia looked over and said, "Just pay for the food the next round of drinks is on the house. I haven't seen anything that funny in years." She looked over at Julie and they spoke briefly before Sarah came back behind the bar and Patricia went upstairs.

Julie leaned over and in a hushed voice said to the barmaid, "Another of my special coffees my dear. Light on the coffee if you please."

All thoughts of making plans and looking at sketches and notes had disappeared from their minds while they enjoyed their lunch.

The two girls came out of the toilet and went over to the table. Liz put the back of her hand to her brow and said "Theo, my hero." Theo stood and took a bow. Greg looked over at his son trying not to show the pride he felt at his son's courage. The several years Theo had spent going to kick boxing classes had certainly paid off. Pity he didn't have the time to continue with that and his other sporting activities.

The Beresford Walkers noisily entered the bar just as the Knights were saying their goodbyes to Julie and the staff at the pub. Julie's coordination wasn't very good by this point and neither was her balance. She tried to drink her 'coffee' with one hand and wave with the other, which was a bit too much for her stability. She fell backwards. One of the walkers tried to catch her but was caught off balance. He went sprawling on the floor where Julie landed none to gracefully on top of him.

"Oops a daisy must be that bug that's going around," Julie said with a tremor in her voice. Not really thinking she tried to drink the rest of her pick-me-up, forgetting that she was lying down and also balancing precariously on a very unhappy walker. The cup emptied its contents all over her face and was dripping from her hair onto the face of the poor man underneath her. Ned and Greg rushed over to help her and her victim up. Once they'd got her on her feet, Greg said with a serious look on his face, "I think we'd better escort you home. That bug must have affected your balance Miss Tattershall."

Ned and Greg stood either side of her, holding her up, "More water with it Julie, more water ma dear," Ned said as they helped her out of the door, Julie's feet never actually touching the floor.

Audrey and Louisa helped Julie into bed once the two men had carried her into her flat. They put her on her side and as they went downstairs they called into the chemist shop and Caroline agreed to look in on her.

The two families started to walk to their respective homes. After a few minutes they spied a familiar figure in the distance getting out of a police car. Robin Sergeant stood by the side of a middle-aged uniformed police officer as they compared notes. The older officer who'd been on duty at the castle since midday drove off.

Robin waited at the Gatehouse where the Belle sisters lived, perching himself on a stone seat next to the large gates leading to the castle.

Liz and Holly broke into fits of giggles as they walked up the lane towards Robin. When the group drew closer Robin took off his hat, smiled and said, "Good afternoon. DS Sergeant is on his way over he should be here in thirty minutes or so. I'm on duty until around 7pm. Is there anywhere you feel needs my attention? Anywhere you think leaves you vulnerable that you would like me to concentrate on?"

"You could focus on our kitchen," Liz said fluttering her eyelashes.

"As far away from the castle as you can get, how about the stables," Greg looked at Robin grimacing.

Liz and Greg had spoken at the same time, which was more than a little confusing. "Perhaps we'll leave the answer to my question to the head of the household. That way I may be able to remain as one whole person instead of trying to morph into multiplex man and split myself in half. After all I'm only a police officer not a superhero, but I am working on it." Robin looked over at Ned who was smiling at his eldest sons antics and the humour Robin had displayed. He was getting to quite like this young lad, unlike his son who obviously had disapproved of him at first sight.

"I think they are both right. The stables are right next to the road and it wouldn't take a great deal of effort to climb the wall there during the day and maybe hide inside until dark. That will be a thirty minute walk there and back and a few minutes to check inside. After that I suggest you join us for a coffee, by that time Bob, sorry DS Sergeant will be here and you can report to him. How does that sound?"

They all agreed that was the most sensible solution to the dilemma of trying to please both Greg and Liz, although Greg didn't seem happy, he reluctantly agreed.

Robin started out for the stables accompanied by Pete and the dogs; Greg went to get more clipboards and reams of paper. When he got back, he looked around the room, "Where's Liz and Holly?"

"They've decided to go with Pete and take the dogs for a walk," Bobby said grinning.

Greg really wasn't happy, but Louisa diverted his attention by asking to see his plans for the future of the castle. His face lit up as he spread several pieces of paper across the kitchen table with a scribbled idea on each one, which took his mind off the Liz and Robin situation.

Everyone else busied themselves while they waited and wondered what Bob Sergeant wanted to discuss with them. Perhaps some of the mysteries would at last be solved.

CHAPTER 17

A light bulb moment.

Detective Sergeant Bob Sergeant stood on the doorstep and rang the doorbell. A couple of minutes later Ned was inviting him in. "You can just come around the back if you like Bob, we see more of you than we do most of our family," Ned said jokingly.

The officer followed Ned through the reception room down the hallway and into the kitchen, the journey took a few minutes and he thought how much more convenient his studio flat was. He could make it from the chair in the living room to the front door in less than twelve steps and you could walk around the circumference in about thirty seconds. On his return to the village, he had managed to get two studio flats in a converted Victorian property, one for him and one for Robin. At twenty three, he thought his son could do with a bit of privacy, but he still wanted to keep an eye on him. Robin had been his life since his wife left he felt sad that the lad was growing up and would probably be married with children soon. He just hoped Robin would choose a wife more successfully than he had done.

Robin, Pete and the girls arrived back a few minutes before Ned let Bob in. Liz was being very flirtatious until her father walked in the room, at which point she totally ignored Robin. Greg was not fooled and asked her if she'd had a good walk with the dogs. Everyone could see the colour rising in her cheeks much to the amusement of Robin.

"It was ok. A walk, is a walk, is a walk. We didn't meet a mass murderer or see an alien spaceship landing if that's what you mean?" She said gaining a little more confidence as her mother sat down beside her.

"No need for sarcasm young lady. It's the lowest form of wit. Your father was asking you a perfectly simple question, you could give him a perfectly simple answer," Louisa said reproachfully.

"Ok, Ok, Ok. Yes I had a good walk thank you," Liz said, furious with her mother for showing her up in front of Robin. Anyone would think she was a child instead of being a mature woman.

When Ned and Bob arrived in the kitchen everyone was sitting at the table. Bobby stood up and offered the officer a chair, while he joined Pete and perched on a high stool by the kitchen work surface.

Once the pleasantries where over and done with Bob Sergeant cleared his throat, putting on a sombre voice he said. "Your skeleton."

"Yes Bob?" Audrey leaned forward and so did the rest of the family.

"We think we've identified it. Can't say officially yet so this is off the record so whatever I say must be kept between ourselves. It's not to leave this room." Everyone nodded their heads in agreement. Theo crossed his fingers just in case he needed to use the information later.

"We found a ring on the little finger of the left hand. We looked at several pictures of past owners and the tech lads found a picture of the Duke of Beresford with the exact same ring on his pinkie finger. He seemed to disappear off the planet around 1922. The ring was a family heirloom, handed down over generations to the head of the family. Now we know it wasn't handed to the Duke's son, because the title was never transferred to him. He died and was buried in the churchyard ten years later in March 1932 to be exact. Terrible accident, he fell headfirst down the stairs and broke his neck." Bob was interrupted by the sound of a chuckle.

Audrey had her back to Bobby and swung around to look at her youngest son, "Not a laughing matter Bobby, have some respect," she said sharply.

"What? Why me? Why do I always get the blame?" he threw a piercing look around the room.

"Because it generally is you Uncle Bobby, you have a strange sense of humour." Holly looked at him with a meaningful expression.

"Maybe so, but on this occasion I am so snow white it's a wonder I'm not making you all snow blind," Bobby said sulkily.

Audrey looked around the room and closed her eyes, she could sense there was a presence and it made her feel very uncomfortable, sighing she said. "Any idea how he died and what his full name was?"

"His name I believe was, Bertram Aynsley Beresford. Sorry it's impossible to say with any certainty how he died, the only thing we can do is run a test on the bones to see if it was poison, but that would be a long shot, it's very expensive and the governor is complaining about outgoings at the moment. The skull was intact, there was no obvious damage and it is in quite good condition, no holes or cracks. There is some indication that the back had been broken in several different places consistent with a fall, so we're going to go with that as the cause of death for the moment. They're doing tests to date the bones to be sure the skeleton does belong to the old Duke, but it's going to be a few weeks before we get the report back. The death took place over ninety years ago so they're not looking at this as an urgent case. It probably was murder judging by the sealed rooms. Whoever did it had tried to cover their tracks, but they would have died years ago."

"Just as a matter of interest, we were told that the Duke's wife was committed and died in a sanatorium some years after her son died. Have you any information on that?" Audrey tried to look nonchalant, without much success.

"Seem to remember something was said about that when the tech boys were filling me in on the details. I could be wrong but I think she died in the mid 1930's and the castle was empty until 1939 when the army took it over, not sure what happened after that. I suppose you could look around the churchyard or ask the vicar," Bob replied.

"Oh yes, we must do more research on the castle, I'm sure it has a very interesting past." Audrey said innocently.

It was getting late, about 7.30pm when the officers left. "Anyone want food?" Celia said getting up from the table and stretching.

They all agreed that after that huge lunch they couldn't face a large dinner, "Ok I'll put out some cheese, biscuits, salad and pickles, you can just help yourselves when you're ready." Audrey said.

"Anyone got any plans for the rest of the evening?" Greg helped himself to a packet of crisps from the cupboard.

The only person who had any commitments was Audrey. She was going over to the Gatehouse to see the sisters at about 8 o'clock, taking some of the journals with her; they were going to work on them together. She went into the library and pushed the journals into a small attaché case she'd found propped up against the shelving a few days before.

"Are you there Bertram?" Audrey whispered. "I know you're around somewhere you old scoundrel. Come out, come out, wherever you are." There was no response, so she thought he must have used up all his strength chuckling in the kitchen.

Something caught her eye at the very top of the shelving. It was a black ball of smoke. "Cinders is that you?" she peered upward not sure if her eyes were deceiving her. Two large green eyes glowed in the dark cloud. "Hello Cinders what are you doing up there dear?" She looked around to make sure the door was closed, and she was alone.

Cinders floated down a couple of shelves and kept bouncing off a book. "Oh you must be getting the hang of this ghost thing Cinders that book seems to be moving." Audrey moved towards the steps resting them on the shelving near to where the cat was still bouncing. She climbed up gingerly and reached for the book, which indeed had moved forward an inch or so. "What a clever pussycat you are, well done, I'm so proud of you." As she pulled out the book, and thought she heard a very quiet purrrrr. "I wonder what this is, The Hobbit, JRR Tolkien. Mmmm this is bulky even for Tolkien," Audrey said climbing down and putting the book on the desk, opening it up an old exercise type book was revealed. "Ah hah! The missing journal, I'll take it with me."

She said goodbye to Cinders, trying and failing to give her a stroke as her hand passed through the black cloud. When she got to the door, she held it open. "Come on darling don't want you trapped in here." The black ball stopped for a second and then vanished, floating through the wall and into the next room. Audrey laughed aloud at her stupidity.

"Laughing to yourself; isn't that the first signs of aging?" Pete said as he passed the door with Theo, they were heading towards the games room.

"Yes it is, the stage after that is madness, I turn into an axe wielding child killer, so just watch out young man." Audrey continued to laugh as she went in the opposite direction to the boys, entering the reception room and going out of the front door with her attaché case, which had the journals in it, including the missing one that Cinders had just found.

Five minutes later Audrey joined the Belle sisters, they were sitting around their dining table, all the journals spread out in front of them. May took a bottle of tonic water with elderflower out of the fridge and poured herself and June a glass each. Before they could put the bottle back April took it and added it to two glasses of gin with ice that she'd poured for herself and Audrey. "Mmmmmm I just love a tall glass of G & T, makes me feel as if it's summer." April said as she took a sip.

"It is summer," May said retrieving the bottle and returned it to the fridge.

"I know that. I'm not stupid, but it makes it feeeeellll like summer, which is more important than it actually being summer." April replied, taking another sip and closing her eyes with pleasure.

"Just how many have you had sister?" June said, looking into April's eyes.

"Don't know dear, I'm not counting, I'm on holiday." April smiled.

"You're retired April, you're always on holiday," May said with a little exasperation in her voice.

"Exactamundo dear, exact a mundo," April's smile turned into a laugh, which seemed to be infectious because everyone joined in.

After a few minutes they composed themselves. Each taking a journal they started to make notes. It was still very difficult, even with a magnifying glass the writing so faded only a few words per page could be deciphered.

Audrey put her pen down and started rubbing her eyes, "Oh by the way Cinders is back and so is Bertram."

"I expected Cinders to make an appearance at some point she was just that sort of cat. Who is Bertram?" May said taking a sip of her tonic.

"Bertram is the skeleton we found. They have identified it as Bertram, The Duke of Beresford, but it's a bit hush, hush at the mo, it isn't official yet. I have the feeling he is our mischievous ghost who's always chuckling."

"You think he's back, after your display the other day?" June ripped open a large box of vanilla custard tarts.

"I'm not absolutely sure it's the same ghost, the one who controlled the lift seemed to be quite sinister. I don't think I did a particularly good job. I think I just weakened him. The chuckling ghost just seems to be amused at the whole situation, very playful, almost childish." Audrey reached for a custard tart from the plate June had put on the table.

"Why do you think he's chuckling again?" April cut a custard tart in half and popped one piece into her mouth.

"Because Bob, DS Sergeant came by, to tell us who they thought the skeleton was. He mentioned the Duke's son falling down the stairs to his death. Everyone in the room heard a giggle. We blamed it on Bobby but I really don't think it was him. I wouldn't put it past Bertram to have tripped the lad up or pushed him," Audrey took another drink of her G&T to wash down the crumbly pastry.

"Maybe it was revenge. It might have been the son who murdered Bertie?" May said closing the box of tarts and putting them away, in an attempt to stop June scoffing the lot. As she was putting the box back in the cupboard, she noticed chocolate muffins. May was very partial to a chocolate muffin or two; in fact, May was just partial to chocolate. She turned with the muffins in her hand and put them on the table.

"What did you call him, May?" Audrey sat up as if a light bulb had just been turned on in her brain.

"Bertie, that's what they call people named Bertram," May replied.

They all looked at each other. Each one of them spoke at the same time "I've seen that name," they said in unison. The notes that Audrey and the sisters had made from the journals were quickly flicked through.

"Yes there and there." Audrey turned over another page, "Let's look at the last journal there are only a dozen or so pages written on."

Audrey sat with the latest journal in front of her. The others stood behind looking over her shoulder. "Well I never." Audrey ran her hands over the last few of pages. "That's why the journal disappeared, it was hidden."

"I agree," said May, "I think at some point we need to face the culprit."

"Yes, but perhaps now isn't the time. Let's spy our chance." June said helping herself to one of the muffins, much to May's annoyance.

"Mmmm yes, I think we could have some fun with this ladies, I'll get typing tomorrow and do a rough draft of what I think actually happened. Then we can all have a look at it before we go to the WI meeting. See what you think. I can always alter a few things if you don't agree. In the meantime I think these journals should go in our safe. Don't want them disappearing again do we?" April gathered all the paperwork together shuffling it into some sort of order before taking it out of the room and into the study, returning after a few minutes.

We have a busy day tomorrow. Choir practice in the morning and WI in the evening." April said as she was walking into the dining room, "Think I'll turn in, after I've just had one more drink," she poured everyone a drink and joined the other ladies at the table.

Don't forget we've got the Indian Dancing Celebration on Friday night. I think we need to remind Mrs Gahir, she's probably forgotten. Have you got everything ready to decorate the church hall May?" Audrey said popping a couple of cubes of ice in her drink.

May looked at her 'to do' list. "I'm sure everything is under control, food is being delivered by The Roshni, they're bringing the hot food and setting it up in the kitchen. We have enough hot holding trays and slow cookers to keep things warm. The woman dancers will be changing in my bedroom and the men in the spare room. I have all the bunting and balloons. Ordered them off the internet, very reasonably priced, they came yesterday. I think we're all set, any other suggestions?"

“You seem to have everything covered May.” Audrey replied.

“How about music, so we can all have a boogie after the Indian dancing?” May was sitting on the floor doing yoga exercises.

“Really May, I do find it extraordinarily disturbing talking to you while you’re in that position.” April had her head to one side trying to make eye contact with her sister.

“It’s really good for you, makes you more flexible and it extends your life apparently,” May said going into the cat position.

“Well if you must, but could you turn around, I find it off putting talking to your bottom,” April’s face was a picture, her nose screwed up as if she had a nasty smell under it.

May turned around and decided to stay in the Buddha position while her sister was so grumpy.

“There’s going to be people there from every age group, so I’ve recorded some 50’s and 60’s music. Louisa is doing 70’s to 80’s. Liz is recording some modern day so we just need a few from the 80’s and 90’s, can you sort that May?” Audrey said squatting on the floor and trying to adopt the Buddha position, not quite making it.

“Pete, Bobby and Greg are going to take it in turns to be the DJ. I can’t wait for the Indian dancing lesson. It’ll be a bit like Indian Line dancing only with Sitars and Tablas instead of twangy guitars.” Audrey gave up with the Buddha position and got up. She started trying to do some Indian dancing with the shaky head movements. All the other ladies joined her, squealing with laughter at their feeble attempts.

“I’m hungry, anyone for toasted cheese ladies?” June was the first one to give up and started towards the kitchen.

Audrey’s mobile started to ring, “Oh its Mr Gahir, Mrs must be in bed,” she took the phone into the other room to talk to the postmaster, coming back a couple of minutes later, “he wants to see me, I’ve told him to come over here in a couple of minutes and I can talk to him then.”

“Really Audrey this is all very deceitful,” June said reproachfully.

“Yes but fun,” Audrey said laughing.

“Do you think Mrs Gahir knows anything”? April said in between bites of her supper.

“Obviously she suspects something, but just what is occurring, I don’t think she has a clue,” Audrey said “but it will all be in the open soon enough.”

CHAPTER 18

The Chocolate Thickens.

"White Rabbits, White Rabbits, White Rabbits." The words echoed around the castle as everyone greeted each other on the 1st of the month. "I wonder what this month's going to bring us." Audrey said, confident that whatever it was, it would be lucky. After all, ten people saying the magical words had to bring more good fortune than just two people saying it.

All of the family were gathered around the table when a little tap on the back door made everyone turn around. Ned shouted, "Come in."

Mandy Riley popped her smiley face around the door, "It's only me."

"From over the sea said Barnacle Bill the sailor," Ned greeted her, much to everyone's amusement.

The whole family shouted, "White rabbits, white rabbits, white rabbits."

Mandy looked startled, her eyes wide, not really knowing if she'd entered an asylum instead of the family's kitchen.

"It's ok Mandy, we always say white rabbits three times when we first see people on the 1st day of the month, it's supposed to bring good luck." Audrey got up to get another cup out of the cupboard.

"And does it work?" Mandy still had an unsure smile on her face.

"Well, when Nana and Grumpsy said it a few months ago they won the lottery," Holly said getting the young woman a chair.

"Oh, white rabbits, white rabbits, white rabbits!" Mandy shouted, "If I say it six times, is it extra lucky?"

"It can't do any harm," Pete said, "I'm taking the dogs out in about fifteen minutes, if anyone wants to join me?" He didn't wait for anyone to reply as he strode off into the cloakroom to feed the dogs.

"Anything interesting happening Mandy?" Audrey said putting a cup of coffee in front of her along with a plate of hot buttered toast.

“Not sure really. I’m here until 1pm, but when I spoke to DS Sergeant he said he might need me this afternoon. Don’t know why. Guess I’ll find out when I get back to the station,” Mandy sipped her coffee.

“I’m going to Choir practice in a few minutes, not quite sure why I bother, but James does make the most delicious cakes. It’s definitely worth a couple of hours of my time just to see which ones he’s baked this week. I particularly like the carrot and walnut but May would kill for his double chocolate chip,” Audrey moved towards the door to get changed.

Pete came back in the kitchen again, “Anyone for walkies?” he said.

“I’ll go,” Bobby and Theo said.

“I’ve got to do a patrol, so I’ll join you all,” Mandy stood up.

“Ok, let’s get this party started then,” Pete opened the back door and followed the dogs out accompanied by the three walking volunteers.

Audrey entered the church just before 10am. Everyone was there, James was handing out photocopies of the words to ‘I can see clearly now’ and explaining how he wanted the harmonies to be sung.

He put the choir in three different groups. Pointing to the group Audrey was in he said, “You are group one.” Turning to point at April’s group, he said, “You are group two.” Looking over to where June was chatting to another couple of women he pointed and said, “You are group three.”

“I’ll sing it with May and when I point to your group, you start singing, when I put my hand up in a stopping motion,” he demonstrated by raising his arm, bent at the elbow palm towards them. “You all stop. Let’s try it.”

May and James started to sing.

“I can see clearly now the rain is gone
I can see all obstacles in my way
Gone are the dark clouds that had me blind
It's gonna be a bright”
He pointed to group one “Bright”

His finger turned to group two “Bright”

Group three joined in “Bright” and they all sang

“Sun-shining day
It's gonna be a bright
Bright sun-shining day”

He put his hand up to stop the groups and continued singing with May.

“Oh yes I can make it now the pain is gone
All of the bad feelings have disappeared
Here is that rainbow I've been praying for
It's gonna be a bright.”

“Bright.”
“Bright.”
“Bright.”
“Sun-shining day.”

They all continued in this manner until the song came to its conclusion.

“Well people, what did you think of that?” James didn’t realize what a mistake it was to ask people what they thought; everyone started to give him their opinion, which unanimously was not favourable.

“Ok, hold on there, I can’t understand when you’re all speaking at once. Can we have a volunteer spokesperson?” James asked.

April stepped forward, “It’s a beautiful song and I don’t think it’s fair that we’ve only got a few words and you and May have the bulk of the lyrics,” she stopped abruptly looking daggers at James and May. Everyone else joined in with “here, here.”

“No problem, I’ll get together with May and try to sort out something that we can all agree on. In the meantime how about practicing some old favourites, shall we start with Morning Has Broken, Cat Stevens?”

Everyone agreed and they sang at the top of their voices for another half an hour or so, until most of them were sounding very croaky.

June started to have a meaningful debate with James and Julie, while everyone else looked on with anticipation. They were just waiting for someone to slip up and say something silly so they could tut tut.

It was then that it entered May's mind. That deliciously yummy and seductive chocolate cupcake she'd seen in the fridge when she was putting some milk on the shelf. They always had cupcakes and coffee after their practice, James was a wonderful baker, always coming up with different flavours of cupcakes that really were mouth-watering.

Stop. Don't think about it; just don't think about it. She thought to herself.

She continued to interact between the two tasks, trying to listen to what they were saying and answer appropriately.

Just focus on what they're saying and stop thinking about it.

She cleared her throat and answered yet another question on the new arrangement of 'I Can See Clearly Now', by the late great Jimmy Cliffe.

Deep breaths, that will stop the craving, she thought, *it will pass, it has to, but it hasn't passed, has it*!

Ever since she opened the fridge door and saw that mountain of chocolaty delight, she just couldn't stop thinking about it.

Chocolate. Chocolate muffins. Soft and scrumptious, with a gooey chocolate middle and those adorable chocolate curl decorations, finally topped off with a mini chocolate flake, stop it now. She had the feeling she would burst if she thought about the muffins any more.

"May, are you ok you look a little distant," James said bringing her attention back to the room.

Right focus. "Sorry James my mind was elsewhere."

Stop, she thought.........*Noooooooo.* She screamed in her head.

Or at least she thought it was in her head, until she saw James looking at her with wide eyes and an amused smile on his face.

“I think we could all do with a break,” he said, as though he could read her mind. “It’s been a long morning and we‘ve got a lot done. Whose for coffee and cake?” he said with a deep chuckle.

May needed no second request and threw herself at the kitchen door. In different circumstances, she would have beaten Usain Bolt off the blocks. She flung open the fridge door grabbing her prize muffin. By the time everyone else had entered the room, May could be seen standing in the middle of the kitchen with a look of complete ecstasy on her face, cupcake in her hand and a huge blob of soft chocolate icing clinging precariously onto the tip of her nose.

James and the rest of the choir stood open mouthed at the sight of May, obviously in a world all her own, totally oblivious to the eyes that were fixed on her. The spectators looked at each other and laughed as they saw the funny side of it. Audrey rolled up her sleeves and started ducking and diving, jabbing the air as she made her way to the open fridge. “If there’s a carrot and walnut muffin in there, it’s mine and if anyone tries to take it off me, they will die.” Everyone roared with laughter at the sight of Audrey in her sensible shoes, green tweed skirt and M&S top, crouching over and hopping from one foot onto the other in front of the fridge, hands clenched, fists pumping in and out as if she were shadow boxing.

Most of the cakes had vanished when Caroline appeared in the doorway.

“Sorry to disturb you all, but could I have a quiet word Miss Tattershall?” Caroline said somewhat apprehensively.

“Most certainly dear, we’ll go into the courtyard, would you like to take a coffee with you?” Julie looked at her, trying her very best to be charming.

“No thank you, just a few words please. It won’t take more than a minute or two.” Caroline waited for Julie to pick up her coffee, which was sitting half full on the kitchen counter next to the microwave oven.

“I’ll top up my cup. The kettle’s just boiled, are you sure you won’t partake?” Julie picked up the kettle and filled her cup with the hot water, stirring in another sugar and pouring in a drop more milk.

"No I won't, I'm a little short on time Miss Tattershall. I need to open the shop, I've put a sign on the door saying I'll only be away for ten minutes, and it's nearly that now."

"Off we go then ma dear," Julie said, ushering Caroline through the door, before turning and silently mouthing to the people whose eyes were following them, "needs my help." Her eyes were like slits in her smug face.

As soon as the choir heard the back door close, they dashed over to the window to see what was happening. Patricia pushed and pulled everyone out of the way, barging through the gap she had made for herself, she was peering out of the window trying to hear what was going on outside.

"Can't hear a thing," she muttered, her face pressed up against the windowpane, thinking she could get a better insight if she could see more.

"Oh goodness," they all exclaimed when Julie threw the remains of her coffee in Caroline's face. Even Patricia jumped back in amazement at the spectacle. Julie was looking like someone possessed, the young woman had brown liquid running down her face, staining her crisp white blouse. Caroline turned away from Julie and walked down the path, disappearing through the back gate in seconds.

June ran from the kitchen and through the church hall, in an attempt to avoid bumping into Julie, she tried to catch up with Caroline, but the girl was just too quick for her. By the time June was within hailing distance, Caroline was in her car and going full steam ahead, out of the village. June stood for minute, knees slightly bent, hands on her ample hips. She leaned forward trying to take some deep breaths, to slow her heart rate down. She turned and strolled slowly back to the kitchen of the church hall.

"I really must lose some weight and get fit, this is absolutely ridiculous. My father's far more agile than I am," she said aloud, and then looked around to make sure no one had overheard her remarks.

By the time Julie had reached the kitchen everyone was chatting and busying themselves, washing cups and plates and emptying bins as though nothing had happened.

"Stupid, moronic trollop; she can't even understand my stock system. That piece of trash doesn't deserve the title Pharmacist. I'll get her back if it's..." Julie's voice trailed off as she realised everyone was looking at her.

"Ah Ah" she giggled nervously. "I suppose I'll have to teach her the right way to do things, when I'm reinstated." Julie wasn't fooling anybody; they had all seen the look of fury in her eyes and heard the venom in her voice.

A nervous and embarrassed silence fell across the kitchen. No one knew what to say. Audrey jumped to Caroline's defence.

"I don't know what happened out there Julie, but I'm sure, whatever it was, Caroline didn't deserve that sort of treatment. It was unforgivable. I hope she's alright."

"What about me? No one seems to be worried about me. You didn't hear what she said. She accused me of theft. I think she deserved a lot more than she got and I'll be taking it up with Head Office, as soon as I get back to the shop." Julie didn't show any remorse; in fact, she appeared to think she was the injured party.

They all started to disperse and go their separate ways. James joined the Belle sisters on the short journey home. The sisters had invited him for lunch, as they often did since his wife died a few years ago. Everyone thought he and May might get together, they had been close friends for many years, but May just wanted to be friends, she always said there was no romance only friendship. James was still grieving, but anyone close to him knew he had a soft spot for the carefree and unconventional woman.

Audrey and Patricia followed Julie back to the chemist shop; they could hear her ranting, even though they were several yards behind her.

"Silly bitch, she can't even be trusted to keep the shop open during the proper hours," Julie said, her arms flailing about haphazardly. Unexpectedly she stopped in front of the shop and turned, a big smile appeared on her face as she threw her arms around her friends, before cheerily skipping past the post office and around the back to her flat.

Audrey and Patricia were astonished at her Jekyll and Hyde behaviour.

“I definitely think she needs professional help.” Audrey said before trying the door to the shop.

The door wouldn’t budge and the ‘back in 10 mins’ sign that Caroline had hastily put up earlier was still stuck to the window, the shop was in darkness. Audrey shouted through the letterbox but there was no reply.

“Didn’t June say she’d seen Caroline drive off after the altercation?” Patricia said whilst she looked through the window, her face cupped either side by her hands stopping any shadows disturbing her view.

“Yes, she did. I thought she’d be back by now. I have Caroline’s mobile number in my phone, but I’ve left it at home. I’ll give her a call when I get back, just to make sure she’s ok,” she said, with concern in her voice.

Patricia said her goodbyes and headed towards the pub. She had to take over the bar for a couple of hours this lunchtime, her lazy worthless husband hadn’t been around to take on any of the extra work, caused by the staff shortage. She was sure he didn’t spend all his time at the hospital with his mother. He didn’t even like her, he was definitely up to something and she was sure she would find out eventually. Slowly, slowly catchee monkey. However, just for the time being, she didn’t care that he wasn’t around a lot, he only annoyed her when he was about. Still, she thought to herself, if she could wangle it, she would be married to the son of a Duke. She wasn’t quite sure how she was going to do it, but if anyone could, she could. She started to speed walk towards the door of the pub, eager to have a good gossip with her staff and the customers about what had happened at choir practice. Already she was thinking of ways to spice the story up a bit to make it a more interesting.

CHAPTER 19

Then a hero comes along.

Caroline ran to her car, hastily fastened her seatbelt whilst starting the engine, she drove out of the village towards the police station in the nearby town. It was only twenty minutes' drive, but it seemed a lot longer to the distressed woman. She knew there had been no physical danger when Julie Tattershall had rained abuse on her, she could have disabled the woman with one move, but it still upset her to think that anyone could have said such awful and discriminatory words.

When she'd parked the car she looked at her mobile and noticed several missed calls from Audrey, but her priority was to call head office to explain why the shop was closed, she could deal with the calls later.

Caroline's boss was very understanding about the shop closure, but raised her voice several octaves when telling Caroline she should have gone through the proper channels, someone should have been with her when she approached Ms Tattershall. It was irresponsible and she'd put herself in unnecessary danger. Once she'd ended the call, she burst into tears.

It had been stupid facing the woman on her own but she knew nothing bad could happen, her martial arts training prepared her for any violence and the choir were only feet away. But she wasn't prepared for her own reaction. If anything like that happened again, she would be better equipped to deal calmly and rationally with it.

Caroline made her way to the small police station which was housed in an old detached house right in the middle of the town centre. She'd parked at the local supermarket, walked a few yards to the building and spoke to the officer on the front desk, who greeted her with a friendly smile.

"Sorry" she said apologetically, all her confidence had vanished.

"No need to be sorry duck, just tell me how I can help you." The officer leaned forward, looking enquiringly through the bars, which separated him from the visitor.

Again, Caroline broke down in tears and the elderly officer disappeared, appearing a minute later with a WPC who gently ushered the distraught young woman into a small interview room. She pushed some tissues across the table, Caroline took the box thankfully. The officer didn't speak until Caroline had taken her last few sobs and had wiped her eyes. The desk sergeant tapped politely on the door, he entered and put down a tray with two mugs of steaming hot coffee. Each one had a spoon standing upright in it, sachets of sugar and small tubs of milk were piled high. Once the uniformed man had disappeared, his colleague smiled.

"Madam would you like to tell me what had caused you to be so upset? Come on now, let's have coffee and we can chat about your problems." As she was speaking she emptied a packet of sugar and a tub of milk into her coffee, stirring the beverage slowly, she continued. "However, I can't guarantee the quality of the coffee. The Sergeant is renowned for getting confused between coffee and sludge, but he tries bless him."

Caroline smiled and put sugar and milk in the mug before taking a sip. It wasn't the best coffee she'd ever tasted, but it was piping hot and she'd put extra sugar in to make it palatable.

"I would like to speak to DS Sergeant, if I could please; it's a matter he is familiar with, we spoke on the telephone yesterday afternoon. Rather than go over the whole distressing situation again with someone new, I think it would be better to speak to him."

"I quite understand, but DS Sergeant won't be back in until about 4pm. In the meantime if I could take a few details from you, name, address and a brief outline of your problems, it would save my superiors having an apoplexy at the thought that I hadn't followed procedure." The young woman opened a drawer in the table and withdrew a couple of official looking forms. "This will only take a couple of minutes and once we've finished you can have a walk around the town, or if you would prefer you could stay here and drink more of this atrocious coffee."

Caroline gave her all the information she needed and told her where she was going just in case her confidant came back earlier than expected. She bought a magazine and settled in the supermarket café waiting patiently for the minutes to tick by until she could get all this information off her chest and laid to rest. Caroline kept taking furtive glances towards the entrance and breathed a sigh of relief when a little after 3pm Bob Sergeant walked over to the counter ordered a large coffee and strolled over to join her.

Mandy had been on duty at the castle from early morning and she was eagerly awaiting her replacement. It was starting to rain and she didn't want to seem forward by asking the Knight family for shelter. After all she was supposed to be protecting them not adopting the family. Robin would be taking over this afternoon, which was good. She always had a laugh with Robin; he was such a nice friendly person, so easy to get on with.

Audrey arrived back home and was looking very upset, both Louisa and Celia were concerned, they had just persuaded her to sit down at the kitchen table when they noticed Mandy standing outside in the rain.

Audrey got up and opened the back door, she shouted across the courtyard. "Mandy come in dear you'll get soaked, fancy a cuppa?"

Mandy trotted over, "I really shouldn't, I'm supposed to be on patrol."

Louisa overheard and said, "Well you can patrol the house and after that take the brolly by the front door and patrol The Gatehouse, someone could be hiding in one of the rooms."

They all looked at her innocent face, "Well it's a possibility," she said, eyes wide and a very cheeky grin on her face.

Audrey told everyone what had happened during choir practice while Celia was prepared lunch. They all agreed it was more than a bit weird.

"Have you tried Caroline's mobile recently?" Mandy asked.

"No I don't want to seem as though I'm interfering, I've left her a message saying how concerned I am about her. I think it's up to her to reply when she's ready." Audrey took her empty coffee cup to the sink and rinsed it out before placing it on the draining board.

Mandy received a text message, she looked surprised, "Robin is going to take over a little earlier this afternoon, he'll be here in about an hour."

Holly and Theo were standing in the doorway, obviously their internal lunchtime bell had just rang. "I'll text Liz perhaps she could get off work a little earlier today." Holly had a mischievous smile on her face as she started to text her sister.

"She finishes early on a Tuesday anyway, she'll be back by 3 o'clock," Louisa said getting plates and cutlery out ready for lunch.

"Ohhhh what a shame, she's going to miss precious minutes of lover boy's company." Theo feigned a swoon.

"What's that? Lover boy? Are you trying to tell me something Theo?" Greg appeared in the doorway, followed by Bobby and Pete.

"Oh God no, it was a joke Dad, just a joke." Theo replied.

"Not funny." Greg scowled as he looked at his son.

Mandy discretely disappeared, picking up a brolly from the front door and heading towards the Belle sisters residence to do her 'patrol'.

The family finished lunch just as Greg spotted Robin walking towards the old tied cottages, "I think I'll take the dogs for a quick walk while the rain has stopped, it's supposed to pour down later this afternoon."

"We'll tag along if you" Pete said steering Bobby towards the door.

"Ok see you boys later," Audrey said not acknowledging that she knew just what her sons were up to.

By the time the boys had got themselves and the dogs ready, the police officer had done a quick check in the abandoned cottages and was returning to do a turn around the castle. He bumped into the boys and the dogs in the courtyard next to the orangery.

The brothers stood in front of the young man in a threatening manner, obviously Greg was interrogating him. Audrey left them for a couple of minutes before deciding to intervene. She went through the cloakroom and appeared unseen in the orangery, opened a window and shouted."Leave the nice policeman alone boys. Play nicely."

They spun around, "We are playing nicely," Bobby said shrugging his shoulders, his hands extended palms up, as if proving they were empty.

Audrey, even from this distance, could see the twitch at the corner of Bobby's mouth.

"Robert James Knight. Liar, Liar, pants on fire." She shouted.

Bobby's shoulders dropped as he turned towards his brothers. "How come she always knows? I swear sometimes she's telepathic."

Audrey could only guess what Bobby was saying, but just for a bit of fun she said. "I'm your mother, I know you better than you know yourself."

Even Robin joined in with the laughter at the comment and the look of complete disbelief on Bobby's face.

"Now shake hands boys and be on your way. There's too much to do for you to be chatting." Audrey said returning to the kitchen.

The boys shook hands with Robin. Greg's grip may have been a little tighter than it should have been.

At 5.30pm the women from the WI gathered in the Library. Caroline hadn't joined them. Audrey still hadn't heard from her.

Liz and Holly bought in coffee; they sneaked into the corner and sat on a seat in the bay window, hoping no one would notice them. The chairs had been arranged in a horseshoe shape and the women were facing the door rather than the window this time.

April opened the meeting. "OK ladies before we start on the roster for the clearing and logging of the books, which seems to have been sadly neglected." April turned to Audrey, "Is it alright if I tell them our findings Audrey? I thought it would get the meeting off to a good start." Audrey nodded but couldn't disguise a look of wicked mischief in her eyes.

April continued in a loud and clear voice. "Ladies, we will start off with the journals. As you all know they were found in one of the concealed rooms upstairs. I know it isn't really relevant, but it is quite interesting and I feel it will inspire us to work on these magnificent array of books you see either side of you."

Patricia interrupted. "Get on with it. I've almost dropped off twice."

April carried on, "We have found the last journal!"

Patricia's face dropped and she couldn't suppress a scowl.

April persisted despite the hum of whispering noises around the room. "Audrey had already told the family, we have a transcript of the last few pages, but there still isn't a clear picture, so we've tried to fill in some gaps. Here's what we think happened."

She went on to explain that the tied cottages on the land were full of farmers who had families and because of money; some of the older children were put into service. Around 1920 two of the children, from different families, went to work in the castle, which was then owned by The Duke of Beresford., Bertram but people called him Bertie, he was married and had a son who was a little strange.

The young boy who came from the tied cottages was fifteen, his name was Albert. He was employed as a stable boy and had a crush on the girl who went into service at the same time, she was fourteen and her name was Edith. It was not uncommon in those days for the master of the house to release his passions on the younger members of staff. Bertie took full advantage; he was always chasing the girls around and taking them to his secret hideaway. They couldn't complain or they would have been dismissed and their families would have starved without the girl's wages coming into the home. Edith avoided him until she was sixteen, the cook helped her to hide, it was a long time before Bertie realised she was there. Things got a bit complicated when Edith and Albert, the stable boy, became sweethearts. She didn't dare tell him about Bertie's advances, she knew he would be upset and he could do nothing about it anyway.

Edith, with the help of some of the other staff had played games with Bertie, knowing he liked to dress up in costumes for his cavorting, Edith told him that if he dressed in a suit of armour she would give herself freely. She thought once he was in the suit of armour he wouldn't be able to move and so she'd be safe for a little while. She didn't realise he'd had a suit made of a lighter material and he could move quite easily in it.

She went to meet him but as she opened the door to the steps, which led to his secret boudoir, she heard him scream. When the door was opened, she saw he was laying on the bottom few steps. Standing over him was his son, who was babbling about pushing him down but it was an accident. She and two of the girls from the dormitory, who were standing behind her, could see exactly what had happened.

"To cut a long story short, Bertie never had his evil way with Edith, but she was pregnant. Edith and the her friends the twins, blackmailed Ernest Edward, Bertie's son, and his mother, telling them that the baby was Bertie's and they that they'd seen the boy push his father down the steps to his death. They hung the family out to dry until the money was gone."

"So the baby was the stable boy's?" Mrs Gahir said a little awkwardly because she was sitting right next to Patricia.

"It would seem so, according to one page in the journal, they were planning to run away together, but unfortunately there was a fire in the stables and the boy died." Audrey replied.

"It really is an amazing story, you should write a book," Celia said.

April continued, "We've uncovered more facts about the church. Edith confessed to the vicar's wife about the baby, but told her the Duke was the father. She revealed that she had seen the boy push his father down the stairs. Not too sure how it came about, but I would guess that in order to buy the vicars silence the Duke's wife gave the church a ninety-nine year lease, at a nominal charge of one guinea a year. The Church has been paying that amount since, obviously the church in those days wasn't quite as honest as it should have been, and the gatehouse has been a home for the clergy of St Johns since that day, until the lease runs out in 2021."

April turned to Patricia. “It seems that Roger’s Grandma was a maid and his grandfather was a stable boy.”

Patricia growled.

“There is good news though Patricia, Roger’s great uncle is still alive. He was the youngest of the family and he’s in the Manor nursing home. He has no relatives and he doesn’t know yet that his eldest brother had a child, isn’t that exciting?” June said enthusiastically.

Patricia nodded her head without any enthusiasm at all, deciding to change the subject, she said. “Did you find out who knocked you off your bike and strung the cat up Audrey?”

“No, we don’t know who tried to poison our lunch either. I’d love to know who killed my beautiful Cinders.” Audrey voice quivered.

Julie opened the large carpetbag she’d been clutching since she came in, saying in a very matter of fact tone. “I didn’t kill the cat, the useless creature was curled up on the bed in the porch, dead as a dodo,” she said pulling out a very old revolver. “This was my brothers, it was his old police revolver, left it to me in his will. I didn’t think it would come in useful, but it has.” Her face was blank and her eyes distant, as though she was deep in thought, trying to remember something. “I came to put the chopped daffodil bulbs in some food in the fridge but it took me so long to hang her body on the tree that people had started to move around. That stupid kid arrived and I couldn’t risk being seen, so I come back the next day. The mushrooms were very conveniently placed and the door was unlocked. All my intended victims were elsewhere, it only took me a minute to chop a few mushrooms and put the bulbs in with them. It was most fortuitous that Caroline was here, killed several birds with one stone, or it should have done.” she let out an evil cackle as she laughed at her own joke.

“I thought I’d string the useless cat up to give you all a scare. It’s better off dead anyway, all cats should die a long and painful death. They urinate on my garden, vermin they are, vermin.”

Everyone gasped at her callousness.

“I’m sorry if that offends you, but I don’t much like cats.” Julie said swinging the gun around, pointing it haphazardly at people in the room.

“I understand.” Audrey said in a conciliatory tone.

It’s very hard to think rationally when you have a revolver pointing straight at you, no matter how old the gun looks. It may have bullets in it and it could go off accidentally. If the gun wasn’t loaded, she could be carrying all manner of weapons in the big bag she was clutching to her chest. She was standing just to the side of the door blocking it off, or there might have been an opportunity to make a dash for it, but not all of them could have made it through the door at the same time.

Something caught Audrey’s attention on the shelving above Julie’s head; it was a small black fur ball with large green eyes. Audrey had a feeling she knew what the precious moggie was going to do.

“So what are your plans Julie? What are you going to do now? Why did you want to punish us all?” May said, eyes glaring.

“You all plotting against me. I’m the only one with a degree and you’ve been green with envy for years. You’re dim and duller than dishwater; I’m younger than you and better looking. No wonder you wanted me out of the village, you lot wouldn’t get a look in while I was around. They wouldn’t listen to me at the office; I told them it was you dreary old slags trying to cause trouble by reporting me. None of you have ever been happy about my success. Jealous, jealous, jealous.”

She waved the gun at the terrified women and reaching into her bag pulled out a long shiny carving knife. They watched with strange fascination as the long blade reflected the lights overhead, it all seemed surreal. Julie had a gun in one hand and her bony fingers clutched a knife in the other.

“I have no plans, other than to kill you all. I’ll tell them a voice in my head told me to do it, they’ll commit me for a few years and after that I’ll come back and open the shop again.” All rational had left Julie. She was now in a very dangerous place; all sane thoughts eluding her.

Audrey was trying her best to focus on a way out when she heard a sound in the corridor outside. "Did you hear that Julie? Someone's out there; if they're listening at the door they'll have heard all that."

"Oh my God, do you think I'm stupid enough to fall for that old trick?" She snarled, her face contorted and menacing, her eyes narrowed.

Audrey could see Cinders bouncing against a large book on the top shelf just above Julie's head, it was moving, but very slowly. Then suddenly the bundle of fur floated across the room and bounced up and down for a few seconds before hurling herself towards the book. This time it moved a couple of inches and the book toppled off the shelf, hitting the deranged woman on the head. She dropped the gun and it exploded, the bullet went through Cinders making the furry ball fly in all different directions before coming back together again. Her green eyes blinked furiously, obviously wondering what had just happened.

The door flew open and Robin Sergeant came crashing into the room. In one swift movement he knocked the gun away with his foot, grabbed the knife from the stunned woman and turned her onto her front. He pulled out handcuffs from his belt, grabbed both her hands behind her back and put the handcuffs on. His knee was in the middle of her back holding her wriggling body down.

Bob Sergeant came into the room directly behind his son and with two burley constables right behind him. Robin got up and helped Julie gently to her feet, handing her over to the constables, who checked the handcuffs before sitting her down in a chair in the reception room. Julie may have been stunned, but she was still screaming blue murder at the top of her voice, calling everyone in the room some very rude names and using God's name in a very derogatory manner.

June bent down and looked at the large leather-bound volume of the Bible. "Mmm, God moves in mysterious ways. Julie really shouldn't have taken the Lord's name in vain," she said.

Bob Sergeant nodded to his son. "Well done lad. Good job," he said smiling. He was obviously proud fit to burst.

Robin turned to the women in the room. "Could I ask you ladies to leave the room very quietly and slowly? We need the area keeping exactly as it is. A firearm has been discharged and so obviously there will have to be an enquiry. Perhaps you could lead them into the sitting room Mrs Knight?"

"An enquiry and a medal are needed I think Robin. Ladies please follow me into the sitting room. Perhaps Ned could bring his drinks trolley through. By the way where are Ned and the boys? We seem to be four men and a young boy short in this little gathering." Audrey said heading very carefully towards the door.

An extremely large WPC and an even larger PC took Julie away. She was virtually carried kicking and screaming into the awaiting police car. They managed to get a seat belt on her and the PC drove whilst the WPC sat in the back keeping an eye on the unhappy woman, who was still shrieking obscenities at the top of her voice.

Ned, Greg, Pete, Bobby and Theo had been told to wait in the kitchen. The back door had been locked. The key was given to Mandy who had been standing in front of the door to the hallway, to stop anyone interfering with the operation. Sitting with them was Caroline, who had arrived about half an hour before with Bob Sergeant. The two police officers and Mandy Riley arrived in another patrol car at about the same time. The Police cars were left outside the Gatehouse and the occupants went around the back of the building where they met Robin. He had already filled the family in what he suspected was going on. His father had called to alert him as to what may be happening and so he looked in the library window. It was obvious that something was amiss. Normally ladies of the WI don't brandish guns whilst having a meeting.

Mandy stood like an immoveable mountain. Everyone kept their places and were very quiet, having been told what was happening and it was going to be handled. Even Greg sat quietly, he had no wish to be the one who interfered and caused someone injury, particularly not his family.

DS Sergeant tapped on the door and said. "All clear officer Riley you can bring them all to the sitting room, we're in there."

The boys wasted no time and overtook Mandy, running into the room where they could see all the family and visitors were safe and sound. Much hugging, kissing and relieved laughter went on for the next few minutes until Bob Sergeant cleared his throat. "I'm afraid we'll have to ask you for a key to the library. The room will have to be sealed until we can get our forensic team over here. Do you have a key Mrs Knight?"

Audrey smiled and nodded her head, "Thanks to my team of stock takers and planners I know just where it is."

Celia and Louisa laughed as they disappeared through the sitting room door and headed for the cupboard under the stairs. They opened panelled door revealing a pegboard with numerous hooks embedded in it. At least half of them had keys dangling from them. Each row had which floor the keys belonged to. Celia's hand ran across the hooks marked 'ground floor', before resting on a key tagged 'library'. Louisa retrieved a clipboard from behind the door and against the column marked library, she wrote, out 'DS Sergeant' along with the time and date.

The mother and daughter went back into the sitting room and handed the key over to the police sergeant. While they had been away, Ned had wheeled in the drinks trolley and was busy pouring spirits into glasses. Mandy and Pete had gone to put the kettle on to make tea and coffee for those that didn't want an alcoholic drink. Bobby had appeared as if by magic with several plates of biscuits.

"I'm afraid you will be stuck here for quite a while. Officer Riley's will take some preliminary statements from you. The more detailed stuff can wait until tomorrow, but we have to at least take your names and addresses." Bob Sergeant said apologetically, as he took the keys from Celia.

"Where is Robin?" Liz said looking at Robin's father.

"I'm afraid he had to go straight back to the station ma dear, a firearm was involved and so he has to make a statement and be debriefed. Don't worry he'll be fine, no doubt he'll be back home later for supper." Bob smiled encouragingly at the young girl.

"Why are you asking about him?" Greg said, suddenly being aware of his daughter's question.

"Because he saved us," came the reply, not just from Liz but also from all the other women.

"He was so brave Greg, really. He charged in the room, no thought for himself and disarmed a deranged woman, who was holding not only a gun but a knife as well, he was a real hero." Louisa said looking at her husband, daring him to say another word.

Ned's eyes opened wide. "Really, well if that's the case, we owe that young man a lot. Perhaps we should give him your eldest daughter as a thank you Greg."

"Ned, really not appropriate darling." Audrey looked at her husband reproachfully.

Ned showed Mandy to the games room, where she set herself up with notepaper and pens. Sitting at a card table, she took information from some of the witnesses. Bob Sergeant went into the new dining room to scribble some names and addresses in his notebook.

After a couple of hours all was finished and everyone got their coats and said their goodbyes.

"Oh don't forget ladies, we have the authentic Indian Dancers doing a display on Friday evening. Hope you can all be there. We've got Sam and Ali from the Roshni serving Pakoras and Samosas, and it's all free." June was jumping up and down with excitement.

"Oh goodness gracious me, I'd almost forgotten about that. It seems a lifetime ago you invited me and him indoors to that evening. We will be there, wouldn't miss it for the world." Mrs Gahir seemed to have forgotten that she had fallen out with her husband and most of her friends. She smiled happily as she walked to her car with Patricia.

"How are you dear?" Audrey asked Caroline who had been extremely quiet during the proceedings.

“I’m fine thank you Audrey, just a bit shaken. I am hoping one of the police officers will give me a ride home, I don’t think I could face driving, I’m still a bit shaken.” Caroline sighed and closed her eyes.

“No need for that Caroline, we have a lot of spare rooms. Several of them already made up for visitors. You’re about the same size as Louisa and Liz. I’m sure they could find you something to wear and no arguments young lady; you’re stopping here tonight and having some supper with us.” Audrey steered Caroline towards the kitchen and told everyone they had an overnight visitor.

Louisa and Liz took Caroline upstairs and showed her to a small room next to Audrey’s, on the second floor. While she was having a quick shower, Liz nipped upstairs. She returned fifteen minutes later with everything the young woman needed for an overnight stay, including a beautiful flowered kaftan to wear this evening.

“Come down when you’re ready. You can tell us all the sordid details over supper, I’ll go and see what everyone’s up to. Liz will stay with you; it’s very easy to get lost.” Louisa grinned. She knew how easy it was. She had done it several times in the few months since they’d called the castle their home.

CHAPTER 20

Bringing everyone up to date.

The boys unwrapped a few pizzas and put them in the oven. Celia and Audrey always kept some in the freezer for emergencies. This was an emergency, it was 8.30 in the evening and no one had eaten. There was a large bowl of salad in the fridge which Greg put on the table and he pulled out some salad dressings from the cupboard. Bobby emptied potato wedges onto a tray and popped them in the oven. Thirty minutes later the oven let out its familiar 'ping' and everything was removed. Greg sliced the cooked pizzas and put them on plates. Bobby was in charge of the wedges. Pete returned, he'd taken the dogs out and fed them.

It was Theo who heard the cry from Ned,

"Suppers Up,"

The brother and sister ran at full speed into the kitchen, almost colliding with their mother. Louisa texted Liz to tell them food was on the table.

A few minutes later the two young women entered. Caroline had her dark straight hair in a pageboy style which framed her pretty face. She was wearing a beautiful pink, purple and turquoise kaftan with a pair of cream wedge heeled sandals Liz had loaned her, she looked stunning. Everyone was astounded at the transformation, from efficient, cool, prim pharmacist into a real bobby dazzler; and she certainly did dazzle Bobby.

"Wow," Bobby said mouth open. "You look very, err, um, very oriental."

Everyone smiled. Bobby really had a way with words.

"Close your mouth son, unless you're entering a competition for the best impersonation of a goldfish," Ned quipped.

Bobby ran around the table pulling out a chair for Caroline. She thanked him with a nod, once she was in position he pushed the chair forward a little too fiercely, the petite woman was trapped without a millimetre to spare between the table and the back of the chair. Bobby moved back and took his place in-between Pete and Greg. Both of his brothers nudged him and winked. Bobby's face lit up like a Belisha Beacon.

The family were trying so very hard not to laugh. Some coughed, some bowed their heads and some bit the side of their cheeks. It was almost an impossible task, but they managed it even though many of them had tears in their eyes from the strain of repressing their laughter. Caroline was one of the people who sucked in her cheeks to stifle her amusement. Bobby had been courteous enough to try to do the right thing and so very discretely she moved the chair back so she could breathe without obstruction, saying a little prayer of thanks that her ribs weren't damaged.

"Ok dish the dirt Gert," Theo said leaning forward and looking at Caroline. He didn't want to miss one little second of this. He was left out of things because everyone thought he was too young, it was very frustrating. He was really fed up of being told to disappear. But not this time, he was determined to get the full story come what may.

"My name isn't Gert," Caroline said.

"Whatever, whatever, come on, tell us what happened?" Theo said eyes wide open, his face eager.

"Why don't you and Holly go and play pool?" Louisa said turning to face Theo.

"Because we don't want to play pool. We want to hear the full story, not the version minus all the juicy bits," Holly said in a defiant tone.

Louisa gave up, she was too tired to argue, "Ok you can stay, but no interrupting and whatever is said in this room does not, and I repeat, not go any further, do you children understand?"

Theo and Holly nodded their heads to confirm they did understand.

"Yes mother," replied Ned and the other males in the room.

"Very funny, don't we all wish we were as amusing as you lot. Sorry Caroline please go on, you have to excuse the male contingent of the family. They've had problems getting past puberty." Audrey said frowning at her husband and sons.

Caroline's story only took around ten minutes and wasn't that juicy, much to the dismay of the younger members of the family.

"Head office knew Ms Tattershall had a drinking problem. It was reported to us anonymously, so they sent a secret shopper who confirmed that the lady looked worse for wear. It was established when they visited the post office and the pub and had a little chat with the people on duty. Apparently everyone knew. It was no secret; we had to act immediately for the safety of the community, so they sent me to take over. I'm actually the Regional Manager, but I only live fifteen miles away in Stafford and I was free, so it was the easiest option for them. What they didn't know, which wasn't uncovered until I took a stock check, was that there were quantities of drugs missing, some of them quite dangerous. One substance, the only controlled drug to go missing, was an Anabolic Steroid, which can cause hallucinations and paranoia if taken with alcohol.

I don't think she was aware of what she was doing. Once she was drunk she lost all perspective, probably just started by taking something like an over the counter painkiller for her headaches. I'm only guessing that in her inebriated state she'd got confused and took the steroid by mistake.

I feel so sorry for her, I'm sure it wasn't intentional. Once she's been sectioned they'll ween her off the drugs and she should return to normal in a few months.

"Are there no long lasting effects?" Ned said as he was leaving the table.

"It's hard to say, a lot depends on how long and how much she's taken. There's a large quantity missing, whether she took them or stashed them somewhere is debateable." Caroline bowed her head obviously upset.

"Miss would you like a drink, we usually have a nightcap, could I get you one?" Bobby said following his father out of the room.

"That's very kind of you Bobby. I think a nightcap would be lovely," Caroline said smiling.

"What do you drink in China?" Bobby replied.

"Our national drink is Brandy and coke which would go down very nicely thank you." Caroline had to stifle her amusement. Bobby was trying very hard and despite his unrivalled ability to say the wrong thing at the wrong time, she really did like this kind and gentle young man.

They were all in the sitting room having a nightcap or two when there was a light tap on the window. Greg opened the curtains to see Bob, Robin and Mandy Riley standing smiling at him.

Pete went to let them in. Ned got Robin and Mandy a soft drink and he joined Bob in a large port.

"I know it's late," Bob said, "but I thought you'd like to know, Julie didn't spend any time in the cells. Caroline had already told me what happened and why she thought it had happened, we came over here straight away. We went over the moat footbridge and entered via the back door. Robin had already had a glance through the window in the library; it seemed like a tricky situation that needed a bit of planning. I posted two officers at the front, Robin and I stood listening on the other side of the door, but we couldn't hear very much, everything was muffled, so we were a bit stuck. Then Liz called Robin's mobile and left the phone line open on the table. We were able to hear everything that was being said. It was obvious Julie was unhinged. We informed Stallington Grange to expect a visit and the two officers took her straight over there. The staff sedated her and made her comfortable in a secure room within minutes of her getting there. The two officers are going to take it in turns on guard outside her room until I can get over there tomorrow.

Audrey was busy sending a text message to her friends at the Gatehouse, promising to visit them the next morning, hopefully with Caroline to give them the full details. She had decided that once Julie was feeling better she was going to visit her. Perhaps take some homemade cakes and biscuits to make her feel better.

Mandy yawned. She'd been on duty for over fifteen hours, "Sorry" she said. "Is it alright for me to go Sir? I'm due here again tomorrow at 7pm."

"Yes, sorry Mandy. Really inconsiderate of me going on like that, but I think you can get here a little later tomorrow, say 9am. Once I've established that Julie is securely contained and these good people are safe, then I think our work is done," Bob smiled at the young lady.

"What's happening with the hidden passages? Do you need to keep them taped up or can we go exploring again?" Greg said hopefully.

"Oh, yes sorry, I should have taken the tapes down today, but it's been quite a day. I'll call in tomorrow with some officers and make sure we haven't left anything behind, then you can use the area again." Bob stood slowly. He was feeling his age. All the excitement had worn him out.

As the three officers were leaving Greg spoke, glaring at Robin he said, "Just a minute, how come Liz knew your number?"

"Psychic Mr Knight. She tells me she takes after her nana," Robin winked at Liz as he walked through the door, proud of his quick response.

Greg followed the officers out of the front door. He leaned over, his head close to Robins and said, "Hey Robin, well done. I appreciate your valiant efforts at keeping my family safe," Greg walked down the last few steps and shook Robin's hand. He whispered in his ear, "but leave my daughter alone." he smiled through gritted teeth.

Robin smiled but didn't reply, as soon as he got into the car and was out of sight, he shook his hand to get the circulation back in his fingers.

Bob smiled at him, "He's got a good strong handshake hasn't he?"

"Vice like Dad, vice like," both men laughed. Mandy was unaware of the conversation, she was gently snoring on the back seat.

Caroline was up bright and early the following day. Celia had sponged her suit and Audrey hand washed and ironed her blouse. She'd had fruit and yoghurt for breakfast, so she was all ready to go to work by 9am. "I'll give you a lift if you're ready. I'm passing the village on my way to work." Liz said as she grabbed her bag and coat, "I'm due in at 9.30 so we'll have to get a jog on."

Caroline was on her mobile. She excused herself to the person on the other end and put her hand over the mouthpiece. "Very nice of you Liz, but I think they want someone to enter the shop with me a bit later, something about a full audit and check. It looks like we'll only be open for emergencies, so I'll give it a miss. What time do you finish today?"

"About 3pm. It's a short day. Why do you fancy meeting later?" Liz said opening the door to make a quick getaway.

"That would be great. How about an early meal at the pub around 5.30? We can have a chat." Caroline removed her hand from the phone and started talking to the office again, raising her hand in a little wave to Liz who was just flying through the door.

"I have a feeling they're going to be great friends," Audrey said to Celia. "I think us girls need a meeting a little later. I'm off to the Gatehouse to fill the sisters in on the events of last night after they'd left. Can you grab Caroline and meet me over there?"

"Right you are. I'll get Louisa. I think she's just putting the washer on," Celia said, heading toward the utility room which was the other side of the cloakroom.

Audrey sat in the living room of the Gatehouse with the sisters, explaining the events of last night. When she arrived, April was still crouched over the journals, trying to peace everything together. She'd written several names that seemed to appear quite regularly.

"Edith's two roommates in the dormitory were Daisy and Poppy. They were twin sisters and had come from the next village. Their dad had died down the pit. They had four younger siblings, so the mother sent the two elder girls into service when they were 14, the same age as Edith. Mrs Shufflebotham and Mr Ayre keep cropping up, quite favourably as well. It seems that they were surrogate parents, very strict but fair. The stable boy seems to be a bit of a wimp and there's a white stallion called Spirit. That's as far as I've got. It took me two hours this morning to build this character list." April handed the other three ladies the list of people.

"If when you're looking through the journals, you see any characteristics or things that each one of them did, any titbit of info, just write it against their names. I'm going to do some internet research next week, on the names and the years they were born." April sighed.

"Well April, I think you've done remarkably well in such a short space of time. It should give us a good idea about the staff at the castle and how they were treated," Audrey said looking out of the window to see Caroline, Celia and Louisa walking towards the back door.

"Yes it should, I think we will be in a position at some time in the future to write a book about the Duke and the goings on in the castle," April said.

"What a super idea April, well done dear, we could include the church in that," June said munching on a piece of fruit.

All seven women sat chatting about what was going to happen to the chemist shop and about the imminent Indian Dancing Celebration.

Back at the castle, Liz came running through the back door. Ned was doing his crossword in his special chair in the corner of the kitchen and Holly was looking through the internet on her mobile.

"Where's Mum and the Nanas," gasped Liz trying to get her breath back.

"They were kidnapped by pirates," came the reply from Ned.

"He looked just like Jonny Dep and mum said if you try to rescue her, you'll die by her hand," Holly muttered tapping away at a text message.

"They're at the coven then?" Liz said.

"Yep," replied Holly

Liz turned to go. Holly got off her stool to follow, looking at her sister she said "Don't try and stop me. I'm fed up of being left out of things. I'm almost a woman and I deserve to be treated like one."

Liz couldn't be bothered to argue. It wouldn't have done any good; her sister would have followed anyway.

They both burst into the Gatehouse having run all the way down the path and over the footbridge, jumping over the small fence, which divided the house from the castle grounds.

"Goodness Liz, what's the matter with you? You don't look very happy, why aren't you at work?" Louisa said turning to look at her daughter.

Holly had already gone the full length of the kitchen, opening the fridge she said. "Can I have a drink please? I'm parched."

"Yes certainly, there's some sparkling water in there. Would you like a glass Liz?" May said getting some glasses from the cupboard.

Holly pulled her face, but took the glass of water anyway.

Liz sat down with hers, drank half of it and then taking big deep breaths said, "That cow at the salon has let me go. She said she'd heard we were opening a salon and she couldn't afford to keep me on knowing I'd be spreading the word and taking customers with me. She said she'd give me wages until the end of the week. It was so humiliating. There were customers in the shop and she stood over me while I got my scissors and stuff," Liz finished and sighed obviously trying not to get upset.

Holly's eyes were open wide. At last she'd heard some gossip first hand, instead of being the last person in the whole wide world to know. She really was part of the coven now, she thought, not being able to stop a smug grin spreading over her face.

"Never mind darling, I'm sure we can come up with something, perhaps bring the opening of the salon forward. We'll work something out, don't you worry," Audrey rubbed her granddaughters back in sympathy.

Liz looked at her mother, "But what about my apprenticeship? I only have a couple of months to go and without a placement I won't pass."

"Ok, I'll work on that. My friend Natasha is working in Fenton, her lease is up soon and she doesn't want to renew it. I'll ask her if she will take you on a couple of days a week, just until you are signed off. I'll call the college and clear it with them, but I'm sure it will be fine. Diane the mobile hairdresser is looking for something more stable and I think Lola the beautician will be moving from The Hair Hub once we open," Louisa smiled. She hadn't told anyone that she'd already contacted the team she wanted to work with and they were all eager to join in the new venture.

"So FAMILY AFFAIR is going to be a reality is it?" Celia said proudly looking at her daughter and granddaughter.

"Looks that way Mum, if we can get a backer. Obviously it will take money to start up," Louisa looked over at Audrey.

"Well I don't think we'll have any problems there, but I want a free hair and beauty treatment every week," Audrey laughed as she spoke.

"I have a confession," June said finishing off her second apple.

"Ok we're all ears," Holly said, then clasped her hands over her mouth. She'd promised herself she'd keep quiet. She looked around; no one seemed to have noticed. "Good" she thought to herself, mentally zipping her lips together and throwing away the key.

Everyone looked at June, "Don't laugh; I'm on a diet and I'm going to try to get fit." She sat up straight, waiting for the laughter and put-downs.

"Oh that's great news. We'll help you with your diet, we could all do with losing a couple of pounds," Audrey said patting her tummy. "How about we ask Beth from Slim-Thinkers to set up a meeting in the Church Hall? I'm sure she would if enough of us wanting to join."

"I'm all for that. I have half a stone to lose and I'd be a lot happier if you were healthier June," April said trying to hold her stomach in while she walked over to the kettle.

"Count me in," May chirped, I'm all for healthy living.

"Me too." "Me too." Said Liz and Holly in unison.

"Well I don't need to lose weight, but I could help you with the fitness. I'm a martial arts instructor. I could hold a 'Tia Chia' class and do some kick boxing with you." Caroline joined in.

“That’s a brill idea. The boys could join us, Theo has done a few years kick boxing and I know he’d like to start again,” Holly was getting enthusiastic.

“Greg has always wanted to be a personal trainer. Perhaps he could start by training us. We’d have to rein him in a bit. He doesn’t seem to know the difference between gentle and excessive. I’ve been to the gym with him and believe me, he used to have to carry me out and I couldn’t walk the day after.” Louisa laughed at the thought of what her husband had put her through, before she told him to bog off.

“I could do a beginners yoga class. I’ve been practicing Hatha Yoga for ten years now, as long as you don’t expect anything professional.” May said getting on the floor and adopting the cobra position.

“Well that’s sorted then. We start on a fitness regime, but what’s bought this on June? It’s most unexpected.” Audrey asked looking at the vicar.

Before she could answer, the doorbell rang and June went to answer it. She came back into the room, followed by Bob Sergeant.

“Hello ladies, Ned told me you’d all be here, but I think he was convinced you’d be sitting around a cauldron chanting spells.”

“That’s my husband. He’d love to be with us, he can’t stand not knowing what’s going on. That’s why we’re here and not in the castle kitchen.” Audrey looked at the aging police officer. He was only a little younger than Audrey, but just at that moment in time, he looked ten years older.

“Just reporting back to the powers that be,” he stood upright and saluted, much to the amusement of the women.

“Julia’s on a detox programme. They say it will be at least six months before they can assess her condition properly. In the meantime I don’t know what’s going to happen to the shop and flat. Any ideas Miss Chen?”

“When I spoke to the office this morning they were thinking of clearing out the flat and perhaps asking one of her relatives to store it all for her. Even if she makes a full recovery, I doubt very much whether she’ll be allowed to practice again, but we’ll have to see.”

"She doesn't have any relatives, but we have a cellar under the church hall. Perhaps we could clear everything out and store it for her?" June looked at the other ladies with concern.

"She's in the WI with us. I think it's our duty to help her and arrange a visiting schedule once she's up to it. If you can't fit it all in the cellar we could move it into one of our spare rooms, for goodness sake, we have enough of them." Audrey helping herself to another glass of sparkling water and popping a slice of lemon and an ice cube in.

"Can we get you a drink Bob?" June asked.

"No thanks June, I have to be going, paperwork to sort out. We have the Dukes bones being released in the next few weeks. Not sure what we're going to do with those," Bob said shaking his head.

"If June will perform the service, we'll pay for his burial. It's only fitting he's buried on castle grounds." Audrey sipped her drink and was thinking about biscuits. Thinking was all she could do; she was now on a diet.

"Good idea Aud. Bob are you joining us for the Indian Dancing Celebration on Friday evening? It starts at 7.30." June stood to show the officer out.

"Only if I have a date, I wouldn't like to be attending on my own," Bob smiled looking questioningly at June.

"Oh Bob I'm sure you'll find one. There are quite a few single ladies in the area," June dipped her head and started towards the door.

"June, I'm asking you out on a date. Will you be good enough to attend the celebration with me?"

June looked shocked. She opened her mouth several times, but no words came out.

"Yes she will," April said pushing June into a chair.

"What time would you like to pick her up Bob?" May said her hands on the back of June's neck, to stop her getting up or saying anything.

"Would seven o'clock be ok? We could go for a quick drink at the pub before it all kicks off." Bob looked at June waiting for a response.

"That will be just perfect Bob," April said.

May grabbed hold of the back of June's hair, gently pulling it a couple of times to give the appearance of a nod.

Once he'd gone, June said almost hysterically, "A date? I've got a date. I've never had a date before. What do I do? What do I wear? What?"

"No more questions June, just be yourself. Talk about the school days, you're good at that." May said, releasing June's hair and moving away.

The women looked around at each other, before their eyes rested on June, sitting cumbersomely in her cassock, her hair limp and face pale.

"I think this is the first assignment for 'Family Affair'. I'll do her hair you do the makeup Liz," Louisa looked at June, trying to decide just what she was going to do with the greasy mop. Liz bent down looking at June's skin and peering into her eyes.

We'll take her shopping this afternoon; get her a couple of nice outfits. One for Friday and one for the second date," April looked in her bag for her M&S privilege shoppers' card.

"Wait just a cotton picking minute. What second date?" June exclaimed, "I haven't had the first one yet."

"There will be a second one June. I've got a feeling there will be many more after that." Audrey said, standing she gathered her family together and left the Belle sisters to their tasks. There was a lot to talk about and plan before 'Family Affair' could open.

CHAPTER 21

Bollywood comes to Heathbrook.

The Bell sisters arrived home late on Wednesday evening, after spending the afternoon shopping for June. They couldn't make up their minds which one of four outfits to choose, so they chose to take all four. They called in to see their father Tom on the way back, to tell him the news of June's date and their plans to be healthier. He was happy to think his youngest daughter might be on the verge of a romance and took them all out for a pie and a pint at the Raven Arms.

The Knights had a meeting to discuss the best way to proceed with the new salon. It was obvious that to start the new venture quickly, the castle was out of the picture, the change of use with the local council and the renovations that would have to be done, although that would be the plan for the future. They would have to wait for approval to change some of the outbuildings. Everything had to be planned in detail and approved with the local council; the mayor Joy Potter was a stickler for proper procedure. Greg was over the moon at the thought of being able to practice the art of personal training on friends and family. Immediately he enrolled on a course that would give him a proper qualification.

On Thursday Greg and Louisa took their three children, plus their nephew Jack Jnr to Alton Towers as a treat. They explained just how busy the family were going to be in the next few months and hoped they'd understand if the adults didn't have very much time for them, hopefully getting some help and co-operation from them. Young Jack said he could knock a wall down if they wanted him to, but they'd have to buy him a superman outfit. He couldn't possibly do it without the right clothing. Greg in a moment of weakness agreed to his request, only when he thought about it after, did he feel that he might just regret that decision.

Friday morning everyone congregated in the castle kitchen. The Belle sisters joined them for coffee and biscuits at 11am to go over the plans.

June looked at the biscuits suspiciously. "Aren't we supposed to be doing this healthy thing?"

"These are healthy June; I baked them myself this morning. Beth from Slim Thinkers sent me the recipe, Chocolate Chip and Orange Cookies. As long as we only have a couple as a treat we're still following our healthy living plan." Audrey said proudly.

"These are delicious Audrey, yummy, only a couple?" May pouted.

"Only a couple, just savour them dear, take your time," Audrey replied.

"June, you'll need to be here with your outfit no later than five o'clock, so we can get you tarted up," Louisa said looking over at June with a don't you dare be late stare.

"But I have to get things ready in the hall. There won't be enough time," June was trying to wriggle out of the makeover, but she didn't stand a chance. They'd already worked it out.

"The whole family are going over there now; we will have finished getting the tables ready and everywhere decorated by 4.30pm. Ned, the boys and Theo are going to put the decorations up for us. Holly's asked her friend Jemima to help her to put the tablecloths on. Louisa and Liz will fill the jars we've gathered with the flowers they're picking up from the florist in Cheadle at two o'clock. So that should be plenty of time to decorate the tables, once Tom and Ned have put them in the right positions. Celia and myself will be in charge of putting the stretch covers on the chairs and dressing them with chiffon voiles, which we are going to put around the chairs and finish them off by tying them in bows, like they do at weddings. Theo's in charge of putting balloons on each table, making sure they're nowhere near the candles, which you are putting in jars before you go. Sorted, everything planned to the last detail and Greg has done a work plan and time schedule." said Audrey taking a breath.

"Yes, it's all down on paper." said Greg tapping his clipboard. "We'll be finished by 4.30pm, in plenty of time for us to get ready for the big event.

"What about the dancers," June shouted eyes wide in horror. "You've forgotten the dancers and the other guests who are coming by train and coach."

“No, we haven’t June. Two of Gregson’s mini buses have been to the train station and the coach depot in stoke, to pick up the guests. He’s already dropped them at the hotel in Beresford. They’re going to be picked up from the hotel at 6 o’clock and taken through the back lanes to the church hall. Mr Gregson is going back to the station to meet the 4 o’clock train to pick up the dancers and drop them off at the Gatehouse to get dressed. We have all our spare rooms ready for the dancers, they’re staying overnight. Mr Gregson is going to be on standby from 10pm to midnight to ferry the guests back to the hotel when they are ready. You are going on that date June. You are going to have a good time, is that clear?” Audrey said with some attitude.

Remarkably with a lot of hard work, everything was ready by four o’clock. They looked around and patted each other on the back. The room looked magnificent, bunting and glitter balls were hanging from the ceiling. The tables were dressed in cream and gold. Each one had a candle, flowers and a balloon. Just in front of the stage was a table with a large rainbow cake with figures of Indian dancers on it.

The Staff from the Indian restaurant got to the church hall just before the final touches were being put in place. They’d brought all the food, plates, cutlery, napkins, glasses and hot holding containers, in fact everything, for the celebration to make sure a hundred hungry people would have plenty to eat. June showed them through to the kitchen and told them if they had any problems with space they could use the kitchen in the Gatehouse as well. Sam, the chef assured her they’d already done the prepping, all they had to do was switch on the hot holding containers and warm everything up in the ovens. They’d be back at eight o’clock to start everything and they would be ready to serve the food at nine.

June scrubbed up very well, with the help of Louisa and Liz. She wore a dark blue suit with gold trimmings and a pair of flat black patent shoes to go with her handbag. Her bobbed hair had been trimmed and it now had subtle mahogany highlights. Liz made sure her makeup wasn’t obvious, just enough to make her look more feminine and attractive. Once the girls had finished she looked at herself in the mirror.

"I look quite pretty," she said, tears starting to appear in her eyes.

"No tears June, I don't know how long that waterproof mascara will last. It isn't Halloween yet, so we can't even make that an excuse." Liz laughed.

June walked proudly along the path to her home to wait for her date to pick her up. Her sisters were overjoyed at the transformation. She'd gone from frumpy to fab in just a couple of hours.

Bob arrived bang on time and did a wolf whistle when he saw June. "You look wonderful June, truly wonderful," he beamed as he spoke to his date.

June seemed to have gained a new confidence with her new look. "You don't look half bad yourself old man," June laughed as she looked at Bob. He was wearing a light grey suit with a crisp white shirt and dark grey tie. He held his arm out and June linked him as they strolled up to the pub, laughing and chatting, like a couple of teenagers.

Everything was in place, the guests had arrived and the dancers were on stage just behind the curtain waiting for the cue to start. The lights were off; just the candles glowed on the tables, throwing a hint of light across the room. Everyone was silent as the door opened and Mr and Mrs Gahir walked in. They were dressed up to the nines in their finery.

"Surprise, surprise," everyone shouted as the lights came on, revealing a banner just above the stage saying 'HAPPY 60TH BIRTHDAY'. All the balloons on the tables had 'happy birthday' written on them, some in English, some in Punjabi. The cake in front of the stage had sixty candles, all in different colours. Pete and Bobby opened the stage curtains, revealing colourful dancers, who were led by Mrs Gahir's son. He'd come from his home in London with his wife and children. The music played and the dancers sprang into action, while Mrs Gahir looked on in disbelief.

After just a couple of minutes the music was turned down, the dancers stopped and her son jumped down from the stage. Mrs Gahir looked around to see all her family had gathered around her. They'd come from all over the country and some from abroad to help her celebrate her birthday.

Mr Gahir turned his wife around to face him and said, “Happy Birthday to my darling wonderful wife. This is just a humble celebration we’ve organised for you. You deserve much more. All the people here love and admire you, but none more than me, your unworthy husband.”

Mrs Gahir burst into tears. “Oh no, my wife, are you not happy, do you not approve?” Mr Gahir said with genuine concern.

“These are tears of joy my husband. I thought I’d lost you and all my friends. I am so happy I can only express my feelings with tears,”

“You can thank your friends for this. They have been outstanding; we have been planning it for so long.” Mr Gahir smiled with pride.

“I realise now. The whispering and absences, the mysterious telephone calls, you all had me so worried, but it was worth it for this amazing extravaganza. I will thank them all later. But now, Davinder, we dance.” She held his hand and walked onto the dance floor to join her family and friends in a dance of celebration.

The music started and the dancing began. There was a buzz of excitement and joy as everyone hugged each other and swayed to the intoxicating music. The delicious food was served on time and when everybody had eaten copious amounts of the Indian Cuisine, the dancers came down into the audience. They put people in lines on the dancefloor. Some went back on the stage, some stayed with the people to demonstrate and teach everyone a few moves. It really was like a line dance with a difference.

What a wonderful celebration it was, Bob and June had a waltz towards the end of the evening. Robin and Liz got up from the family table and had a slow dance, to ‘Unchained Melody’; they strolled outside to the enclosed area at the back of the hall. The small fairy lights and the orange lanterns made the whole area look like a fairy grotto.

Robin gazed in Liz’s eyes, “I get the feeling that now this case is over, we’re going to be seeing quite a lot of each other.”

“Do you know Robin Sergeant, I think your right.” Liz looked up at Robin as he put his arms around her and gently kissed her. Liz felt Robin’s touch for a long time after they'd returned to the celebration. She was beginning to care more than she wanted to admit. They turned and walked back into the church hall to the party, which was now starting to wind up.

Ned and Audrey appeared out of the shadows. "I don't think our lives will ever be the same do you Ned?"

"No Audrey, time moves on, children grow up and mysteries are solved."

The noise heightened as the rest of the Knight family joined Ned and Audrey at the tables in the outside area. Most of the people had gone back to the hotel. The caterers were just cleaning away and the Belle sisters and Bob sat down next to Liz and Robin.

"I'm going to start selling African folk art and healing crystals, essential oils, lucky charms and things like that." Everyone watched as May's eyes lit up with enthusiasm as she broadened on her idea of a new business.

April started to discuss the history of the castle with the family. "I think we should have a celebratory drink to toast our good fortune and solving several mysteries. Although I do get this feeling that even now we've sorted a lot of things out, we haven't really, do you know what I mean?"

"The good thing is," Ned continued, smiling. "There's always the mystery of what's coming up next isn't there?"

Everyone sat around the tables all heads turned towards Ned. A smile started to creep onto all the faces, until the smiles turned to laughter and they all nodded their heads in agreement.

"Yes we do have a few mysteries that haven't been solved. Plus we've got lots of plans for the future." Audrey said reaching for her husband's hand.

He lifted her fingers to his lips and kissed them lightly, "I think there will always be mysteries to solve don't you darling?"

Audrey laughed and nodded her head. They looked around at family and friends, feeling very blessed that they had an abundance of both.

You've reached the end of Knights in Shining Armour a Rookery Castle Mystery. I hope you enjoyed this read, look out for Book 2 in the series.

Author's Note

Knights in Shining Armour is the 1st in the Rookery Castle mystery series. Each title should be enjoyable on its own, but the characters do change and develop as the series progresses, so you will find the series more enjoyable if you read the books in order.

This is a work of fiction. Any resemblance that any character may have to any real person, living or dead is coincidental. Similarly, the businesses in the village that are named within the story are also fictional. If they resemble any real businesses, this is a coincidence.

Any historical sites mentioned in the text are all real, but the events that take place at them within this story are fictional.

I do correct errors when they are pointed out to me and every effort is made to ensure that by the time the books are published they are accurate, however sometimes mistakes happen and I apologise.

I enjoy hearing from readers. I'm active on Facebook and would love to have you join in the chat on my page there.

Thank you for choosing to spend time with the Knight family.

Acknowledgments

I am hugely grateful to everyone who has helped me bring this book to you and have worked so hard to make these books the best they can be. The mistakes that remain are, of course, my own. Barbara, Annette, Alison and Mel are wonderful women who have given up their valuable time to share their thoughts on early drafts of my books. I truly appreciate their time and their insights.

Sam, who is an extremely talented artist and has designed the wonderful pictures that grace the cover. www.theartofsambentley.com.

Thank you readers, for sharing the Knight Families world with me.